LIZ JASPER

Underdead

Dear Ania,

Enjoy!

& Liz

CERRIDWEN PRESS

What the critics are saying...

ॐ

"UNDERDEAD is certainly not your typical vampire story, it's better […] I guarantee UNDERDEAD will have you laughing out loud, while keeping you in suspense right up until the end." ~ *Two Lips Reviews*

"Light-hearted mystery with a touch of the paranormal and a hint of romance is a recipe for a just about perfect read." ~ *HuntressReviews.com and EternalNight.co.uk*

"People of any age and from every walk of life will enjoy this intelligently written, humorous take of a normal girl's entry into the paranormal." ~ *Grunion Gazzette*

"This is a funny and fast-paced read that will delight anyone who has ever enjoyed a cozy mystery, a comedy, a romance, or a vampire novel." ~ *BellaOnline*

A Cerridwen Press Publication

www.cerridwenpress.com

Underdead

ISBN 9781419956836
ALL RIGHTS RESERVED.
Underdead Copyright © 2007 Liz Jasper
Edited by Raelene Gorlinsky.
Cover art by Syneca.

This book printed in the U.S.A. by Jasmine-Jade Enterprises, LLC.

Electronic book Publication May 2007
Trade paperback Publication December 2007

Cerridwen Press is an imprint of Ellora's Cave Publishing, Inc.®

About the Author

❧

Liz Jasper lives with her husband and cranky grey cat in Southern California, where she is at work on her next paranormal mystery.

Liz welcomes comments from readers. You can find her website and email address on her author bio page at www.cerridwenpress.com.

Tell Us What You Think

We appreciate hearing reader opinions about our books. You can email us at Comments@EllorasCave.com.

UNDERDEAD

❧

Dedication

❧

To my husband Harrison, who sat down to read the whole manuscript and liked it, even though he "doesn't read books".

Trademarks Acknowledgement

ஓ

The author acknowledges the trademarked status and trademark owners of the following wordmarks mentioned in this work of fiction:

Armani: GA Modefine S.A. Corportation

Barbie: Mattel, Inc.

Bugs Bunny: Time Warner Entertainment Company, L.P.

Denny's: DFO, Inc.

Disneyland: Disney Enterprises, Inc.

Dockers: Levi Strauss and Co.

Emmy: National Academy of Television Arts and Sciences, The Unincorporated Association

For Dummies: Wiley Publishing, Inc.

Hershey's Kisses: Hershey Foods Corporation

Jetta: Volkswagen Aktiengesellschaft

Krackel: Hershey Foods Corporation

Lexus: Toyota Motor Sales, U.S.A., Inc.

Lipton: Lipton Investments, Inc

M*A*S*H: Twentieth Century Fox Film Corporation

Macy's: Macy's Department Stores, Inc.

Obi-Wan: Lucas Licensing LTD

Peet's: Peet's Trademark Company

Post-It: 3M Company

Starbucks: Starbucks U.S. Brands, LLC

Stormtrooper: Lucasfilm Entertainment Company Ltd.

The Far Side: FarWorks, Inc.

Volvo: Volvo Trademark Holding AB Corporation

Yakima: Yakima Products, Inc.

Yoda: Lucas Licensing LTD

Acknowledgements

ॐ

Writing a book can be a hard, lonely task. I was lucky to have family and friends who, with their unwavering support, made it all a little easier.

Special thanks to my mother, for long phone calls that would have bored anyone else and for reading everything I send her with the enthusiasm of an Austen scholar finding the lost sequel to Pride and Prejudice. Thanks to my father for giving me more reference books than anyone should have to lug home in a suitcase — and then offering more.

Thanks also to those who helped even thought they didn't have to: Marilyn (though she has to, now); the Sisters-In-Crime Guppies, especially Mira Sperl and Pat Gulley; and Cindy Sample, who sits in the back and giggles with me at all the conferences.

Thanks to Raelene Gorlinsky, my editor, for wearing a giant red hat to a conference so I didn't miss out on sending this book to the right person. And thanks to Book Passage and the SVRWA for holding good conferences.

And last but definitely not least, huge thanks to my sisty ugler, Laura, for reading too many bits on too short notice and for getting all the jokes, even the bad ones.

Chapter One

∞

I would have shot him then and there if I thought it would do any good, but Roger was such a troll the bullet would have bounced off his thick, ugly hide. Maybe poison...

Becky interrupted my pleasant daydream with a whack on my arm. "Okay, don't turn around and look," she said, "but a guy is staring at you. And he is *hot*!"

"How nice for him."

All I needed to cap off this fabulous evening was Becky's matchmaking. I knew her taste. He probably wore chains and had a Mohawk. Becky herself was dressed in what was best described as slightly toned-down punk, not exactly your typical high school chemistry teacher garb. It went with her spiky hair, which she wore bleached and dyed silver, though a red fringe had been added in honor of the holidays. I should mention that she is Korean, so the dye job isn't exactly subtle. The headmaster turns a blind eye to this display of "personal expression" because she's a first-rate teacher and, at twenty-seven, cheap.

Around us, hip twenty-somethings in denim and black sipped cappuccinos and talked knowledgeably about the band that was setting up in the bar area. But we weren't sitting with them. *We* were at a long rectangular table in the back of the restaurant, where a small balding man in a hideous sweater was lecturing passionately about the insidious evil that was grade inflation. If I'd ever imagined a fate worse than death, this was it—the science department Christmas party.

Becky was staring over my shoulder and had started fanning herself vigorously with a dessert menu. "I mean really, really good-looking."

"Pass," I said from my slumped position. I seemed to have lost the will to sit up straight.

Becky tore her eyes away from the "hot man" long enough to look at me as if I were crazy.

"I'm off really good-looking men," I said.

"Oh please. That's such total bullshit."

"I'm not kidding." And I wasn't, not really. "Extremely good-looking men are always horribly deficient in other areas—you know, like kindness, consideration... It's like they get by on their looks and don't develop a personality." I threw my balled-up napkin on the table. "Either that or God put all their eggs in one basket—they're hot but they're stupid." The last thing I needed after an evening of Roger, our pompous gasbag of a department chair, was to deal with another overblown ego.

"Ouch. Sounds like someone has some old boyfriend issues to work out."

"Already have. Lesson learned—don't date extremely hot men."

Carol had stopped trying to make her sliver of chocolate cake last longer than Moses was lost in the desert, and was following our discussion interestedly from her position between us at the foot of the table. Unlike Becky, Carol looked like a high school science teacher. She was in her mid-thirties with long dark brown hair and the weight of a few too many faculty meeting doughnuts pooling about her waist.

Carol leaned forward. "You know, Jo has a point." Her brown eyes glittered behind her sensible gold-rimmed glasses as she warmed to her topic. "They've done studies that show very good-looking people actually do not tend to be as well developed in other areas—uh..."

Her words shriveled and died under the heat of Becky's glare. "Live a little, Jo! We didn't pick this place for the food, you know." *Ah.* That explained why we were eating at this unexpectedly trendy club a few blocks outside the gentrified section of downtown Long Beach.

"I still can't believe you talked him into this," Becky said.

Carol gave her a stern look over the top of her glasses. "I told him it was rated one of the best restaurants in Long Beach, and it is. I just didn't tell him what for." Her pursed lips twitched and then widened into an evil grin that was the duplicate of Becky's. It looked strange on her sweet face.

"In another hour, the Jungle Cranks will be playing, and this place will look like any other club," Becky said with a dreamy smile. "Roger is going to pitch a fit when he sees it."

That just tells you how clueless Roger is. He probably didn't even know there *were* restaurants outside of Denny's. "I'd like to see Roger pitch a fit," I said, beginning to look forward to the evening for the first time. I glanced at my watch and stifled a yawn; it was getting close to my normal bedtime. "I guess I could stay for another hour or so."

"I'm beginning to think you may be beyond help," Becky said.

Carol shook her head in silent agreement.

"Hey, what are you ganging up on me for?" I said.

Becky scowled. "Well, look at you. Tonight's outfit's not so bad — that skirt shows off your long legs and your sweater's actually in fashion this year and not two sizes too big for you for once — but what's with all the Dockers and Oxford shirts and little matching sweaters you wear to work? I mean you're what, twenty-four?"

I hesitated and then corrected her. "Twenty-two." I didn't like to talk about my age. The last thing I needed was for my eighth-grade students to learn I had only nine years on them. My lips curved up in a sudden smile as I recalled that I was about to have two whole weeks away from them.

Becky's scowl deepened. "You're twenty-two," she said. "You dress like a thirty-five-year-old soccer mom."

"I do not! I just dress more conservatively than you do."

"No, Becky's right," Carol said, eyeing my outfit. "What you're wearing now really is much more age-appropriate. Not that I blame you." She smiled. "I did the same thing when I was your age."

I was trying to work out if she was on my side or Becky's, when Becky attacked my hair. Literally. "Ouch!" I cried, slapping her hand away.

"And what's with the granny bun all the time, for crying out loud?" She examined the bobby pin she'd taken from my hair as if it were a rare artifact. "I'd kill for hair like yours, and you hide it away."

I glared at her and rubbed the tender spot on my scalp. "I wear it up because it gets in the way and tickles my face. But I'll wear it down for you tonight. Happy?" I pulled out the rest of the pins and thick red-gold waves tumbled to the middle of my back. I pretended not to notice as midway up the table, Bob stopped talking sports with Kendra long enough to watch my unintentional imitation of a shampoo commercial. According to the students, Bob's the reigning HTOC (Hot Teacher On Campus). I suppose he's attractive, if you like the beefy football player type. I didn't.

Becky said, "Let me take you shopping and then I'll be happy."

I held out my hand for my hairpin.

"All right." She sighed and handed it back. "It's Christmas. I'll back off. For now. Will that do?"

"Fine." I said it to keep the peace, but there was no way I was ever going shopping with her. My goal at work was to be inconspicuous. I didn't think I'd help the cause by bearing my midriff or whatever was in fashion just now. As a five-foot-ten redhead, I had a hard enough time as it was. You can probably guess what my nickname was growing up. No, not Ariel of *The Little Mermaid* fame. Think more vegetable. And, though my mother says my eyes are a romantic green, they look like plain old hazel to me. So, in sum, giant, hazel-eyed carrot.

Becky reached for the nearly empty margarita pitcher and snuck a glance behind me as she topped off our glasses. "Hot man, still heating up the room, still checking you out."

"Still not looking." I slumped further in my chair. If I sank any lower, I'd be under the table. "Besides, what happened to waiting until Roger goes home before starting the real party?" I said, trying to put her off before she did something awful, like wave him over to join us.

Becky opened her mouth to object, but I cut her off. "I'm not about to willingly provide fodder for the Bayshore gossip hotline." That at least was true. Schools are gossip pits without equal. If I showed any interest in a man, and I mean the *slightest* bit, the rumor mill would have us engaged by the time school started up again. It's like that children's game "telephone". But instead of a phrase getting humorously distorted as it passes from person to person—Jo met a man; Jo met a can; Jo ate a can—the story gets cruelly embellished on each pass—Jo met a man; Jo and a man were holding hands; Jo and a man were making out in the parking lot; Jo and a man were buck-naked in the backseat of a Porsche having wild sex that's banned in ten states.

"Really, Jo," Carol said. "You shouldn't let other people keep you from living your life. People are going to talk about you one way or another." She twisted around in her chair to get a look at the mystery man for herself. Her eyes widened. "It might as well be for a good cause," she said. Then she sighed. I stared at her. Carol? Happily married, motherly Carol, sighing over another man? Who was this guy? I looked doubtfully at the icy liquid in my glass and wondered sourly if they'd put something in the margaritas.

Then I caved.

Pretending I was checking out the band, I shifted around in my chair. "Hot" did not do the man justice. He was the most fabulous-looking man I'd ever seen, and that includes Johnny Depp as a pirate and Brad Pitt in *Fight Club*. He was leaning against a nearby wall, a still figure in black, as distinct as silence in a crowd. Most of the men in the place were dressed in black, but for them it was a statement, a uniform, a pick-up line. This man belonged in it.

Flickering lights from the dance floor slid over his chiseled features, briefly illuminating strong cheekbones before getting lost in the dark hollows below. He had one of those long, lean bodies, with just the right amount of muscle, and dark, slightly wavy hair that hung to his shoulders in a way that made my stomach lurch.

As if sensing my regard, he suddenly turned his head from the shadows and looked directly at me. I did an embarrassing deer-in-the-headlights thing and our eyes locked. His eyes were the most gorgeous blue I'd ever seen. I mean piercingly blue. Meltingly blue. A sharp desire to be closer to him slammed me like a wave.

With an effort, I turned back around, but I could feel his eyes burning into mine as acutely as if he were still in front of me.

Carol didn't say anything. She just stared at him with a goofy smile on her face, her glasses misting softly. Becky had stopped fanning herself and had settled in for the night of viewing too, planting her elbow on the table and resting her head in her palm. I pushed her elbow out from under her chin and she nearly smacked her chin on the tabletop. She blinked her kohl-lined eyes a few times and grinned sheepishly at me. "Not bad, eh?"

I didn't respond. I couldn't—I hadn't yet regained proper speaking powers.

"You should go talk to him," Becky said, giving me a nudge.

"In front of everyone?" I said. "You've got to be joking." My legs felt like jelly. I gave myself a shake. I was being ridiculous, overreacting. Becky was right. If this was my response to the first good-looking man I saw, I really *did* need to get out more.

"Please. There's smart, and then there's stupid," Carol said, coming up for air. "You're going to let Roger and a bunch of old gossipy biddies keep you from a man like that?"

Carol was right. It was time I showed a little backbone. "Not when you put it that way," I said. I risked a glance back in his direction. He was watching the band, giving me a good look at his profile. It was gorgeous too.

Too gorgeous, actually. Sanity returned. I turned around more firmly in my chair.

"Go on." Becky gave me another little push.

I didn't budge. "No way," I said. "There's something wrong with him."

"What? What is wrong with him?" Carol demanded.

"He's boring, he's vain, he has six wives in various countries, he lives in a yurt with fifteen Chihuahuas, he sells deodorant for a living—I don't know, but I stand by my theory. No one can be *that* good-looking *and* have a personality."

"Oh, for goodness sake!" Carol said. "What a load of crap!"

Becky gave her a stunned look at this unexpected reversal of argument. Carol never backed off something that had been written up in *Scientific American*.

Carol continued, on a roll now. "Stop inventing reasons to avoid talking to him. If you want to forgo meeting fabulous men to sit here with the likes of us for the rest of your life, be my guest." Her glasses had slid down her nose and she glared over the top of them at me.

"What she said," Becky said. "Though I don't know why you'd even care if he has *thirty* wives and *eats* deodorant for a living. You don't need to have him around for scintillating conversation—look at him! He's so hot he doesn't need a personality. What do you want to talk to him for anyway?"

"Gotta love liberated women," I muttered. "Equal opportunity chauvinism."

Becky jiggled the empty margarita pitcher. "Now stop yer stalling and go get us another. And while you're there, talk to the man. No, wait. You'll chicken out. I'm going with you."

"Oh, no, what are you doing?" I squeaked as she pulled me up from the table. Roger sent us an irritated frown and I responded with the look all females possess instinctively, the one that says "ladies' room". He cleared his throat and turned away. Unfortunately now I was committed, at least to a trip to the bathroom.

"If you think I'm going to just march up to him and talk to him, you're wrong," I said in Becky's ear as she propelled me out of the alcove. Becky was more forward with men than I was. A lot more forward.

To my relief—and maybe just a *tiny* bit of disappointment—the man in black had disappeared. This didn't stop Becky. She took an iron grip on my arm and steered us toward the bar through the dense band of people who sat five and six around tiny tables near the dance floor. When we reached the packed bar area, its wooden floor already tacky with spilled drinks, she paused and looked around. "Oh good, he's right over there."

My backbone deserted me. She gave my arm another tug, but I dug in my heels. "I don't *think* so," I said.

"Don't worry." She spoke soothingly, as to a nervous dog, "We're just going to the bar for another pitcher. And when we get near him, I'll just give you a little push into him."

"Becky, don't you dare! That is so high school."

"Shhh." She dropped behind me and fastened her fingers lightly on my waist.

I stopped and turned around to face her. "I mean it, Becky, don't you dare."

She gave a disappointed sigh. "Spoilsport. All right. Fine. Scout's honor." She held up her hands in a mixed gesture of supplication and Scout salute.

I sighed. "I will talk to him *later*, Becky. I promise. The second Roger's gone, okay? I'm not that stupid."

"All right, all right."

"Now, can we go back to the table?"

Her dark eyebrows disappeared up under her spiky red bangs. "Of course not. We have to get that pitcher while we're here, or Hot Man will think you came over just to get a closer look."

"Oh, for crying out loud."

"C'mon." She pushed me in the direction of the bar, holding on to me as if I might do a bunk. Which I would have, had we not been boxed in by the crowd.

I ignored the man in black and fixed my attention on a random point behind the bar. It wasn't any sort of flirtatious coyness—I was legitimately embarrassed. I mean he had caught us staring at him, and now we were heading in his direction like lovesick groupies. Well, to the bar, really, but he didn't know that. As we were even with him, I felt Becky's hand leave my waist to tug my arm. Furious, I ignored her and pushed forward. She gave my arm another, stronger tug. As I half turned to tell her to knock it off, I was pulled off balance and spun around. But instead of frowning down into Becky's mischievous brown eyes, I was glaring at a man's chest. A very nicely built man's chest. I tilted my head up and met blue eyes, the blue of the night sky just before the sun totally disappears.

The censure for Becky died on my lips as I got lost a second time staring at the hot man.

His eyes crinkled slightly at the corners, and he broke the fraught silence with a simple hello. His voice was low and gravelly with an accent I couldn't quite place. It made my knees weak. I've always been a sucker for an accent. *Oh, no.* I was definitely in for some trouble with this one.

Chapter Two

ഔ

"I hope I didn't alarm you just now," said the man in black, "but you looked like you needed rescuing from your dinner party."

The kitschy disco ball above the adjacent dance floor started to spin, showering him in twinkling fragments of color as if gift-wrapping him in fairy dust. I felt a giggle bubble to the surface and ruthlessly tamped it down.

"You've come to save me from certain-death-by-boredom? How wonderful." I stretched out a hand. "I'm Jo. You must be Prince Charming. How nice to finally meet you."

"Not quite." His lips twisted briefly in a wry smile. "Will." His handshake was good and firm.

"Jo's an unusual name for a woman," he said.

"It's short for Josephine," I admitted. *Why had I told him that?* I never told *anyone* that. Even my bank knew me as "Jo".

The band had launched into a funky, ironic rendition of an old disco tune and the crowd around us surged with enthusiasm. I had to place a hand against the wall to keep my balance.

"It's getting a little crowded in here," Will said, raising his voice to be heard over the din. "Maybe we should go out to the back porch where we can talk?"

He pointed toward an open doorway at the back of the dance floor where a heavyset bouncer stood guard, but my attention was turned in the other direction.

Becky had scuttled back to our table. She and Carol were pointedly looking elsewhere and Roger was fully absorbed in whatever he was saying, but the rest of my colleagues were getting restless. Hunky Bob was pointing to the band with one beefy hand and Kendra's new blonde highlights glinted as her head swiveled to follow. After four hours of talking nonstop sports, they'd picked *now* to run out of things to bore people with?

I gave in to the inevitable. It was one thing to be talking to Will while waiting in line for the bar, quite another to be seen leaving with him. Even if it was only to the back porch.

As I opened my mouth to decline, a strong jab pushed me off-balance and I lost my footing. Will caught me and held me upright.

"Are you all right?"

"I'm fine, thanks…"

He was holding me at a respectful distance, but really, twenty feet was too close to this man. His beautiful blue eyes had darkened with concern and I felt a strange recklessness. My nosy, gossipy co-workers could take pictures for all I cared.

"Maybe some air would be good," I said. The words seemed to tumble out on their own.

The crowd opened up for us as if by magic and Will steered me out into a relatively private nook another couple had vacated. The porch area was about the size of a four-car garage and enclosed by two-story tall cypress trees. It might have been claustrophobic but for a clever arrangement of potted green ficuses and red Japanese maples that divided the area into smaller, inviting alcoves. Everything was strung with those fat multi-colored bulbs that had been big in the Seventies. I'm sure the effect was supposed to be ironic or retro or something, but to me it just looked pretty and festive.

I knew all this because conversation had ceased between us and I was looking everywhere but at him. We were practically alone out there, and with this man I definitely needed a chaperone. I snuck a glance at Will from under my lashes. He seemed far away, an odd look on his face I couldn't interpret.

The silence became too much for me and I had to say something, anything—so long as it was witty, clever and engaging.

"I'm afraid I'm not very good at small talk," I said.

Jeez.

"That's all right, we don't need to talk." He gave me a lazy, slightly wicked smile that made me clutch the railing for support.

For some reason I couldn't explain—maybe I was on auto-stupid-pilot—I did the only thing that could make it worse. I launched into a long, unnecessary explanation.

"I've never been good at small talk; I never know what to say. That's why I usually avoid this sort of place. You're not supposed to discuss anything controversial, intellectual, or personal. Pretty much anything worth discussing is taboo. Why can't people talk about something interesting when they meet, like…" I threw up my hands. "I don't know, what book they're reading? Instead you're stuck with insipid and inane topics like the weather and *that* hardly varies in Southern California. Oh, never mind," I said, a little confused myself at how it had come out.

Will regarded me narrowly, as if I were a kitten that had suddenly sprouted horns, and took a step back. *Great.* Maybe, if I was lucky, the Earth would open up and swallow me whole.

When he finally spoke, it was the last thing I would have expected.

"If you cannot think of anything appropriate to say you will please restrict your remarks to the weather." Then he smiled, a genuine full-blown grin. I let out a breath I hadn't known I was holding and relaxed back against the railing.

"I see you know your Jane Austen. I suppose you saw the movie."

"I read the book, too."

"You're kidding, right?" I'd never met a man—a straight man anyway—outside the occasional English teacher forced to include Austen in his curriculum, who had read *Sense and Sensibility*, much less was willing to admit to it.

"Had sisters, growing up." He shrugged and lean muscles moved under his shirt.

"Tell me then, Jo, who finds small talk inane, have you read anything interesting lately?" He spoke nonchalantly but watched me keenly, as if my answer mattered.

All I could think of was the half-finished mystery on my nightstand and the pile of Regency romance novels I bought for a quarter at the library and hoarded in a pile under my bed for particularly nasty days. Judge me when you start teaching thirteen-year-olds.

"What genre?" I asked, stalling shamelessly.

His eyes took on a challenging glint. "I've been reading some intriguing works by Rousseau on the nature of society. But we can discuss whatever *genre* you like."

French philosophy? Great. *That's what you get for being such a babbling prude*, I told myself. No doubt it was karmic payback for my stupid theory about *his* intelligence. "Why don't we start with Jane Austen and work our way up to solving the world's problems."

I half expected him to turn away in disgust, but he laughed good-naturedly and we proceeded to discuss books. As he appeared to have read everything ever written, the conversation drifted all over the place. The enclosed porch filled and emptied several times, though I barely noticed the other people. We might have talked for ten minutes or ten hours.

I was lightly lampooning his theory that Utopia could exist outside the pages of literature when the conversation took an abrupt right turn.

"Do you believe in destiny?" he asked.

It was the worst pick-up line since "Hey, baby, what's your sign".

I didn't realize I'd said the words out loud until he gave a small shake of his head and said, "You misunderstand me. I'm asking whether you believe our lives are governed by fate or free will."

I let out a breath of relief. He hadn't turned into a freak on me, after all. "Free will," I said, "though it's less a well-formed philosophy than wishful thinking. If I didn't think I had some choice in what happens to me, I wouldn't want to get out of bed in the morning."

In reply, he muttered something in Latin.

A light bulb went off in my thick skull. Not that I understood Latin. I didn't. But I *was* familiar with people suddenly shifting into the dead language. I'd seen it at work a hundred times. My eyes narrowed. "You're an English teacher," I accused him.

"No."

"Philosophy? History?"

"No." He shook his head. "I just read a lot."

"What *do* you do then?"

The laughter seemed to fall from his face, and I wondered if I had inadvertently brought up a sore subject.

"I guess you could say I'm in…Human Resources Management. Nothing exciting. And yourself?"

"I teach middle school science, but my background's in ecology."

My degree is officially in biology, but I had loaded up on ecology classes because the labs were mostly held outdoors. I discovered early on that I much preferred wearing heavy boots and tromping around in mud to the more traditional latex glove and petri dish route. I liked studying outside so much that I'd signed up for astronomy and geology classes as well. Of course, there's a price to pay for a self-indulgent education.

Mine was that the only job I could find upon graduation was teaching earth science to eighth graders.

"Ecology," Will said. "That's a subject I know little about. I so rarely get out during the day. It's only at night that I have the flexibility to study things that interest me." His voice was flat, the animation I'd glimpsed earlier gone.

Great. In addition to being financially useless, my educational interests repelled men. I shifted the conversation back to books.

"I like to read Thomas Hardy novels at Christmas," I said. "They're so outrageously depressing that even if you have to spend your holiday hearing about your aging relatives' medical issues, and then go home to find your tree on fire and all your presents stolen by pirates, you still can't help but feel as if you're having the best Christmas ever."

This got him to laugh again and his eyes, lightened to a brilliant sapphire, met mine in shared amusement before the humor in them gave way to something else. My breath caught as he stepped slowly, purposefully, into the space that separated us. I was dimly aware that the band had started up again after a short break and the porch had emptied. Completely. We were alone out there.

He spoke in a low gravelly voice that intensified his faint accent. "You're not at all what I expected." He reached forward to capture a long lock of my hair and watched it slide slowly through his fingers as if mesmerized. "Gold and orange and red, like the sunrise." He traced a finger lightly down my cheek. "You're as lovely as daybreak."

He closed the remaining distance between us.

I'm a "third date, first kiss" kind of girl but that night I didn't care. Soon—too soon—he broke away abruptly and studied me for a long silent moment at arm's length.

An odd mix of triumph and regret seemed to war across his face, but before I could decide what I'd seen or ponder what it meant, he pulled me tightly against him and I was lost once again in his kiss — until a sharp, ravaging pain jerked me out of my hormonal fog. I wrenched myself away and took a staggering step back. *What the hell did he think he was doing?*

He had bitten my neck.

Hard.

I wanted to yell for help, to give him an earful of what I thought about weirdoes who bit people, but the words froze on my lips. I just stood there staring wonderingly into his eyes, those blue, blue eyes as he pulled me toward him. I was terrified yet curiously unable to move away, as if I were in one of those dreams when you try to run and nothing happens. He pulled me closer, closer, and as his lips hovered an inch from mine, the simmering attraction between us caught fire again and I forgot about running away altogether. He lowered his teeth again to my neck and bit again.

The pain woke me partially out of my stupor and the years of self-defense classes my father had made me take kicked in, giving sudden strength to my limp legs. Almost automatically, I pulled a knee sharply up into his groin. He gave a startled cry and loosened his grip for a brief moment, but almost immediately grabbed my shoulders and yanked me back toward him. But the break had been enough. My mind cleared, as if someone had poured a bucket of cold water down over me.

Instead of resisting, I shifted toward him. It caught him off guard and he was forced to step back to keep his balance. I used the opportunity to crack an elbow into his jaw. It was all I needed. Clutching a hand to my throbbing neck, I ran blindly for the door back into the bar and ran smack into another hard chest. I let out a strangled scream.

The owner of the chest, a tall, brown-haired man with intense light grey eyes and a crooked nose, pushed me away and held me at arm's length. His eyes raked my face and seemed to linger at my neck, though I was sure he couldn't see what I could only imagine as the world's nastiest hickey, since my hand covered it.

"Are you okay?" His voice sounded harsh, urgent.

"I'm fine," I said. I forced myself to remain calm as I scanned the dining area urgently for Becky and Carol. They were still at the table, a half-full pitcher of margaritas between them. They didn't seem to have moved since I left them.

I realized the man was saying something to me. I brushed off his polite concern and hurried back to our table. Gathering up my long hair in one hand, I pulled the thick mass around my neck and let it hang down the front of my chest. I have a lot of hair. Anything on my neck that needed to be hidden would be.

Becky was waiting eagerly for a report. I bent to collect my purse. "I'm going to head home," I said.

"So soon?"

I pitched my voice louder and said to the group at large, "I'm sorry I have to leave early, but I'm not feeling too well. I think I'm coming down with something."

Becky's grin faded and her brow furrowed as she exchanged a glance with Carol.

Roger spoke portentously from the head of the table. "I'm not surprised. Many people, especially the new teachers, are only able to hold off a cold until the holidays."

His smug response got my back up, but now was not the time to deal with Roger.

Carol was watching me with a concerned look. "I'll drive you," she said, standing up. "I'm parked just down the block."

I forced myself to speak lightly. "No, you stay and have fun. I'd planned to take a taxi anyway—it's only ten bucks, I live so close." It was only a partial lie—I definitely planned to take one now. After a few more minutes of saying goodbye to everyone and fending off offers of company I didn't want for the ride home, I managed to escape. I wasn't kidding when I'd said I felt crappy. My neck hurt, my stomach was churning with a potent combination of disgust and tequila, and the room was starting to spin. Fortunately, a taxi was waiting outside the restaurant and the driver handed me neatly inside.

I managed to give him my address before slipping into darkness in the backseat.

Chapter Three
ဢ

Bright rays of morning sunlight jolted me back into consciousness like a slap in the face. Never before had I felt so reluctant to be alive. My head hurt, my body hurt—even my eyes hurt, as if the lids were insufficient protection against the light. With what seemed like an absurdly large amount of effort, I shifted my head back into the shadows and opened my eyes.

My mind wasn't working very fast, or very well, and I took things in slowly. The first thing I noticed was that the small, sparsely furnished room needed some serious maid service. The small bedside table and wide matching dresser were simple, cheap and nearly invisible under their heavy loads of picture frames and unfolded laundry. Unframed posters, an erratic mix of impressionist art and nature scenes, splashed color on generic white walls. A stack of books listed determinedly toward the door, as if trying to escape back to the orderly seclusion of the library. Maybe they knew they were overdue. I did. The library had left messages.

While I had gone through the sluggish process identifying my own bedroom, the sun had crept back across my face with the sly grace of a water buffalo. I pulled a pillow over my head and tried to go back to sleep, but it was abundantly clear I wasn't getting any farther before I consumed a handful of aspirin and a bucket of water.

I hauled myself out of bed and stumbled across apartment-beige carpet toward the adjoining bathroom that seemed miles away from my bed instead of just ten feet. *I am never drinking tequila again*, I promised myself fervently. *Never ever*.

I squirted a rather crooked line of toothpaste onto my toothbrush and went to work scouring the cotton out of my mouth while I drummed up the courage to stop avoiding the mirror. If I looked anything like how I felt, there would be an ogre looking back at me. I rinsed my toothbrush, carefully patted my mouth dry with a towel, and then risked a peek.

Ooh, even better. Two ogres. I closed my aching, bloodshot eyes for a moment and regrouped, trying to ignore the dizziness that suddenly swamped me. When the room stopped spinning, I rubbed my eyes and tried again, squinting a little against the fuzziness.

I was all that was lovely. I looked like a carrot-topped banshee. My face was flushed, my hair was a tangled mess and my neck was throbbing. Will's kiss—and its creepy denouement—came rushing back. *How had I forgotten that? What else had I forgotten?* I began to panic. It had finally occurred to me that I didn't even remember coming home. I looked down at myself. I was still dressed in the clothes I had worn to dinner.

How many margaritas had I had? It was hard to gauge— Becky had kept our glasses filled from the pitcher, but I thought it had probably been only two, maybe three. Surely not enough to cause a blackout! I shoved my hair aside and craned my neck to inspect the spot between my ear and collarbone where that jerk had bitten me. I could swear he'd left teeth marks. I probed the area gently with one finger. It came away wet. The wound was seeping a bit—he'd actually broken skin.

Eew! Eew! Eew! I did a little gross-out dance, the sort until then I'd only seen women in cartoons do when they encountered a mouse, and reached for my first-aid kit. Soaking a cotton ball with antiseptic, I scrubbed furiously at my neck and thought about Will. I had joked with Becky and Carol about good-looking men having drawbacks in other areas, but come on! I wasn't sure if I had been a victim of kinky S&M foreplay or some sort of Goth thing run amok. What kind of weirdo bites a girl during their first kiss? Who did he think he was? Dracula?

I threw the cotton ball in the trash and gave another cry of disgust. The hair near my wound was matted and sticky with blood and his saliva – a minuscule amount, maybe, but as a trained biologist, I am fully able to gross myself out on a microscopic level. I had to get myself to the emergency room immediately. Right. And spend the next four hours hung over in a cramped and crowded waiting room only to have a doctor laugh at me for being paranoid. I could see it right now. They'd send me home with a teensy-weensy adhesive bandage and tell me not to kiss strangers in bars.

I pulled off my clothes instead, threw every item into the wicker hamper and showered, washing my hair obsessively three times. When I got out, I felt much better. I put a cheerful yellow bandage strip over the wound on my neck (so I wouldn't have to look at it) and dressed in my oldest, comfiest sweats. Coffee, I decided firmly. Lots of it. And maybe pancakes. And bacon—ooh, maybe a steak! Nice and rare. Thinking of food cheered me up a little. Was it odd that I wanted a bacon cheeseburger, hung over as I was? No. That was the one thing normal about today. I always wanted food. Yawning, I padded down the short hallway to the living room, opened the connecting door and screamed.

A strange man was standing near the couch, watching me intently and holding what looked like a small club. A voice in my head yelled at me to run, but I stood there, frozen with fear, until a gust of wind came through my bedroom window and slammed the door shut behind me, trapping me in the room with him. I jumped and shrieked and grappled frantically behind me for the doorknob.

He spoke. "Wait! Miss Gartner! I didn't mean to scare you. I'm the taxi driver. Ah, Gavin Raines?"

He did look vaguely familiar. He was a tall, athletic-looking man in his late twenties with brown hair and a hooked nose that looked as if it had been broken once or twice.

"Taxi driver." I repeated loudly, to cover the sound of the doorknob turning behind me.

"I drove you home last night?" He spoke earnestly, willing me to remember. "You, um, passed out in my cab. You were holding your keys so I helped you inside, but I didn't want to leave you like that, without the deadbolt, it wasn't safe—anyone could have gotten in..." His voice petered out uncertainly.

Anyone did. "Are you always this chivalrous to your customers?"

His glance dropped to the floor. I took a half step back and silently pushed the door behind me open a little wider. "Well, no." He sounded embarrassed. "It's just, well you look a little like my younger sister, and..." He looked up and his eyes met mine. They were a curious light grey that struck some chord of memory. I was sure now that I had seen him before, but the memory went no farther than simple recognition.

He said, "I'm sorry. I'm new at this. I just started the job last week—I'm just doing it part-time while I finish my dissertation. Here, let me show you my ID... Er, I didn't realize I was still holding this." He put the club down on the table with a little self-deprecating grimace and dug into the back pocket of his jeans.

My suspicions had returned in full force. I pointed to the club with my free hand and the other tightened on the doorknob behind me as I readied myself to dive back into the bedroom at the first sign of homicidal mania. "What do you have that for anyway? Given how I remind you of your little sister and all, I'm surprised you felt you needed it."

To my surprise he smiled widely. "I didn't. Bring it in I mean. You did. It's usually kept under the driver's seat—all the cabs have 'em. It must have rolled into the back. You were holding it when I carried you out. Here." He held out his ID card.

When I didn't move to take it, he put it on a table between us and stepped back. I reached forward and picked it up. I had to squint to read the tiny writing. What was *wrong* with my vision? Did I need reading glasses? Had all the studying and grading finally caught up with me, or had I just discovered a new and exciting side effect of the truly horrible hangover?

"UCLA, huh?" I said, pushing the unpleasant thoughts aside. "What're you studying?"

"American history—the colonial era. Actually, more like pre-colonial. I'm interested in how the diseases Europeans brought over—not just the human diseases, but the ones their livestock transmitted to the native animals—may have decimated the native populations, making it easier for Europeans to gain a foothold…"

"How interesting," I said, cutting him off. The man spoke in run-ons. I hoped his writing was more concise or he was going to need that taxi job, and I didn't think he was going to last long in that profession if he pulled stunts like this.

I handed back his ID in silence, not wanting to say anything that might trigger more conversation. I wasn't scared of him anymore and my thoughts were shifting to more pressing concerns, like my head. It had begun to throb in earnest and I desperately wanted to stick it in a bucket of ice water. I also wanted my coffee and my breakfast, but what I wanted, most of all, was for Gavin to go away.

"Well, I'll be on my way, then," he said, as if reading my mind. "And, um, I'm sorry if I startled you."

I followed him to the door. "It's okay. It was…" I paused to choose my word—*weird* came to mind. "Considerate of you to stay until I could lock the door myself."

"It was no problem, really." He stood awkwardly at the door. "Well, goodbye."

I squinted my eyes painfully against the near blinding brightness of the clear December morning and scanned the street. "Where's your cab?"

"Just over there." He pointed toward a blue Jetta with a black Yakima bike rack strapped to the top.

"That's a cab?"

"I have one of those removable lit taxi signs for the roof—it plugs into the cigarette lighter and hooks onto the bike rack. I took it off last night—regulations say we can't park taxis overnight in residential areas." He shrugged at the strangeness of city regulations, flashed another quick, sweet smile and jogged across the street toward his car. As he drove off, he stuck an arm out the window and gave me a cheery wave.

I held up a hand in a more subdued response and as I watched him turn the corner, something niggled the back of my brain. I didn't bother trying to get a fix on it, knowing from experience it would be a waste of time. It would come out on its own if I focused on something else for a while. I went back inside, my head pounding anew with each step, and headed for the coffee maker.

It was five minutes after he'd left that I remembered my car was still parked downtown. Under normal circumstances, I'd walk, run or bike the five miles. But today? "Ain't happening," I said aloud. Kicking myself and sighing, I hauled out the phone book and called a cab.

I'm a chatty person on the phone; more than once my father has chided me for getting too personal with strangers. But I can't help it. I get nervous when I can't see someone's face when I talk to them, so I babble. I must not be the only person to do this, for the dispatcher listened patiently as I explained, in more detail than was strictly necessary, why I needed my car.

"And of course I didn't think to ask your driver, Gavin Raines, for a ride—"

"Who?" said the dispatcher.

"Uh, Gavin Raines?"

"We don't have any drivers by that name, miss. You sure you have the right cab company?"

"Yes, I'm sure. He's new — he and another driver are sharing a cab. A blue Jetta? With a bike rack?"

"Sorry, miss, you must have the wrong cab company. Our drivers all use the company's yellow minivans."

"Oh."

"Miss? You still there? You still want a cab to pick you up?"

"What? Oh. Uh, yes, thanks."

When the taxi came it was, as promised, a yellow minivan. Not to be confused with a blue Jetta.

The driver and I had a very interesting chat about taxi regulations. I learned that the city of Long Beach authorizes a finite number of the medallions that permit a taxi to work. I even got a rundown on the cars used by the city's cab companies, lots of Fords and Chevys, mostly large sedans and minivans. Not a German compact in the bunch.

I didn't know who Gavin was, but I did know who he wasn't. He had lied to me, this stranger who had spent the night in my apartment while I lay passed out in my room. It gave me the creeps all over again, enough that I stopped by the emergency room on the way home after all. I leveled with the doctor and got the full work up, including tests for any of the diseases that might have spawned the vampire myth and AIDS. It might have been a little late in the day for me to start worrying about strangers and strange diseases, but better late than never.

Chapter Four

༓

It's a myth that teachers never get sick. What people really mean is that teachers *shouldn't* get sick. Because when they do, it means they've succumbed to some super virus, something that has passed from student to student, mutating along the way into something truly hellish. And that's what I had—the flu from hell.

After I'd gotten back from the emergency room and inhaled the supremely large meal I'd promised myself, I'd gone back to bed and stayed there, huddling under my covers with the lights low and the blinds tightly drawn—for three days—getting up only for *the necessary* or to choke down a few crackers or some ginger ale.

I felt so terrible that I would have thought I'd contracted something nasty from Will—except the hospital lab results had all come back negative. So it was either the flu or a particularly gnarly hangover, and I went with the first option. I mean, I can make a case for a two-day hangover, but three? No, I'd gotten whatever had been going around school. Once again, my evil students had found a way to suck the joy out of my life. *Some vacation!* I bit down a wave of nausea that left me weak and shaking. When I could muster up the energy I pulled the covers up over my head and lay there feeling miserable and very, very sorry for myself.

I might have stayed that way indefinitely but for my mother, who called around ten in the morning to inquire why I hadn't yet arrived. "Why weren't you at Mass?" she demanded, reminding me I had been expected to meet my parents for church the night before and then go home to stay with them through Christmas day.

I explained I had caught a nasty flu. "I'm going to have to miss the festivities this year," I concluded, pulling the receiver under the covers with me. "I'm too weak to drive."

"You are *not* missing Christmas," she insisted.

"I'm probably contagious. I don't want to get anyone else sick." *Call me Martyr Jo.*

"Nonsense. I never get sick," she said firmly, "and your father's as strong as an ox."

"I'll try to drive over Christmas morning," I said, closing my eyes tightly against another wave of nausea.

"I will not have my daughter driving around town sick on Christmas morning." I heard the faint but unmistakable sound of car keys jingling. "I'll come get you. You can rest here. I'm sure you'll get better with someone to take care of you."

I groaned in protest and got a dial tone in response. I pushed the phone, a cheap holdover from college, back on its duct-taped cradle and fell back asleep.

A hand shook me gently awake. I cracked open an eye, saw something glowing and red and shut it again. I was having that nightmare again, the one where I'm in the castle with Bugs Bunny and that furry red monster.

The hand shook again, more forcefully this time. I opened both eyes.

"Mom?" I croaked, narrowing my eyes against the brightness of her hair, which an errant ray of light peeking through a gap in the blinds had turned to fire.

"Why aren't you packed yet?" she asked. "Let me feel your forehead. You're not running a fever, in fact, you feel cold. Did you put a compress on it?"

"Huh?"

"And why it is so *dark* in here?" She threw open the blinds.

I cringed against the bright light. "Hey," I protested.

She clicked her tongue. "No wonder you're not getting better," she said, opening a window. "Fresh air, that's the ticket. Didn't you learn anything at all in those biology courses?"

"God, have you always been this cheerful?" I muttered crankily, watching helplessly as she bustled around the room automatically tidying as she looked for luggage and clothes, like a whirlwind, only better coiffed. A full scale tornado wouldn't have the ability—or the temerity—to disturb my mother's hair, presently dyed a virulent red. I'm not kidding. You should see what they can do with hair dye these days. I don't know if it's her or her hairdresser, if it's boredom or creativity. Someone needs to rein someone in, that's all I'm saying.

I should explain a little better—you might be getting the wrong impression. My mother is beautiful. I mean really stunning. She's tall, fashionably lean and fashionably clad, perfectly manicured and has cheekbones to die for. Even without the *very* red (actually, it was more magenta), perfectly styled hair, she would stand out in a crowd.

Despite the same general build and a certain obvious family resemblance, we look nothing alike. But we could. My sweats could be exchanged for form-fitting designer duds. My long, gold-red hair could be fashionably cut, colored, and styled. With contacts, I could even change my eye color from the hazel-green I'd inherited from my father to my mother's vivid blue.

Part of me lives in mortal fear that some day her bevy of beauticians will hijack me off the street and submit me to the plucking, pulling, cutting, coloring, and lord knows whatever else it takes to "be seen in public" these days. My mother, on the other hand, lives in hope for such a day, and I'm not sure she is above engineering it should my "outdoorsy" phase go on much longer.

"Did you say something, dear?" She was arm-deep in my underwear drawer. She held up a thong and looked at it with a quizzical frown before tucking it quickly back in the drawer.

She moved on to my closet. "I'll put together a few things. Now, where's that sweater your father and I got you last Christmas?"

Back at Macy's, where I had traded it for a great new pair of khakis. "I dunno, Mom," I lied.

"Well, surely you have *something* appropriate in here *somewhere.*" Apparently I did, for soon she was packed — I was packed — and it was time to go.

I pushed myself to a sitting position. "God, I feel horrible," I said, slumping against the headboard.

My mother came over and tilted my face up. Her face was creased with concern. "Oh, Jo dear. What happened to your face?"

"What do you mean?"

"It's all red!" She touched a finger lightly to my cheek. "And you have scaly patches!" Her pitch rose at the horror of it.

Then her eyes widened and she sucked in a breath in sudden understanding. "Oh, honey, you've been victimized by a cut-rate chemical peel, haven't you? It's scandalous, the way *anyone* can open a shop these days. Honey, if you wanted a facial, why didn't you ask? I'm sure Johnny would have made time for you. Is this why you didn't come to Mass?"

What? "I did not get a chemical peel," I said, jerking my face out of her hands. "I'm sick," I said. "Sick. You know, with the flu? I can't eat, I have a raging headache, I'm so exhausted I can hardly sit upright and my whole body feels as if someone hit me with a baseball bat while I was sleeping!" I glared at her, as if she herself had crept in during the night and done the whacking.

She ignored my outburst, eyes intent on my face. She looked both curious and horrified, like a specialist confronted with a rare disease. "Have you been moisturizing properly?"

"I have been moisturizing with abandon," I lied. I hadn't washed my face in two days. "My face is fine. I'm fine, or I will be. I'm just sick. A few more days' sleep and I'll wake up fine, you'll see."

I wondered, as I said this, if I should have gone along with the horrible skin problem scenario after all. Flu couldn't keep her away but maybe she'd leave me in peace if I had nice, contagious facial fungus?

It was too late. Through sheer power of will, she had me bundled, head and face wrapped in a scarf ("You'll get permanent scarring if you go in the sun like that. The UV rays are strong in LA, even in December. And with your fair skin...") and in no time, I was back at my parents' house, tucked into the twin bed in my old room.

Despite my dad's repeated threats to turn it into a gym, my room hadn't changed since I'd last inhabited it, aside from being scrupulously clean. The same lightly flowered blue and yellow wallpaper adorned the walls, the same mix of childhood favorites and textbooks filled the bookshelves, the same well-worn antiques passed down from my great grandmother furnished the room. Even my bedspread was the same, a cheery hodgepodge of bright colors that looked like something Andy Warhol might have designed after some major partying. It goes without saying that my mother hated it.

Next to me on the bedside table lay a steaming tray of soup and toast triangles. The food remained untouched until my mother came in and started spooning chicken soup down my throat. I gagged and tried to push her away, but she was relentless, and stayed until I had finished the lot. Only then did she let me sleep, promising—threatening?—to wake me up in an hour or two for hot chocolate.

"You look like a crushed insect," she said, brushing away my feeble protests to be left alone. "If you don't eat, you'll get even sicker. And you are not ruining Christmas for the rest of us because you are too stubborn to eat a little soup." Soothing, almost, my mother's particular brand of love and guilt.

Almost before she turned off the light and closed the door lightly behind her I fell back asleep, but it was not the peaceful, dead-to-the-world sleep I usually had when I came home. I dreamt of darkness, of long passageways, and oddly, since I had forced him out of my thoughts, of Will. Actually, that part of the dream wasn't so bad. Not so bad at all.

* * * * *

By the day after Christmas, I had chicken soup coming out my eyeballs and was feeling well enough to be anxious that school was starting up again in less than a week. I had a scant six days left of my two-week vacation, at least three of which would have to be devoted to catching up on grading and prepping the last topic of the semester—*moon phases*, the highlight of every thirteen-year-old's life. A little voice in the back of my head reminded me I also had the semester exam to write, but I managed to ignore it.

Figuring on at least one day of procrastination left me with basically tomorrow to cram in the great vacation I had planned. I needed to get out of my parents' house right away.

My mother came in my room with a breakfast tray and unaccountably agreed. I should have known something was up when she further announced that she had taken the morning off from her frighteningly successful real estate business to take me home. (She could sell ice cubes to Eskimos, as the saying goes, though frankly she would never waste her time with something so low commission.) She even helped me pack.

I dozed in the car, awakening when she shut off the engine to the façade of a building I'd never seen before. I blinked. "This is not my apartment," I said brilliantly.

"I made an appointment with Dr. Nagata for your face."

I opened my mouth automatically to protest her highhandedness, but the words never came out. I was worried about my skin, too. It hadn't cleared up and the red scaly rash had spread to my hands and neck. It was spreading so fast I could swear it had gotten worse in the car.

After a careful examination, and a bunch of tests to which I was too tired to pay any more than the vaguest attention, Dr. Nagata ordered me to stand outside on the sunny landing. He stood with me, watching my face and his watch with equal concentration. "Umm, hmm," he concluded after a couple of minutes. "Just as I thought." He escorted me back into the private room and bade me sit.

Regarding me over his half glasses with that stern compassion doctors do so well, he told me the problem, explaining the results and implications of all the tests he'd done.

He misread my blank, disbelieving stare as confusion and added, "What it boils down to, Jo, is you have become allergic to the sun."

"Oh, no," my mother said. Yes, of course she had insinuated herself into the room with me. "You mean like that poor little girl on *60 Minutes* who can't go out in the sun or she'll die?"

What? What kind of designer quack had my mother taken me to? Was he even a real doctor? *Allergic to the sun*, I mean, really! "I've gone out in the sun my entire life," I said, "and have never had a problem before. 'Allergic to the sun' seems a little extreme. Are you sure it's not a simple allergic reaction to my face lotion or some sort of side effect of my flu? The problem *is* coincident with my cold, and it's not only my skin that has been affected. My vision has been a little blurry too."

"I'm sure," he said. "In fact, it might be the other way around. The flu symptoms you had might have been your body's way of responding to the allergy, and I'm not surprised your vision is a little blurry. After all, the cells covering your eyes would be sensitive to the sun's rays as well."

At my mother's gasp, the doctor paused and turned toward her, as if to offer support. My mother has that effect on men, but their instinctive efforts to prop her up are completely unnecessary. If anyone can take care of herself, it's my mother.

I must have made some sort of noise, for the doctor turned back to me and said, "I realize it sounds odd. Frankly I'm a little hesitant in calling it a sun allergy, because as you said, it's rare, it's unlikely, and to be frank, it's rather unheard of for someone to develop it so late in life. But as Holmes said, 'Once the other stuff has been ruled out, whatever's left, however unlikely, is the answer.'"

Evidently, the good doctor couldn't make it as an English professor and had gone into medicine instead. As my mother and I sat silently contemplating my sunless future in respective states of horror and denial, he spelled out the rules, which boiled down to no exposure to the sun, not even through a window.

"You're kidding, right?" I burst out. "How am I supposed to get around? Wear a ski mask in the car? What about my job? There's not a room in the school that doesn't have some light coming in through the windows."

Dr. Nagata listened patiently to my whining, even venturing an opinion that yes, the ski mask wouldn't be a bad idea so long as I wore a really good sunscreen under it, though he would supply me with something a little better. He went to a supply closet in the corner of the room and after a few minutes' rummaging returned with a small, clear package containing something beige and squashy.

My mother poked suspiciously at the lump of cloth. "What is that?" she asked, curling her lip in disdain.

"It's a top of the line face mask. Lightweight, stretchy, molds instantly to any face shape, and best of all, it's rated SPF 75," he said, beaming as if he'd pulled out the cure for cancer.

"You'll need to wear it any time you're outdoors during daylight hours (though, of course, it would be best if you avoided daylight altogether), and any time you're in a sunny room."

"So—all the time?" I said.

My mother looked horrified. "Surely, she can get away with sunscreen when she's inside."

"Well, now." He spoke jovially, as if all we needed was little perspective. "I suppose it's not really necessary once the sun goes down. And if you're in a dark room during the day, a high SPF would probably be sufficient, but I think you'll find the mask so comfortable, you'll wear it all the time. I think it's really rather sharp."

He took our silence for agreement, but my mother and I were just too appalled to contradict him. He wrote me a prescription for some seriously heavy-duty sunblock and another for something to soothe my skin. He also gave me a note for the headmaster explaining my new "disability", and advised me to use copious amounts of aloe, and then his nurse herded us out the door.

* * * * *

I spent the rest of the day alternating between freaking out and total denial, before surrendering to the common denominator—self-pity. I hate to admit it, but as I discovered to my great shame that afternoon, I am weaker—and more concerned with my appearance—than I'd ever thought I would be. My mother had rubbed off on me.

I was so upset I had to go out for emergency fries. I ordered a double bacon cheeseburger to go with them and ate every scrap. Then I went home and worked my way through about a pound of chocolate.

About the time I reached for the mint chip ice cream, I began to feel claustrophobic, probably from being so fat in such a small apartment, and forced myself to go out for a walk. I didn't care that it was after nine at night. In fact, I almost wished someone would put me out of my misery by sticking a knife in my back or shoving me under the wheels of a truck.

Questions without answers shot though my mind again and again. How would I live? With these insane restrictions, I didn't know if I could keep teaching. How had this happened? Why me? I hadn't wanted to say anything to Dr. Nagata in front of my mother, but I couldn't help but wonder if the emergency room doctors might have missed something. Maybe I had a rare disease they hadn't tested for! Maybe Will *had* infected me with something. It was a little science fiction urban myth, but maybe he hadn't bitten me out of misplaced lust or lame Goth fantasies; maybe he had some disease that made him bite me *and* could explain my sun allergy...like some mutated form of rabies! I don't think the emergency room had tested me for anything like *that*. Did I need to go back? Had I been unusually thirsty lately? I made a mental note to look up the symptoms of rabies and to do a full Internet search on obscure diseases. Will had an accent—he must have traveled around a bit. Maybe he'd picked up something in some dark corner of a forgotten forest in Eastern Europe. Been bitten by some insect or animal—wasn't that kind of how AIDS had started?

As my thoughts got weirder and more absurd, I walked faster and faster, fueled by anxiety and my umpteen-thousand calorie snack. I walked at warp speed for over an hour, not paying much attention where I went.

Once or twice I thought I heard footsteps behind me but I didn't see anyone when I turned to look. Frankly, I didn't much care if someone accosted me. I almost relished the thought of taking out my stress on someone fool enough to tangle with a well-sugared woman on the edge.

By the time I'd circled back and my apartment was nearly in sight, I was exhausted. I hadn't fully recovered from the flu and this was far more exercise than I'd gotten in the last seven days combined, but my freakout was over. I had come to terms with Dr. Nagata's diagnosis and no longer felt the need to research every disease in the world in an attempt to prove him wrong. All I wanted to do now was crawl into my bed and go to sleep.

I was about to turn down my street when I noticed a small, dark car cross an intersection a couple blocks up. I couldn't be sure of the car's color, but I was pretty sure it had a bike rack on the roof.

Gavin?

The car had had its right turn signal on and would drive right past me, up on the next block. My fatigue was forgotten. I made an abrupt ninety-degree turn and ran up a side street for a closer look at the car, but I hadn't gotten more than halfway when the car whizzed by, little closer than it had been the first time.

"Damn!" I said when I could catch my breath.

I turned and headed home. It only took a few steps before I was sure the car had a bike rack. By the end of the block I had convinced myself it was Gavin's car.

Was he stalking me?

I *had* worried about Gavin after I'd learned he'd lied to me about being a taxi driver, but only a little. With all that had happened lately, I hadn't really given him much thought. I thought about him now.

He'd had the run of my apartment that night while I lay dead to the world in my bedroom. I hadn't noticed anything missing, but for all I knew, he'd gone out and made copies of my keys. Maybe tonight he'd gone back in! As these chilling thoughts ran through my head, I became aware of my footsteps echoing loudly in the still, cool night air, like an auditory beacon for muggers and weirdoes. It wasn't long before I had that strange feeling again of being followed. I picked up my pace.

I was only two blocks away from my apartment, but it might have well have been two miles. The quaint stucco houses and duplexes usually charmed me with their whimsical architecture. But tonight all I saw of the arches, recessed doorways and winding staircases were dark looming shadows large enough to hide a homicidal maniac *and* his chainsaw. I stepped off the sidewalk and walked down the middle of the empty street. Just in case.

As I passed the dark, silent alley behind my apartment building, my downstairs neighbor flicked the light on in his bathroom. Pale yellow beams radiated from his tiny opaque window into the alley, illuminating a small area near the dumpster. Something there caught my eye: a faint gleam of leather, as from a man's shoe, moving smoothly and silently from the penumbra of light back into the shadows.

My heart thumped loudly in my chest and my mouth went dry. I wanted to run, but I knew I couldn't risk it. I didn't have enough of a head start. My only recourse was to act naturally, pretend I hadn't seen anything, and hope whoever was hidden in the alley wanted to stay that way as much as I wanted them to.

I rounded the corner of my apartment building at a slow saunter and managed to get as far as the mailboxes before I gave in to panic and ran full tilt up the stairs to the second floor. I fumbled badly with the locks, turning the key in the wrong direction before I finally got the door open. Once inside, I slammed the deadbolt and latched the security chain that my dad had installed the day I moved in. Though I wanted nothing more than to run to hide behind my couch, I stayed by the door and tried to quiet my breathing as I listened for footsteps or breathing on the other side.

I couldn't hear a thing. After a few minutes my heart stopped pounding as if it were trying to escape from my chest, and I got up the courage to peek around the edge of the blinds. I didn't see anyone out there, but turning my back to the shadows *in* my apartment made the hair on the back of my neck stand out. *Was someone* in *my apartment?* Making as little noise as possible, I crept over to the chair where I had dumped my purse earlier, pulled out the cell phone and carefully dialed 9-1-1. Keeping my finger hovered over the *Send* button, I picked up the heavy flashlight I keep on my bookshelf in case the power ever goes out and went through my apartment.

I looked in every room and behind every door, checking every possible hiding place, including my tiny joke of a linen closet that has built-in shelves a mouse couldn't stand on, and under my bed, as if someone could possibly have squeezed in with all the crap I store there. When I was finally satisfied I wasn't harboring any murderers, I turned off the phone, put the flashlight back on the bookshelf and collapsed on the couch.

It was definitely time to bust out the mint chip ice cream.

Chapter Five

ಐ

"Are we watching a movie?" my students asked excitedly as they entered the classroom Monday morning after the holidays and saw the curtains drawn. It was a temporary solution to my problem, at best, as the ill-fitting, cracking curtains only blocked part of the light. Don't ask me what they were made of. Plastic? Polyurethane? Old toilet paper rolls and kindergarten paste? I wasn't sure what I would do when lunchtime rolled around and direct sun came streaming in through the gaps.

That's denial speaking—I'd have to wear the mask, of course. I just didn't want to.

"No, we are *not* watching a movie," I said to the usual chorus of boos and whines. There was a brief moment of silence while I drummed up the nerve to tell them about my sun allergy. I took a deep breath, blocked off my emotions as best I could, and threw myself to the wolves. The response was overwhelming. I'd never seen my students so excited inside the classroom.

"No, I am not the elephant man."

"Yes, I do have to wear that mask on my desk when I go out during the day."

"No, I am not planning a new career as burglar, but that's a very good idea and I certainly will consider it."

"Yes, the test will still be on Friday."

Little monsters.

By the time I got through my first-period class I felt like a delicate prairie wildflower after a stampede had gone through, but it was just the beginning of that morning's hell.

Earlier that morning, before school, I had gone to speak to the headmaster about my sun allergy. After listening to my tale of woe, he had patted me on the shoulder and told me he had every confidence some arrangement could be worked out, that there was no reason why we couldn't find places for me to teach that didn't subject me to direct light.

My grateful smile faded when he went on to tell me I would need to work out any changes to my schedule or classroom with my department head. Rotten Roger was the last person I wanted to discuss my sun allergy with. He was the last person I would want to discuss *anything* with.

But it had to be done or I would be That Weird Teacher With The Mask for the rest of my career. Roger and I both had the second period free. I pulled back out the note Dr. Nagata had given me, took a deep breath, and forced myself down the stairs to Roger's classroom.

Fifteen minutes later I returned to my classroom and collapsed in the chair behind my desk. I stared at the black-topped lab benches, unaccustomedly aligned from a holiday cleaning in two straight lines, à la Miss Clavel in those *Madeline* books I loved as a child. Roger's unsympathetic words repeated over and over in my head. "If we changed your schedule—even if it could be done, which I doubt—not only would it create problems for many students and several other faculty members, but it would be unfair to them as well. Why should so many people have to suffer to accommodate your dermatological problems? If it troubles you so much, perhaps you should take a leave of absence until it clears up."

A bell rang to signal the morning break, and seconds later Carol appeared at my door carefully balancing three cups of coffee. Though her usual smile was very much in evidence, the mild brown eyes behind the gold-rimmed glasses were dark with concern. Becky appeared moments later, a little out of breath from running all the way up from the chem lab. I did a double take. Her bleached silver and crimson hair was back to its native black.

Carol handed the coffee around. "We thought we'd save you a trip down to the terrace, limit your sun exposure." Her cheerfulness seemed a little forced. I didn't bother to ask how they'd found out about my sun allergy. I would have been surprised if they didn't know.

Becky shut the door behind her and cut right to the chase as usual. "This way you can avoid all the curious stares and questions." She grinned and added, "It'll give everyone more time to make stuff up about you. By the end of the day, you should have your pick of diseases *with* accompanying stories of how you got them."

Their good cop/bad cop, or rather sympathy/screw 'em, routine had its usual cheering effect. I took a grateful sip of coffee. Well, not too grateful. "God this stuff is worse than I remembered," I said with a grimace.

"Had to get it from the lounge," Carol explained, apologetically. The cafeteria put out an industrial-sized urn of coffee on the terrace for the teachers at morning break and at lunch. Anyone who wanted caffeine at odd times was stuck with whatever was left in the coffee maker in the faculty lounge. It was barely tolerable if you caught it fresh brewed but more often than not, you were stuck with a noxious bitter syrup that had been condensing on the burner for hours.

Becky hitched a leg on a lab bench after automatically checking first to make sure it was clean. "So what's with this disease you've contracted?"

"Sun sensitivity," I said dismissively. "What's with your hair?"

She shrugged. "Grandparents. They're pretty old school."

"She does this every year. Goes conservative for a few weeks," Carol said.

"Re-ally," I said, intrigued by this unexpected display of conformity. I tried to imagine Becky in a twin set and failed.

"It's just hair," Becky said impatiently. "Stop trying to change the subject."

I gave in and explained Dr. Nagata's diagnosis and that he had prescribed no sun exposure. "And I mean zero. I'm taking a great risk here, only wearing SPF five thousand, inside, with the curtains drawn, on the shaded side of the building. "I held up the mask disgustedly with one finger, as if it smelled, and admitted I would have to wear it that afternoon when the sun hit my west-facing classroom.

Becky was horrified and gave Carol a meaningful look that said "Do something!"

Carol did. "I have the computer room reserved this week, but I don't really need it today. Why don't you teach your afternoon classes in there until we figure out a longer term solution—if you're not doing a lab or anything that needs space?"

It was a windowless room down the hall with a whiteboard and room for twenty. "No, that's perfect, thank you." My eyes got suspiciously bright and I reached for a tissue to dab them. I swear, I'd been a weepy mess since I'd contracted that stinking skin allergy.

Carol pretended she didn't notice and turned the conversation away from me. "Have you been following the articles about the missing woman?"

"I don't think so. What articles?" I said.

"Ooh, I did," Becky said, shivering theatrically. "I read about it on the plane. Creepy!"

Carol said, "A woman reported missing around the holidays was last seen at that restaurant we went to for our department dinner—"

"The same night we were there!" Becky said.

Carol nodded. "She was last seen talking to some man with dark hair."

I felt sick. My hand moved automatically to my neck, fingering the bandage hidden under my turtleneck. The wound wasn't healing well. I really should have showed it to Dr.

Nagata when I'd had the chance, but I had been too embarrassed to discuss how I'd gotten it in front of my mother. I chided myself for being paranoid. It wasn't even infected, just healing slowly, doubtlessly because of my skin problem.

"Did they give a description?" I asked.

"I think they said she was tall, with brown hair," Carol said, misunderstanding who I meant.

"Don't worry," Becky said dryly, watching me. "It wasn't Hot Man. The description didn't match and no one could have forgotten what *he* looked like. Speaking of Hot Man...what happened that night?"

Before I could form an answer, the bell rang signaling the end of the break. "Saved by the bell," Becky said, giving me a knowing look. She opened the door to the roaring wave of students clambering upstairs for third period science. "Don't worry. We'll catch up on that subject later. I want *all* the details," she said, and followed Carol out.

* * * * *

At lunchtime I ate one of my emergency energy bars at my desk, flushing out the meal with tap water from the sink in the back of my room, and some crackers left over from a lab. I knew I was being cowardly, but I'd suffered through gawking and questions from three classes worth of students already, and didn't feel the need to prove anything by submitting myself to more gawking and questions from my colleagues.

When I was sure the hall was empty, I took out my grade book and ducked across to the computer room with the virtuous intention of updating my grading program. After a few tedious minutes of entering grades, however, I gave in to my curiosity and went online to read about the missing girl.

Becky had been right, the description of the man didn't sound like Will. It was a very generic description of a dark-haired man, and I agreed with her opinion that no witness—no female, anyway—could have forgotten Will. I breathed a sigh of relief. He might have been a little out there for me, but at least I hadn't made out with a felon.

* * * * *

The science department always met the first Monday of the month, holiday or no holiday. When classes were over, we duly assembled with varying displays of stoicism, grumbling or noble suffering, except for Roger who seemed particularly excited today, doubtlessly with the anticipated pleasure of cutting short my indifferent career. Carol came in last, late and out of breath. She gave me a surreptitious wink as she assumed her usual position on my left, and then studiously ignored me as Roger opened the meeting.

"The first order of business," Roger began after a glance at his typewritten agenda, "is, once again, the supplies budget. I remind you that all receipts must be turned in before the semester ends. That's two weeks, people. I encourage you all to order now what supplies you will need for the third quarter."

Frustrated, I closed my eyes and counted to ten. It was abundantly clear Roger had filed me under New Business; he was going to make me wait until the end of the meeting. Torturing me that way was just the sort of power abuse he delighted in. If he was lucky, we'd run out of time before we could discuss me. I'd either have to suffer for another month or be the reason why everyone had to reconvene another day, conveniently ensuring enough animosity toward me that he could push forward whatever draconian plan he devised.

My discomfort must have been apparent, for Carol put a restraining hand on my arm under the table.

"Roger," she said briskly, in the firm, no-nonsense voice that made her students sit up and listen, "I think we are all clear on the budget issue by now. I move we discuss the emergency issue of how to accommodate Jo's disability."

Roger's heavy eyebrows formed a deep V over his small black eyes. He raised his voice a little and replied irritably,

"New Business is always discussed at the end of the meeting, Carol."

"Pressing issues preempt Continuing Business, and are discussed at the beginning of the meeting, Roger," she corrected.

"I'm with Carol," Becky said. "I move to table the budget discussion so we can figure out a way to help Jo."

Grandmotherly Mary Mudget looked up from her knitting. Mary taught seventh grade science and, despite a rather crisp demeanor, was the sort of teacher so beloved her students came back to visit her years later. The emerging pale pink sweater was for one of their progeny. She fixed Roger with a stern look. "Second."

Bob's handsome blond head jerked up as he pulled his attention away from the coaching diagram hidden in his notebook. "What's wrong with Jo?"

I was getting tired of being talked about as if I were a pesky line item in the budget. "I've got a sun allergy," I said. "I can't be exposed to any sunlight, even through a window, or I get all red and crusty."

"It is not appropriate to discuss one's personal medical issues in the department meeting—"

"No way, man, that sucks!" Bob said sympathetically, ignoring Roger. "Even if you wear sunscreen?"

"Even if I slather myself in a thick white coating of zinc oxide."

"That's awful! So you can't even bike to work anymore or anything?"

"Bob, Jo, can you please continue your personal discussions after the meeting?" Roger said. The fluorescent track lighting turned Roger's olive complexion a sickly green and he looked even more like a swamp thing than usual as he glared at us.

"This is more important than the stupid budget, Roger," Bob said.

"Yeah," piped in Kendra, putting down her own coaching diagrams.

Touched by (nearly) everyone's concern, I looked away and blinked a few times, willing myself not to show weakness in front of Roger.

"Jo's room is fine in the morning, I think," Carol said, taking control of the meeting, "until around eleven when the sun hits that part of the building."

"She can switch rooms with me," offered Alan. "I'm on the other side of the building and have the opposite sun pattern." Alan was the rather studious African-American physics teacher. He taught just across the hall from me, but I didn't know him very well. He kept to himself. Carol says it's because he's avoiding all eye contact until the open season for college letters of recommendations is over.

"Impractical," Roger said dismissively. "Her room's not set up for physics labs."

"Why not my room then," Kendra said.

"Her rooms not set up for physical science labs either," Roger said, looking almost cheerful. He seemed to enjoy shooting down ideas.

I began to panic in earnest. On my salary, I could barely afford my tiny apartment, and had no savings to speak of. If I lost this job, I'd have to move back in with my parents.

Unexpectedly, it was not Carol or Becky, but Mary Mudget who leapt to my rescue, the knight with the iron-gray bun. "Well then, why doesn't Jo teach biology in the afternoon? The semester ends in two weeks; it will hardly be a continuation issue, and she does have a degree in the subject." She spoke mildly, as if we were discussing nothing more important than our spring vacation plans, her knitting needles clicking away in a blur of pink Angora. "Taking over my seventh grade classes is a little tricky because earth science is not my forte, but she could certainly switch with Bob and teach tenth grade biology."

Roger gaped at her. He taught a mix of seventh and ninth grade science, showing his commitment to both Upper and Lower School and his versatility as a teacher. Because self-promotion comes as naturally as breathing to Roger, this had all been made clear to me within five minutes of meeting him. However, despite all the self-aggrandizing pomp, everyone knows he wants biology, the plum of high school science, but that was Bob's job. Bob had a Ph.D. from Berkeley. Don't ask me what Bob was doing teaching high school with those credentials. If I had 'em, I'd be out of there faster than you can say "big paycheck".

The idea that I, a green teacher, would get Roger's coveted biology class turned the man's face a deeper shade of red than my own sun-damaged one. "No!" he burst out. "It is inappropriate. The students, the parents..." he sputtered angrily.

"I think Roger's right," Carol said. She pitched her voice a little louder to cover my gasp of surprise. "It would be best for Jo's students if she continued to teach them."

Well that was something, I thought. At least she had implied I was a good teacher as she let me down.

She pulled some photocopied pages from her notebook and handed a copy to Roger. "I have three estimates for true blackout curtains for Jo's room. They don't let in any visible light and block a hundred percent of UV rays. But they do let air circulate."

"Amazing what these new materials can do," murmured Mary Mudget.

Roger frowned and tossed the estimates on the table. "Too expensive," he said dismissively.

"Actually," Carol said with smile that was just this side of a smirk, "they're not. We have money in Jo's budget for half, and Maxine will pitch in the balance from the Middle School President's discretionary fund."

"It's about time someone could teach Astronomy properly in that room," said Mary Mudget approvingly. "It's always been too light in there to do constellations and eclipses properly."

And with that, before Roger or I knew what had happened, we had fixed my problem.

An hour later, after the meeting had adjourned, Becky and Carol followed me into my room, "to measure the windows".

I began rifling through my junk drawer for a tape measure, but Carol stopped me with a gentle hand on my wrist. "Don't bother. They've already been measured and I sent in the order as soon as I got Maxine's okay." Her eyes twinkled a little wickedly, but it may just have been the light reflecting off her glasses. "We even sprang for rush delivery, since you start eclipses this week. They should arrive in two days."

I pushed my junk drawer shut and threw my arms around Carol.

"It wasn't just me," Carol said grinning happily. "Mary helped box in Roger with that little dog and pony show."

"I helped too," Becky said, "by shutting up. And I want you to know how much a sacrifice it was to let Mary say the part about your teaching high school bio."

I was so elated by the news that not even wearing the face mask could bring me down. Instead of waiting until dark like I had planned, I put on the awful mask and followed Becky and Carol out. Between the flu and my sun allergies, I hadn't been outside much during the day and just seeing the sun yellowing near the horizon, casting gold highlights onto the silvery blue water, cheered me enormously. For the first time since Dr. Nakata had delivered the bad news, I felt that things were going to work out okay.

The drive home was short and pretty. Bayshore Academy occupies the tip of a flat finger of land that runs along the ocean, beach on one side, bay on the other. The school had been built for pennies back when Long Beach was an unfashionable, flood-prone backwater. Its simple stucco buildings had probably been considered cheap and déclassé at the time, but I found the contrast of their near blinding whiteness against their red tiled roofs rather elegant and I adore the flowers everyone seems to plant against stucco—big, bright spills of magenta bougainvillea, tall, reaching columns of purple-blue morning glories, and fat hedges of yellow daisies and fragrant mock orange.

I live three miles down the beach in a cute little neighborhood of sweet little cottage-style beach homes that, thanks to the recent real estate boom, now go for a cool million. I didn't live in one of those. I lived in a tiny apartment on one of the crowded apartment-row streets tacked on the outskirts of the sweet little neighborhood.

I had to fight for a parking spot four blocks away, and by the time I made it up to my apartment I was giddy with hunger. I dumped my book bag at the foot of my desk and made a beeline for the fridge. After a quick inventory, I discarded plans for a healthy salad and made myself a giant, rare roast beef and horseradish sandwich that I inhaled standing over the sink.

I flopped on my old tweedy loveseat in a post-prandial stupor and snuggled down under an afghan knit by my grandmother to watch the second half of an old Fred Astaire and Ginger Rogers movie. It was a rare night that I didn't have papers to grade and I planned to enjoy it. When the movie was over, I flipped lazily through the channels and settled on the local news.

The networks had gotten hold of a picture of the missing woman. When they showed it, I got up in surprise and moved closer to the screen. They had called her a brunette in the Internet article I'd read at lunch, but she wasn't, not really. Her hair was auburn, a very dark red. She was tall, about my height, about my weight. Had another reporter covered the story, he or she might have described her differently. They might have described me.

A chill ran through my limbs, taking my happy mood with it. I grabbed my heavy flashlight from the bookshelf and did a quick intruder-check of the apartment, turning on all the lights as I went.

There was no one there but me. Of course. I settled back down on the couch for about a second before I jumped back up and turned off all the lights.

I huddled in the dark for a half hour wondering anxiously if the flickering of the TV was too obvious a sign I was home before sanity was restored. I gave myself a good tongue lashing for being so ridiculous. My fear wasn't born of anything more dangerous than self-pity. I had been spending too much time hiding indoors lately and it was taking its toll. So I couldn't go outside in the daylight. So I had to drive to work instead of biking, or running along the beach. So did most people! Sitting inside fretting and feeling sorry for myself wouldn't change anything. I needed to get out of my apartment and exercise something other than my imagination. It wasn't even seven o'clock. It was perfectly safe, certainly no worse than sitting alone and scared in a dark apartment.

Full of bravado, and calmed by the number of dog-walking families out and about, I ran full-out for two miles before I turned around and jogged back at a more sane pace, taking a different route for variety's sake. As I turned down a side street to approach my apartment from the other direction, I saw a small, four-door car that looked terrifyingly familiar. I crossed the street to get a closer look. It was, as I had suspected, a blue Jetta. It had a bike rack on top.

But this time I wasn't scared. I was furious.

I took some deep breaths and told myself to calm down, to approach this rationally, to think it through before I plunged a foot into his door and caused damage I couldn't afford. I didn't even know if this car belonged to Gavin Raines. But if it did — and I thought it did — what in blue blazes was he doing here?

As if in answer, the description of the purported Long Beach Abductor popped into my head — about six feet tall, dark hair, brown eyes. Gavin, I remembered, had grey eyes, not brown, but that was an easy mistake to make in a dimly lit restaurant, on par with dark red hair being recalled as brown. I leaned down and quickly read the license plate, made just visible by a distant street light, and committed it to memory. Just in case. Then I ran the short distance back to my apartment and locked myself in.

The evening news (which I watched with all the lights on, even the one in my closet) had an update on the missing girl. The good news was the police had found her. The bad news was she was dead.

The footsteps I thought I'd heard on my walk the other night and the person I thought I'd seen in the alley took on sinister new meaning. So did Gavin's repeated appearances in my life. I thought back to his story and reconsidered all the gaping holes and absurd rationales that I had cowardly ignored. What had I been thinking, not calling the police after a complete stranger had spent the night uninvited in my apartment? Even if I had initially believed his story about being an overly conscientious taxi driver, it hadn't been more than a half hour before the real taxi service had debunked it. Having the flu was no excuse for stupidity.

I spent the night sleeping with one eye open, one hand wrapped around an old baseball bat. By morning, my fear had been replaced with resolve. No more huddling inside, no more freaking out over "what if". I was going to check Gavin's story. Today.

I didn't have a convenient friend who could run plates for me. I had to do it the good old-fashioned way. As soon as school was out, I was going to the police.

Chapter Six
ℬ

I handed the completed forms to the uniformed desk sergeant. He accepted them absently, his focus clearly on other things.

"Look," I began, and then stopped. I forced myself to switch to a more respectful salutation. "Excuse me, Officer, ah, Brady?"

"Yes, miss?"

It was a start. "Officer, I'm very concerned about this man. I believe he is stalking me."

His response was cut short by another officer who came by to ask him a question. The station was busy, but this was ridiculous. I stared intently at his head, willing him to pay attention to me. Eventually, he turned back. "Yes, miss?"

"The stalker?" I said to jog his memory.

"I have the papers you filled out right here, miss. I assure an officer will get right on it, the moment one is free. But I must tell you, miss, we're very busy. Since a crime hasn't been committed, I'm afraid I have to inform you your alleged stalker is low on our priority list."

"Can't you at least run his plates? Make sure he isn't a psycho? He drives a blue Jetta. It has a bike rack on it. Yakima."

The officer's pale blue eyes focused on me for the first time. I must have looked as desperate as I felt for he took pity on me. "You say you wrote down the license plate number?"

"1CJI110," I said, reciting from memory. "I wrote it on the form."

"Hold on please, miss. Just one moment."

He left and had a quick talk with another officer, who came forward and looked at me curiously. "Hi, Miss…"

"Gartner. Jo Gartner."

"Miss Gartner. Follow me, please." He took me to a small, windowless office and gestured at the utilitarian chair in front of a messy desk. "Someone will be right with you," he said. He disappeared back into the bowels of the Police Department.

I gave myself points for having had the initiative to get the license plate number. It just goes to show what a little ingenuity and persistence can do for you—it had gotten me from the bottom of the waiting list to the top.

Ten minutes passed. Then fifteen. As the clock ticked past the twenty minute mark, I began to wonder if they'd stowed me there just to get me out of the way. Just as I'd drummed up the courage to go find the officer who'd put me there, the door opened to admit the back half of a plain-clothed officer. It was a rather nice back half, as things go, but that didn't keep me from becoming impatient as his conversation with whomever was in the hallway lagged on.

No sooner had the last words fallen from his mouth than he was moving again. He had gotten half the distance to his desk in two great strides before he realized he wasn't alone.

He stopped dead and stared at me. His face blanched slightly under his tan, bringing his bent nose into stark relief.

I stared back. "You!" I sputtered. I stood, collected my purse and headed for the door.

This roused him back into motion. "Jo? What the hell are you doing— Hold *on*." He grabbed my arm and escorted me back to the hard little chair. Then he shut the door and stood squarely in front of it.

"What are you doing here?" he demanded.

I glared at him, outraged. *He* was taking that tone with *me*?

"Well, Officer, er..." Drat it, I couldn't remember his last name. "Gavin, if that *is* your occupation and your name—"

"Detective Gavin Raines," he supplied politely. An unsaid *At your service, ma'am* hung in the air. My temper ratcheted up a couple notches.

"*Detective*—" I corrected waspishly. "I am here to report that a man pretending to be a taxi driver is stalking me. He broke into my house and spent the night uninvited on my couch. He drives a blue Jetta with a bike rack and I have seen it parked near my house the past few nights. The good news is I am now able to positively identify him for the desk sergeant and will take no more of your time." I stood up again but didn't get very far with my grand exit because Gavin was still blocking the door like a sentry.

I planted myself two feet in front of him, and if a glare could have burned a path through him, mine would have. "I'll probably get a medal, since it appears he's also masquerading as a police officer and a graduate student. You might even pick him up on false ID charges. A minor infraction, I know, but you know how the police are these days, honesty above all, and—"

His composure finally broke. "Sit down!"

He closed his eyes and leaned back against the door. "Sit, Jo, please."

I sat.

"Ah, hell," he said, rubbing his temples. "How did you— Brady's got desk duty, doesn't he? Probably recognized the plates right off. The next time his wife kicks him out, he can stay in a hotel." He fixed me with those unusual grey eyes. "Let me explain."

I crossed my arms and leaned back defiantly in my chair. "It better be good."

He spoke quickly, all trace of the bashful graduate student gone. "Four people, two women and two men, have been abducted and murdered in the past two months, all of them last seen in downtown restaurants. We believe the abductions are related, part of a," he hesitated slightly, "gang initiation. We had a tip some members of this gang might be at the club the night you were there. When I saw you come in from the porch, visibly upset, clearly having been in some sort of skirmish, I wondered if you had narrowly escaped becoming the next victim. I checked the porch area to see who you'd been with, but it was empty, and I was concerned he might be waiting for you out front, intending to follow you home.

"When I went back inside, you had left the dance area. Fortunately, I found you back with your colleagues, overheard you telling them you were going to take a taxi. I had my car pulled around and took you home instead. You know the rest." He shrugged.

I mulled this over quietly. "How did you get the UCLA card?" It wasn't the question I thought I'd ask.

"My alma mater. I banked on your not noticing the date sticker was missing, and you didn't. I saw all the science textbooks on your shelves and figured you'd relax if I told you I was a grad student. I chose something far enough outside your field that you wouldn't ask questions." He gave a quick smile. "The 'dissertation' was based on an article I read in a magazine at the doctor's office."

I didn't return the smile. "How very clever of you." I got to my feet. "Now, if you're quite through mocking me, I have papers to grade."

This time he slowly stepped aside. I was halfway through the door before I realized he wasn't going to let me pass. As I stood, trapped, he reached out a hand and slowly pushed back my hair to reveal the bandage strip on my neck. His grey eyes burned into mine. "You should be more careful," he said.

I pushed him aside and left the way I had come, my sensible low heels making angry clicking noises on the linoleum.

I sat in my car in the police station parking lot, practicing yoga breathing until I was calm enough to drive. As my temper cooled, I reviewed what he'd told me. Not much, I realized. He'd carefully left out any and all useful information. But then, he hadn't asked *me* anything of importance, either. Not a single question about Will. Surely, since Will had somehow managed to leave the back area before Gavin arrived, the detective would have wanted a description at least. The more I thought about the past ten minutes, the less they made sense.

I began to get angry again, this time at myself. Why did I keep letting the man spin me gossamer tales? I should have stayed there and made him tell me more. I had a hundred questions I hadn't gotten a chance to ask because he'd gotten me riled up and I'd dutifully stormed out like a fool. But as badly as I wanted answers, I wasn't about to go back in there. He'd won this round, but I wasn't done with Detective Gavin Raines. Not by a long shot.

* * * * *

Despite my resolve to keep a cool head, I was disappointed when I got back from my run that evening and saw no signs of Gavin or his Jetta. I was still angry enough to hanker for another run-in with the detective. After a long hot shower and a quick dinner, I sat staring at a stack of ungraded papers for twenty minutes without making a single mark before I gave in and went back out to look for the Jetta. I walked around the block twice before I accepted that Gavin wasn't coming.

Why? Why would he stop staking out my place *now*? *Nothing that man did made any sense!* I headed back up the stairs to my apartment, but instead of going in I sat on the top step to mull things over. As I sat staring out to the street, a gold Ford Escort drove by, slowing slightly as it passed. I recognized the car because I'd parked next to it at the police station.

Gavin might not be following me anymore, but one of his minions was. Probably Officer Brady, if I read Gavin right.

After another slow turn around the block, the car parked a little way down the street. No one got out. It was so obvious a stake-out it was almost an insult. I wondered if it was deliberate.

I sketched a wave to the officer and went back inside, sat down at my desk, pushed my students' papers aside and began to plan. Really plan. This was war. If they were still watching me, they must think I was withholding information. That or I was still on the murderer's list. And yet all Gavin had done was tell me to be careful.

I didn't think much of the police work on this case. They hadn't exactly done a stellar job with the other four victims, had they? Gavin had as good as admitted the last girl had been abducted right under his nose.

I needed to protect myself. And if the detective wasn't going to level with me, give me the information I needed to arm myself, I would just have to go get it. The stalkee was becoming the stalker.

Chapter Seven
೫

The next evening I waited until the sun went down before heading back to the police station. The darkness fit my mood and my purpose. As it was about the same time I'd gone the day before, I expected Gavin would still be at work, and I was right. After a little hunting, I found his Jetta in the back lot reserved for officers. I parked on a side street, gathered my "to grade" folder in case I had a long wait and ducked into the coffee shop across from the station.

The coffee shop was one of those old mom-and-pop joints that looked as if it had been around forever and probably had. Under its load of framed, signed portraits of grinning customers, the walls were a comforting color of coffee whitened with cream. Padded booths covered in well-worn avocado-green vinyl lined the perimeter. The rest of the place was crammed with an irregular assortment of heavily varnished tables, bumped out of alignment by the legs and hips of customers trying to squeeze by. A heady smell of coffee, grilled onions and bacon filled the air. The place was busier than I would have expected.

As I hovered uncertainly a few feet inside the door, a passing waitress told me the drill—table service and dinner at the booths, coffee orders at the counter. Ignoring the rumbling of my stomach, I opted for the latter and scanned the menu board while a crusty old proprietor waited, his pencil stub hovering impatiently over a small, plain white pad of paper. Normally I would have ordered a latte—they were on the menu—but it would have taken more courage than I possessed to bring up foam preferences with that man. I ordered a plain black coffee.

He slapped a thick white mug on the counter, told me refills were a quarter and moved on to the person who had queued behind me while I dallied. I was headed toward the window to scout for a table when I felt a tap on my elbow.

I turned to see a familiar blond head. "Bob?" This was the last place I expected to find anyone from ritzy Bayshore, even another teacher.

"Hey, Jo," he said, greeting me with a friendly smile. "Looks like my secret's out." He gestured toward the thick stack of papers he'd been grading. "I come here to grade. It's the only coffee shop I know of that the students don't go to."

Poor Bob. I wouldn't be surprised if some of the more assertive female students followed him home. I gave him a sympathetic pat on his burly shoulder. "Your secret's safe with me," I assured him. "Is this place always this busy on weeknights?"

"Only on Blue Plate Special Tuesdays. Entrées are half-off before six. Otherwise it's dead as a doornail."

Before he could ask me what I was doing there, a short, athletic-looking woman in her early thirties hailed Bob from the doorway and headed toward us.

Bob performed the introductions. "Rachel, this is Jo, our eighth-grade science teacher. Rachel used to be my assistant soccer coach, but she's head coach over at Polytech now." He gave her an exaggeratedly martyred look and then clapped her good-naturedly on the back. "It was a huge loss for Bayshore, but I'm not surprised someone snapped her up, she's a great coach! We all miss her terribly."

Rachel's plain face glowed from the praise but she modestly shook her head. After she and I exchanged the usual pleasantries, she pointed to her watch and said to Bob, "We should get going, the game starts in half an hour and there might be traffic."

"Is it that late already?" Bob quickly stacked the papers he'd been working on and stowed them in a soft canvas case.

"We're going to check out the competition," he told me. "Silton Prep has a good soccer team this year, Bayshore will probably face them in the division finals. Wanna come?"

God, no. "Thanks, but I'm swamped. Lab reports." I held up my bag, glad I had thought to bring some along. "I'll take your table, though."

When they left I did a quick survey of the parking lot to make sure Gavin hadn't slipped away while I was chatting, and then settled down to do some work. I got through a scant handful of the lab reports I needed to grade that night before an eye strain headache kicked in. I really needed to go see an ophthalmologist about some glasses. Even if, as I still chose to believe, my "sun allergy" was only a temporary condition, papers waited for no man. The thought of all the finals I would have to grade once the semester ended made me decidedly queasy. I turned away from my papers with a sigh and stared out the window. Gavin was getting into his car.

Drat it! I shoved the labs back into my bag and ran to my car, but by the time I made the light, he was gone.

* * * * *

The rest of my week of stalking went much the same way — that is, badly. On the second night I tried hanging out in my parked car instead of in the coffee shop, but after a police cruiser circled the block twice, slowing each time it passed, I gave up on that plan and went back to the coffee shop. The third night, I managed to catch up with Gavin, only to lose him again after two blocks.

The coffee shop, meanwhile, was quickly on its way to becoming a Bayshore hangout. A few days after seeing Bob there, I ran into Kendra, literally. I was rushing out a little before six, intending to get to my car before Gavin got to his, and collided with her in the doorway.

"Kendra! Hi. Sorry I almost mowed you down there," I said, steadying myself on a newspaper rack. "Are you okay?"

"I'm fine." She had changed from her usual teaching uniform of neatly pressed khaki pants and cotton shirt into dark sweatpants that flattered her lean physique. She probably had come straight from working out or coaching. As usual, she made me feel like the worst couch potato. "Where's the fire?"

Through the glass door behind her, I saw Gavin's blue Jetta exit the parking lot. "What? Oh. I don't think I put enough money in the meter," I lied.

She checked her watch. "You should be fine. You can park for free after six, you know."

"I know, but I've still got a couple minutes to six by my watch. I'd better check that meter in case the meter maids are trying to get in a few last tickets before the shift ends. You can have my table if you want." I pointed over to where I'd been sitting, and rushed out, leaving Kendra standing a little bemusedly in my wake.

Gavin was long gone.

The following Monday, I arrived at five-forty-five and made loops around the block. I almost missed seeing Gavin. He was leaving early.

I pulled into a bus zone until he passed me, let a few cars get between us, and then pulled out after him, feeling like a P.I. from the movies. Until I lost him. I cursed my incompetence until I realized where he was going—my apartment. It was merely his night for a stakeout. I stopped driving like a lunatic and just headed home.

Gavin wasn't there. After some more cursing and a few ever widening loops around town, I found him—or rather, his car parked near the local sports bar. I wasn't sure if he was there for business or pleasure, but there was only one way to find out. I parked and went in.

He wasn't at the bar or in the pool table area, which meant he was either in the men's room or had gone out to the back deck. The bartender was already giving me odd looks—

apparently I was as bad at lurking inconspicuously as I was at tailing—so I decided to try the back deck first.

It was a weeknight—no cover charge—and cold. They hadn't hired a bouncer to man the back door so there was no one to notice or care as I opened the door just wide enough to slip through.

It didn't take a brain surgeon to realize my clandestine efforts were totally unnecessary. Gavin wasn't there. In fact, I was alone except for two strangers making out as if *they* were alone, which they had been until I came out to watch. I felt as much like a voyeur as it sounds. Even more, I felt stupid. I stepped farther back into the shadows and prayed they didn't see me.

I was about to go back inside when the man let out a shrill, almost feral scream, fell to the ground and didn't get up again. His date didn't move to help him, just stood watching as he gave a last gasping breath and lay still. It had all happened so quickly I hadn't had a chance to help him.

I finally found my voice. "Oh my God, is he okay?" I stepped out of the shadows and hurried toward the fallen man. My sudden appearance startled the woman. She whipped around to face me and I let out a gasp of horror. There was an ugly smear of dark lipstick around her mouth. To my surprised and panicked brain, it looked like blood. She took a step toward me and then stopped, turned away and disappeared over the railing.

I felt his presence before I saw him.

As if mesmerized, I turned. He stood, tall and dark, on the edge of the platform as if waiting for me. Our eyes locked and my anger toward him melted away as if it had never been, leaving only the aching desire I remembered too well.

"Will," I said in a hushed voice.

He was just as piercingly handsome as I remembered, his body just as long and lean, his eyes as hauntingly blue. The little voice urging me to flee withered and died. I wanted him more than anything, with every particle of my being. I took a step toward him and then another until I stood before him, close enough to feel the warmth of his skin, to see his lips form my name as he reached for me.

As I lifted my foot to take the final step into his arms, something crossed my vision and struck Will in the chest before ricocheting to the ground with a clatter.

Will's eyes glittered with anger as he whipped around to see who had hurled the missile. I turned too, in time to see Gavin hurtling toward us, a long thin rapier in his hand. Will reached the inside pocket of his jacket and pulled out a knife.

"No!" I cried, watching helplessly. Will spared me a glance and in the next second was gone.

Gavin lowered his weapon, which I could now see was not a knife, only a wooden facsimile of one. "Was the 'no' for him or me?" He scowled, breathing heavily, and his grey eyes were hard with anger. He picked up the object he'd thrown at Will and sheathed the wooden knife in it with an angry *snick*. I recognized the innocent-looking result as the odd baton he'd held the morning after he'd spent the night unbidden in my apartment.

I opened my mouth, but no sound came out. I backed up until I felt the hard wall behind me. I clung to it like a drowning person clings to land. "I don't know what's going on…" My voice shook so much I barely recognized it as my own.

Gavin ignored me. He knelt by the fallen man and checked for signs of life.

I had forgotten about him. A sudden wave of guilt pierced the bubble of shock that had enveloped me. "Is he okay?" I asked in a small voice.

"He's dead." Gavin pulled out his cell phone and punched a button. "Yeah," he spoke quietly. "Another one. Same M.O. No, male. I don't know either." He flipped the phone shut and slid it back into a pocket. Still kneeling by the dead man's side, he bowed his head and let out a deep breath. "Dammit."

I inched closer. "What happened to him?"

Gavin looked up at me for a long moment and then rolled the man over.

At first all I could see was the blood. It was everywhere, on his neck, his face, saturating his shirt front. So much blood could only have come from one spot. My hand automatically reached up to touch my own neck as my eyes rested on the dead man's matching wound.

"Come here," Gavin instructed, grabbing my arm and pulling me down. I squatted awkwardly next to him, trying not to touch the man on the ground. Gavin's voice was harsh. "Find his pulse." When I balked, he repeated, "Find it!"

With shaking fingers, I reached down and touched the man's wrist. "Nothing." I spoke in a whisper.

"Is he breathing?"

Gavin's grip was like iron. I bent closer, listening for any signs. "No. He's dead."

Gavin let me go. "Remember that."

I stood up, stumbling a little in my haste to put some distance between us. Gavin remained where he was, watching me silently, waiting for me to speak.

I swallowed and said shakily, "If this is some sort of weird goth cult—"

"It's not a cult and you know it," he said calmly, getting to his feet.

"They're a bunch of crazy people, then," I said, taking a step back. I tried not to look at all the blood, but I couldn't stop staring at the man's neck. I wished desperately I had never come. I wanted to go home, to forget. Tears slid down my face but I didn't move to brush them away.

Gavin closed the gap between us in a couple angry strides and ripped the adhesive bandage half-off my neck. "The man who did that to you is perfectly sane, as is the woman who killed this man."

I shrank under the sudden onslaught. "I don't understand."

"Well, figure it out, dammit! It's not that hard!"

Behind Gavin, the dead man suddenly stood up and lunged for us like something out of a horror movie. It might have been comical if it weren't so frightening. Before I was done screaming, Gavin had turned, unsheathed his wooden knife and plunged it into the man's chest. The man blinked and subsided back to the ground.

I opened my mouth to scream again, but no sound came out. Gavin said harshly, "Go home, Jo."

I stood uncertainly, unable to move, mouth agape, eyes wide with fear.

"Now, Jo. Backup will be here any second. It will be better if you're not here."

I got home somehow — I don't remember driving — and locked the door tightly behind me. I sat huddled on the couch in the dark, waiting.

Chapter Eight

ॐ

Some time later, minutes, hours, I didn't know, a knock on the door got me up again. I shuffled slowly to the front door on feet that felt like lead. My hand moved automatically to the deadbolt, but I didn't unlock the door. Instead, I opened the peephole door that I hadn't used since the day I'd moved in and chuckled over its quaintness. A neat dark head filled the small view area.

"Jo. It's Detective Gavin Raines." The voice matched the vision.

Slowly and methodically, as if I were directing my own actions from some remote location, I relatched the tiny, eye-level door, released the deadbolt and let him in. Gavin shut and locked the door behind him and flicked on a light. In silence, he examined my face. Apparently he didn't like what he saw.

"Aw, hell. C'mon," he said, and steered me into the kitchen. "Let's get you something to eat. Sit here." He pushed me into one of the two chairs at the kitchen table and put water to boil on the stove while he rummaged around the cupboards. He pulled out hot chocolate mix, found the rum under the sink that I kept on hand for splashing into fruit cobblers and quickly and efficiently doctored a mug to his satisfaction. He pushed it toward me. "Drink. All of it."

It wasn't very hot and I downed it in a few gulps, like an obedient child.

"Feel better?"

Actually I did. I moved to stand up, but he pushed me back in my chair. "Not yet. You'll need some food in you or you're going to fall flat on the floor and I've had enough ambulances for one day. Got anything in here to eat?"

"I think I have some hamburger in the fridge." Ignoring his protest, I stood up again. "Let me do it. I need to do something to keep from—" My voice broke and he stepped aside.

I pulled out a package of hamburger, some condiments and some pre-washed salad mix and put them on the counter. "If you want to make yourself useful, you can cut the tomatoes and make the salad."

He regarded me closely for a moment and then ripped open the salad bag and dumped the contents into a bowl I'd left in the dish drainer. For a few minutes, we worked in silence. It wasn't a companionable one. As I formed the hamburger patties and put a pan to heat on the stove, my brain slowly began to function again and I reviewed the events of that evening. And what Gavin had said.

I slapped the hamburgers in the pan and then turned to face Gavin. "Why didn't you tell me?" I clenched my fists and moved closer. "You knew about those weirdoes and you didn't even warn me! I could have been next! What's wrong with you?"

"I did warn you," he said evenly. "I told you to be careful."

"Please! You tell someone to 'be careful' when they cross the street! When a crazy homicidal maniac takes a shine to them, you do a little more!"

"I did do a little more. I had round-the-clock shifts set up to watch you. Still do, to some degree. But you're an uncertain factor. I didn't know which side you were on. I still don't."

"What do you mean by that?"

His composure started to break. "Fine. If you won't say it, I will. Your would-be boyfriend, Will, is a vampire. Not a man pretending to be a vampire, not a member of an extremist Goth cult, the real thing. The local leader. He tried to recruit you.

Did you ever wonder why I spent that night on your couch, holding a stake? I didn't sleep—every second I expected you to come out that door and go for my throat, like tonight's victim did. But you didn't.

"Will tried to kill you, but he failed," Gavin said emphatically. He reached over and this time was successful in ripping off my adhesive bandage. It began to bleed.

I clapped a hand to my neck. "Stop that!"

"Don't bury your head in the sand and pretend he's an ordinary killer. Look at yourself! You can't go out in the sun without risking a third-degree burn, your vision is so damn blurry you could barely read my student ID the morning after he bit you, and you have teeth marks on your neck, marks that won't heal!" Disgust limned his voice.

He threw a dishtowel on the counter. "You're practically a vampire already!"

"Well, which is it?" I yelled back, removing my hand and letting the blood slide down my throat. "Am I a vampire, or aren't I?"

"I don't know. Neither! Both! Will *failed*. You didn't succumb, you fought. You didn't die, you survived. You didn't become one of them. But you're not normal. He changed you. You went right to the knife's edge, but you didn't tip either way. You tell me what you are!"

When he stopped, silence rang in the kitchen as loudly as his voice had been. We glared at each other for a long moment.

Then I laughed. "Don't be absurd. Vampires don't exist. You may be a policeman, but you're not a 'normal' one either— you have a very vivid imagination. The only thing wrong with me is that I've caught some sort of bug that gives me vampire-like symptoms. There's probably even a medical term for it, Vampire Syndrome or Dracula Flu."

I relaxed back against the counter, calmly wiping away the angry tears that had pooled in my eyes when Gavin had spoken. I got a fresh bandage out of a drawer to stop the bleeding on my neck. "Just listen to yourself! 'Will is a real vampire and he tried to recruit you!' Pu-leeze! You watch *way* too much TV, Detective."

His grey eyes glittered angrily, but he didn't say anything.

I began to form the rest of the hamburgers into patties for another meal and I went on, mockingly. "And it gets even better. Despite what the doctor says, you know better. I don't actually have a sun allergy—no, no, *that's* too far-fetched. The real reason for my skin problems and everything else is that I nearly became a vampire—only the head vampire couldn't manage to convert me properly, so I'm not quite 'Undead'. I'm merely, what, 'Underdead'?"

I began to laugh so hard I had to bend over and clutch my middle. Gavin didn't respond, said nothing, just watched me. When I was able to stand back up, I shook my head at Gavin's ridiculousness and went back to making hamburger patties with the leftover meat. Still chuckling, I pulled a small bit of raw hamburger meat off one of the patties, balled it up in my fingers, swished it around it in the pink liquid that had collected on the packaging, and popped it into my mouth, delighting in the flow of raw juices over my tongue.

A second ball of raw meat was on its way to my mouth before I realized what I was doing. Gavin looked away and went to the stove to flip the burgers before they burned. I sat down with a thump.

"I think I'd like mine rare," I said, and burst into tears.

After a mostly quiet dinner, Gavin flipped into professional mode, asking me questions while I made chocolate chip cookies. I'm a bit of a stress baker. That night, I automatically started out with a double batch.

I plunked a plateful by Gavin's elbow. He helped himself to one in the absent manner of someone used to eating sandwiches out of vending machines while writing reports. He took a bite and stared at it in surprise. "These are good." He helped himself to another. "Maybe it's a good thing you're not dead, after all."

"Don't eat all those or you'll get fat," I replied nastily.

"Not me." He patted his flat stomach. "I'm carb loading. I've got a biathlon coming up."

Hearing about something so normal—something I could no longer do—was sobering. I put down the spatula and sat heavily in the chair across from him. "Do you have any more questions for me?" I nodded toward the notebook he'd been writing in.

"No, I think I'm done for now." He closed the notebook and tucked it in his pocket.

"Well, I have some questions for you."

Gavin eyed me a little warily as he leaned back in his chair and crossed his arms loosely over his broad chest. "All right."

I paused to organize my thoughts, but it was hard to pick a single question from the multitude flashing around in my head.

"You said," I began hesitantly, "that Will is the head—er—vampire, but how do you know that? I thought you hadn't seen him before tonight."

"That's right, I hadn't. But if you recall, he made his position quite clear. He was training that female tonight—she responded instantly to his command to leave. Vampires live under a very rigid hierarchal system. It's a necessary counterbalance to the hedonism that drives them. Without clear leadership, they would rampage, killing without restraint."

"Isn't that what they want? I mean, wouldn't it be better for them if there were more vampires?" From what I'd read and seen on TV, vampires were always trying to take over the world.

Gavin nodded in understanding. "You'd think that, but it's not really how they work. They need two things to survive—fresh blood and secrecy. Every time they kill, they open themselves to persecution. Look at what's happened here. They've been in Long Beach only a few months and have killed only a handful of people, and yet the police are already closing in on them."

All that matter-of-fact talk of blood and killing made me feel sick. Nonetheless, I pressed on, determined to get the answers I needed. "Are there many of them?"

"I'm not sure, but from what I can tell it seems to be a fairly small group. They may have splintered off a larger one, seeking to establish a new base, or they could be a traveling group."

"A traveling group? Like gypsies?"

He nodded. "Some groups move continuously from town to town, coming and going before anyone really realizes they're there."

"I—" I swallowed. "It never occurred to me that there were so many of them."

"There are and there aren't. Many places are just too small and close-knit to support a vampire population, even a traveling one. As I said, secrecy is vital to their survival, and their particular mode of killing invites a lot of scrutiny. Besides, from what I can tell, there's a difference between feeding off someone and recruiting them. My theory is that the traveling groups exist to recruit new members. After a while, they either return to their original group or take root somewhere new, somewhere with a large population where they can feed without drawing too much attention to themselves. No one really notices or cares if a bunch of vagrants go missing."

"That's disgusting! Horrible!" I felt sick. It was like something out of a bad sci-fi movie where aliens come down and start sucking people's brains out while the oblivious neighbors continue going about their daily lives, taking out the trash and watering the lawn and such.

"Yes, it is."

The evening's events replayed in my mind. "I know this seems silly…" I stopped in confusion, but Gavin's patient regard encouraged me to go on. "Why didn't that man disappear? Go poof! in a cloud of dust, like they do in the movies."

I expected him to laugh at me, but he just looked thoughtful. "They do, sometimes. But not always. I think it has something to do with age. The stake to the heart kills the life force. When that's gone, what's left is a body that may have been dead minutes or centuries. Without the life force to preserve its condition, the corpse reverts to its real age."

Eew.

He stood up. "I need to get going. I was expected back at the station a half-hour ago." He went around my apartment making sure all the windows were locked. "Don't open them while it's dark out. And don't let anyone in." His eyes held mine. "Be careful."

Then he left.

I'd rarely felt so alone and so vulnerable. I was suddenly swamped with horrible images from that night, and even more frightening, visions about my future. Cartons of blood instead of milk in the fridge; my cozy apartment replaced by a dark, dank cave; my bed replaced by a coffin; my friends, even my parents, coming after me, en mob, carrying torches and vials of holy water, wearing crosses and garlands of garlic, and brandishing wooden stakes. Moving as if thus pursued, I rushed back into the kitchen, scrabbled around my cabinets for whatever chocolate products I had left and started making an elaborate chocolate mousse cake.

It was a fussy recipe that demanded my full concentration. After a while, my terror began to subside. I cracked eggs, sifted flour and grated chocolate and became less frantic. By the time I had something to put in the oven, I had pushed all the things I didn't want to think about into some dark corner of my mind and shut the door. My only recourse, I had quietly resolved, was to go on living as I'd had. If, as Gavin had said, I was balancing on a knife's edge, I was going to do my damnedest to make sure I stayed on the right side.

Chapter Nine
❧

"Mrs. Miller wants Jasmine transferred out of your class."

"What? Why?" I gripped the arm of the visitor's chair in the middle school principal's neat office until my fingers turned white. Oh God. They knew. Of course they knew. It was all so obvious I might as well have walked around school with a "V" stamped on my forehead and a "Hi, my name's Jo and I'm turning into a vampire!" badge pinned to my chest. Only an idiot—like me—would believe something as ridiculous as someone contracting a toxic sun allergy in their twenties. I should never have gone back to work. I should have gone to a bat-ridden cave where I belonged. Stupid. Stupid. Stupid.

"She thinks you're a leper," Maxine said.

"I—what?"

"And since leprosy is contagious..." She sighed loudly and leaned back in her leather chair. "I'm so sorry to put you through this, Jo. I wouldn't have told you, but I think you have a right to know. I have, of course, told Mrs. Miller that she is a gossipy old harpy whose daughter is lucky to have a teacher like you. In the nicest possible way, of course." She grinned and for the first time I saw the human underneath the glossy professional veneer.

"Of course." I smiled back.

A little while later, I left Maxine's office and headed toward the cafeteria for lunch in a much happier frame of mind. Maybe things would work out, after all. No one actually believed in vampires, ergo no one would guess what was really happening to me. I even toyed with the idea of taking off the small bandage I wore under my turtlenecks and letting my neck go commando, but only for a moment. The last thing I needed was for my students to think I had track marks on my jugular. All things considered, I'd rather be a leper than a junkie.

I stepped into the girl's bathroom and a high school student I didn't know did a double take at the mirror as she left—and I lost my head completely.

I pulled a tube of hand cream out of my purse and rubbed it all over the mirror so everyone's reflection would be blurry. When I was done, I went into my classroom and locked the door behind me. My stomach growled in protest and I fed it a stale candy bar. I couldn't go to the cafeteria. It wasn't safe. Not for freak like me. What if someone saw me drool over meat packaging in the trash?

The only thing that kept me from going completely insane that week was the fact that my students were even more stressed out than I was. The semester was ending and they had finals, or as they thought of it, tests that would determine whether they got into Harvard or died alone, impoverished and unloved in a gutter.

By the time I'd calmed them down enough to prepare them for the test, and written it, and graded it, I found I had managed to work, literally, through my fears. Or at least repress them. I no longer jumped at every noise, slept clutching a baseball bat, and fought back a rush of tears when someone so much as mentioned the word "hamburger".

There's an adage about a window opening when a door closes, and like most adages, I found it to be true, if not in any way I would have expected. Once I stuffed all things vampire behind some closed door in my brain, I promptly started worrying about all those other things I'd managed to ignore. And on the top of that list was parent-teacher conferences. Rightfully so.

* * * * *

"You are an incompetent, ignorant, new teacher! Who are you to give Howard a D?"

Howard's dad stormed out without waiting for an answer. I reached a shaky hand to wipe the sweat off my face and tried to look on the bright side. He hadn't killed me. I could only hope poor Howard fared as well when his father learned his brilliant son had outright failed his math and English classes.

I glanced down at my agenda, for reassurance more than anything else, as by now I had it memorized. My next appointment was with Chucky Farryll's mom. We'd sat together on the bus on the fall field trip, and if a busload of eighth graders doesn't make you friends for life, I don't know what does. This one would be easy.

I was starting to relax when Mrs. Farryll stormed in, waving one of her son's tests. I winced when I caught sight of the big red F. I really had to stop giving those out.

"It's all that Coach Bob's fault!" She slapped the test down on the table between us.

I stared at her nonplussed. Bob? What did the tenth grade biology teacher have to do with Chucky's earth science test?

"My son is a better soccer player than *any* of the kids on the varsity team, but Coach Bob won't let him join the high school team until he's in the ninth grade. Chucky is so upset, he's purposely failing his classes so his father and I will let him transfer to the public school—they'll let him play varsity there." She pursed her lips and waited for my response.

"I see." I spoke slowly, not quite sure how to respond. This was way out of my jurisdiction. "I'll be happy to do what I can to help Chucky improve his grades, of course…"

"I knew you'd understand," said Mrs. Farryll. She dabbed her eyes and smiled tremulously. The clock ticked loudly and she glanced up at it. "Oh!" She got to her feet. "I need to get to my next appointment. Social studies is in that pretty Spanish building with the big arch and all the red bougainvillea, isn't it? Thank you so much for your understanding in this matter."

She shook my hand. "Chucky's father and I do appreciate your help. We'd do anything to keep our son here. It's such a wonderful school. He does so enjoy your class, Ms. Gartner."

She stuffed Chucky's failing test back into her purse and bustled out without waiting for a response, not that I had one to give, other than a blank stare. I was totally confused. What had I just agreed to? Oh well, if Chucky's mom wanted to arrange some sort of tutoring schedule between his teachers, I'd find out soon enough. Maxine was good about masterminding that sort of thing. I checked my agenda again. Four more to go. Yippee.

A blast of musky perfume preceded my next parent by a good twenty paces. Subconsciously, I must have gotten an inkling of the woman who went with it, because I was more or less successful in schooling my features when she posed against the doorframe dressed like a Frederick's of Hollywood runway model. Okay, maybe I exaggerate. She *was* wearing more than bra and panties, but not much. Even her outerwear was the sort of thing most people, or at least most Bayshore parents—up 'til now, I'd have said all—would have worn *under* their clothes.

She was gorgeous in a come-hither way that would send the average male babbling and drooling. Her pretty heart-shaped face was impeccably made up, her silky long blonde hair tumbled over her shoulders in the artless way only skilled blow drying can achieve, and she had cleavage that looked too big for such a petite frame. She also looked far too young to have a thirteen-year-old, unless she'd gotten pregnant the very second she hit puberty. Maybe she was the stepmom.

I realized she was studying me as intently, only she didn't take pains to hide it. It was pretty clear I wasn't what she had expected, either.

"Ms. Gartner?" she asked doubtfully, in a low, husky voice.

"I am she." I gave her my most welcoming professional smile. "And you must be Mrs. Beckworth?"

"Oh, yes. Yes, of course." She spoke absently, still staring at me. Then she smiled widely and sauntered into the classroom, hips swinging. Boom-shiska-boom-shiska-boom. "I've heard so much about you," she said, posing momentarily near a counter.

She didn't sit down, just wandered around looking at the planet dioramas the students had made for the solar system unit, though her glance frequently shifted back to me. I felt oddly as if I were on display at a zoo, *Homo sapiens-teacheramus*.

It was time I took control of the meeting. "Jodie is doing quite well, Mrs. Beckworth. She earned a B+ on the final and an A- for the semester."

She nodded absently and wandered to the windows, looking at the blackout blinds. She fingered one assessingly. "What are these for?"

"They block sunlight."

"Does it help with— I beg your pardon, but your face looks badly sunburned."

I kept the smile on my face with an effort. "They're very useful in the space unit—the room becomes good and dark when the lights are off."

"Umm," she said, her attention fixated on the curtains.

"We have a few minutes left, Mrs. Beckworth. Is there something in particular you wanted to discuss?"

She turned and gave me a sudden wolfish grin that made my skin prick. "Not really, Ms. Gartner. I just wanted to meet you. You've been *such* a topic of conversation at home these days." She laughed, a musical tinkling noise, and left with a swing of her hips.

A moment later, Bob poked his head in. "Who was *that*?" He wiggled his blond eyebrows.

"Mrs. Beckworth," I said, waving my hands around in an attempt to dispel some of her perfume. I gave up and joined Bob in the hallway for some fresh air.

"She's a parent?"

"Yep."

He gave himself a shake. "Hey, some of us are going for a beer later. You in?"

"Only if you make it a row of vodka shots. I don't think beer is going to be strong enough to take away the pain of this evening."

"That bad, eh?" He slung a sympathetic arm around my shoulders. "Hang in there, kid. It gets easier after you've been here for a while. In the meantime, I think we can arrange a beer and a bump for ya."

"All right, then. I'm in."

We heard footsteps on the outer stairs. "Sounds like my eight o'clock is here. Better go." Bob headed back down the hall to his classroom and I sighed and turned back into mine.

I soon wished I hadn't. My next conference was so horrible I had to finish it in the middle school principal's office. It was the only way to get the parent to stop yelling. Maxine, looking as if she was genuinely thrilled to see us, winked at me as she ushered us inside with a practiced smile, a blend of compassion and steel that I really needed to learn before the next conferences.

Twenty minutes later, even Maxine was getting nowhere. She was just suggesting we continue the meeting on Monday, after everyone had had time to cool down, when we heard a loud crash from the second floor of the science building.

Maxine and I politely excused ourselves and walked out of her office, but the moment we turned the corner, we raced upstairs.

Alan, the physics teacher who taught just across the hall from me, was standing outside my room, his dark face blanched. "It's Bob," he said in disbelief. "He's dead."

"What? But I just—" I looked in my classroom and saw Bob, sprawled unmoving on the floor at the foot of one of the heavy lab tables, now pushed out of its neat alignment. Remains of the test tubes and beakers I'd left to air-dry on top of the table lay scattered under and around him. Blood pooled in a dark puddle on the floor from a wound at the side of his head.

"He must have slipped somehow and hit his head on the corner of the table." Alan shook his head in confusion.

I pushed past him and bent down to feel for a pulse at Bob's wrist.

"Alan, call 9-1-1. Now!" Maxine commanded. Alan stood dumbly for a moment and then headed at a run toward the computer room where we had a phone with an outside line. Maxine took a few steps into the room, stepping gingerly over the broken glass. "Anything?" she asked softly.

I shook my head, not wanting to speak lest the sound of my voice override any faint signs of a pulse. Frowning, I let go Bob's wrist and pushed aside his collar to check his jugular. With a small cry, I pulled back my fingers. On the side of his neck, above his collarbone, there were two tiny triangular-shaped cuts. I quickly schooled my features to hide the sickening angst that burned in my gut.

"What?" Maxine said urgently.

"Nothing." I reached for the opposite side of his neck with a logical detachment I did not feel. "He's got some cuts from the glass on the other side, that's all."

The room got very quiet. I repositioned my fingers anxiously a few times without success. I got heavily to my feet and looked at Maxine, but she seemed to know before I said it.

"He's gone." I leaned heavily against the back counter. "We're too late."

Kendra came into the room, panting slightly from sprinting upstairs. She heard my pronouncement, and gave a cry of protest. Heedless of the broken glass on the floor, she ran to Bob's side and began administering CPR.

Maxine opened her mouth to protest, but in the end said nothing. We stood watching Kendra rhythmically pump Bob's chest, knowing it was a lost cause, but unwilling to stop her in case we were wrong.

Becky appeared in the doorway and gave a shocked gasp.

"What happened?" she mouthed, catching my eye.

I shook my head and shrugged helplessly.

A door slammed open somewhere behind Becky. She glanced back and then moved out of the doorway to make way for the paramedics. One of the EMTs automatically took over from Kendra, who joined me at the back of the room, tears streaming down her cheeks. When she noticed Bob's blood on her hands, she gave a garbled cry and began scrubbing it off in the sink.

The EMTs stopped their resuscitation efforts before Kendra had finished cleaning her hands. Bob was dead. More than that, he had been murdered. In my classroom. I knew who had done it. The bite marks identified the man who took Bob's life as surely as a fingerprint. Will.

Chapter Ten
ରେ

The police arrived on the heels of the emergency medical crew. After a review of my classroom and a quick meeting with the headmaster, the senior officer began asking us questions, beginning with those of us who were huddled around my classroom and continuing on to the rest of the science teachers. Our department is housed on one side of a sprawling two-story stucco building, with a well-insulated theater providing a buffer between us and the English department on the other side. It was doubtful anyone outside the science department wing had heard the glass break, and since no one had come forward to prove that assumption wrong, the police contained their investigation to us. Unfortunately for the investigators, all the science teachers had been busy with some facet or other of parent night and were just as bewildered.

As improbable as it would seem, not one of us could have been party to Bob's "accident"—as they were still calling it, whether through ignorance or by design I didn't know.

Even Alan, who automatically came into a lot of questions by virtue of being first on the scene, had been seen by no less than me, Maxine, and the irate parent as he walked past the administration building seconds before we'd heard the glass break. Maxine and I (and the irate parent) alibied one another. Roger had been in the men's room; Kendra, who had been facing the men's room while talking to Mrs. Mudget in the hall, had seen him go in. Becky and Carol had been in parent conferences.

Despite several hours of questioning, the police made little headway into the mystery of Bob's death. Bob, it seemed to them, had died alone. By accident.

I knew differently.

It was nearly midnight before they had finished with us, but even then we weren't free to go home. The entire department was herded, tired and cranky, into the headmaster's office where a subdued Headmaster Huntington faced us, flanked by Maxine and the high school principal. In a calm, authoritative voice, he told us how the next few days would go.

There would be an emergency all-school assembly first thing the next morning to announce Bob's death. Since my classroom was uninhabitable, to say the least, I would teach next door in Bob's classroom. Bob's classes would meet in the library with a grief counselor for the remainder of the week. A long-term substitute would be hired as quickly as possible to finish the rest of the school year, but the headmaster voiced his trust that he could count on us to pitch in if necessary, in the meantime. A memorial service would be held Friday evening, to accommodate those with after-school obligations like sports finals and music recitals that couldn't easily be postponed.

When asked about Bob's death, the headmaster advised us we were to free to say it was an unfortunate tragedy, how very sorry we were, that it was a terrible loss to the school. We could share, within reason, our grief. However we were not, under any circumstances, to discuss the "incident" itself. Police orders.

"Can we tell them Bob was murdered, or are we supposed to pretend we believe the police's line about it being an 'accident', and this being a 'routine' investigation?" Becky asked.

I looked sharply at her, wondering what she knew.

Roger spoke up before the headmaster could respond. "If the police feel it is an accident, it is," he said rudely. "What makes you think you know better than the police?"

"Oh, use your brain, Roger, if you have one," retorted Becky. "Bob's wound was on the left side of his head, the table he is supposed to have bumped it on was on his right. Either he was an amazing, gravity-defying contortionist, or someone attacked him. He's dead, ergo murder."

"Surely you're not suggesting one of *us* killed him—not someone in the *science* department," Roger said, aghast.

I wasn't sure if he objected to the idea that one of us would have harmed Bob or that a science teacher would lack the rudimentary spatial logic to prevent such an obvious blunder.

"I'm not accusing anyone," Becky said wearily. "I don't have the foggiest idea what happened, how it happened, or who helped it happen. Frankly, I don't particularly want to think about it. The fact remains, however, and whether we like it or not, Bob *was* murdered."

The headmaster held up a restraining hand before Roger could respond.

"If indeed, as Becky has suggested, Bob has died under suspicious circumstances, we can best hope to right that injustice by helping the police in any way we can. To that end, we, Bob's friends and colleagues, will not discount what the police have said, regardless of our own views on the matter. The speculation and gossip that would undoubtedly result from the premature identification of Bob's demise as murder would dilute legitimate evidence and hinder the investigation."

He looked around the room, making sure each one of us understood the seriousness of talking out of turn. "Unsubstantiated rumors will hurt Bob, his family and loved ones, and our school community. So, whatever our personal opinions, we will not discuss them with students, in or out of class, with each other, or even with friends outside of school. Is that clear?"

Becky gave a tight nod that seemed to satisfy the headmaster, and the rest of us dutifully muttered our acquiescence.

As I moved to follow the crowd out, the headmaster touched a hand lightly to my arm and asked me to stay.

I took a seat in a plush chair opposite Headmaster Huntington, who proceeded to spend the next twenty minutes scaring me shitless.

He didn't mean to of course, he was just concerned for my safety. But listening to him hint around the fact that since Bob had been killed in *my* room, I should be extra careful, if I didn't have the heebie jeebies before, I certainly had them then.

When he was done, he considerately walked me to my car and waited until it had started before heading back across campus to the adjacent headmaster's residence. As I put my old grey Volvo into gear, I glanced at the dashboard clock. Assuming I went to bed the second I got home and slumbered docilely through all the nightmares I was sure to have, I was looking forward to four and a half hours of sleep.

It might have been the extra fatigue born of knowing this that I idled so long in front of the parking lot gate before realizing it wasn't opening. I pulled up the emergency brake and got out of the car. Fred, the aging night guard, was prone to napping in his cozy little booth. His ineffectiveness was a mild joke among the faculty members, and while normally I was inclined to rather admire the guy's ability to sleep, it didn't seem so funny now. I rapped on the window and peered in. Fred wasn't there.

"Dammit!" Why did he had to have picked now of all times to leave the booth. "Where could he be?" I said aggravatedly. My fatigue had crept up a couple notches and I was getting cranky. I didn't want to wander around the stupid school looking for the stupid security guard at one-stupid-thirty in the morning. Lord knew where or when I'd find him if he had actually gone on his rounds for once.

Just as I was seriously considering getting back into the car and using it as a battering ram, I noticed he had left the communication window ajar. I pried it open the full three inches allowed by the safety latch and stuck my arm in as far as it would go.

I was an inch shy of the gate switch. Getting on my tiptoes, gained me another half inch. Just as I was debating whether I should force the window or repark the car so I could get a boost on the bumper, I heard the guard coming around the corner of the administration building.

"Fred," I called out, stepping away from the window and rubbing my armpit to get the circulation back. "Can you let me out, please? I need to get home." I forced my features into a pleasant smile as he stepped out of the shadows. But it wasn't Fred.

"Oh, no." I whispered, backing up until I felt the guard box against my back. *Please let the guard come back, please let the guard come back.*

"The security guard is taking a little break right now," Will said lightly as he rapidly closed the distance between us. I braced myself and wondered how I was going to fight him off this time—if I was going to fight him off this time—when he abruptly stopped a few feet from me.

"Jo," he said rather formally, "I would like to talk to you."

An unexpected note of contrition in his voice made me stop flinching and look up at him.

"I want to apologize for Natasha."

"Natasha?" I repeated stupidly. I had no idea what he was talking about.

"She had no right to interfere with your work," he said somberly. "She wishes to express her regret."

I hadn't noticed there was someone waiting in the shadows until she suddenly appeared a few feet to my left.

"Arhgh!" I cried indistinctly, jumping and clutching my chest.

"Oh, dear." The woman's husky voice dripped with mock apology. "I hope I didn't scare you, Ms. Gartner."

"Mrs. Beckworth?" I said, confused. I recognized her cloying perfume and wondered why I hadn't noticed it sooner. She practically bathed in the stuff.

Will chuckled indulgently. "No, that was Natasha's little joke." He gave a slight jerk to his head and she began to apologize dutifully if not sincerely.

"I'm sorry for interrupting your parent conference," she said. "I just wanted to meet you." She favored me with a look of contempt that Will couldn't see.

"That's better," Will said approvingly. "We want Jo to feel a part of our family."

"That's okay," I said sincerely.

"Now run along, Natasha," Will said dismissing her. She gave him a sweet smile and a seductive bat of her heavily mascaraed eyelashes, but the look she directed at me was not nearly so pleasant. If Will hadn't been there I would have been in big trouble. Of course, I was still in big trouble. She sauntered away, hips swinging. Boom shiska boom shiska boom.

It was a wasted effort on her part—I was the only one who watched her walk away. Will's attention was focused squarely on me. His deep blue eyes took on a look of concern as he stepped closer to me and gently pushed a lock of hair out of my face. A traitorous flare of desire intermingled with my terror and I forgot to breathe.

"I saw the ambulance and the police here earlier, coming out of your classroom," he said softly. "Was it a friend of yours?"

That was not what I expected him to say. It didn't even really make sense. How could he have seen that? And did he sound—was he—worried about me? I dismissed the thought as quickly as it had come. Romanticizing about a vampire was the last thing I needed to be doing. I refocused on the matter at hand.

"He taught in the classroom next to mine. I— How did you know it wasn't me?"

He took my hand and pressed it to his chest. "I know," he said. He ran a finger slowly down my cheek, following its movement with his eyes. I felt the tingle to my toes and stood there for a moment in breathless anticipation until his finger moved to gently touch the bandage on my neck, and I was able to make myself remember who—what—he was. I yanked my hand out of his and took a half step back. It was as far as I could go. The window ledge of the guard booth dug into my back.

Will smiled lazily and took a half step forward. My breath caught as his fingers deftly removed the pins that held back my hair. It cascaded in a shimmering fall down my back. As if mesmerized, he wound the fingers of one hand through it, and slowly leaned in. I closed my eyes.

"Teeth marks," I blurted out accusingly.

"What?" Will's movement toward me was checked and his hand stilled on my cheek.

"Teeth marks," I repeated. "There were teeth marks on Bob's neck. I could see them, distinctly, even through the blood. You did that to him," I said, my voice catching.

"What?" he said. "I did not!" He looked appalled.

I gave him a hard, disbelieving stare, but he just stood there unflinchingly, with a quiet dignity.

"You..." I hesitated, suddenly filled with doubt. Had Gavin talked me into something that wasn't true?

Will didn't say anything, just waited curiously for me to finish. It was that hint of a smile that made me say it out loud.

"You're a vampire!" I blurted out. "Aren't you?" I added uncertainly when he didn't immediately respond.

Something flared deep in his blue eyes. He inclined his head in the barest sketch of a nod, and that little bit of doubt I had clutched like a safety jacket disappeared.

"But I did not touch your colleague." He adjusted impeccable shirt cuffs. "Why would I choose to spend eternity with that man? I do have standards you know."

"One of your minions then," I said sharply, "Natasha."

"No," Will said firmly.

At my disbelieving stare, he relented. "It's true I usually don't recruit the males—I let the girls handle that. They quite enjoy it, it's a power thing for them, I think. But they didn't hurt anyone here, not without my permission."

He leaned closer, his eyes glittering fiercely. His voice turned harsh, commanding. "And I assure you, Jo, I did not give it."

"No, beautiful, the only one I want here is you." He pulled me roughly against him and kissed me hard, expertly, thoroughly, sending shock waves through every part of my body. Just as his kiss began to linger, he put me gently away from him. When I opened my eyes, he was gone. I touched a shaking hand to my neck, but everything was intact. I was more confused than ever.

Chapter Eleven

ဢ

By some stroke of luck I got a parking spot right in front of my place. Maybe it wasn't luck—it was getting so close to dawn I wouldn't be surprised if some of the early commuters had already left for work.

As I reached my apartment, I heard footsteps coming up the stairs behind me, but I didn't jump or scream. I was expecting him. I finished unlocking the door before turning to address my visitor. "Hello, Gavin." He wore comfortably worn jeans and a lightweight runner's windbreaker over a blue button-down shirt creased from a day's wear, as if he'd gone home from work and gotten only as far as changing his pants before having to leave again. "Come on in."

The invitation was a formality. He'd already followed me in. He shut and locked the door behind him, and turned to face me. "I'm sorry to bother you so late." He gave me a once-over and his forehead puckered in a slight frown. "It's just—"

"You saw the teeth marks, too." I tossed my keys onto the table near the door, and they slid right off the pile of unopened mail and onto the floor. I left them where they lay and headed for the kitchen. It had been a helluva of a day on top of one helluva past few weeks, and I needed a snack.

My kitchen was fairly large (though maybe it just felt that way compared to the rest of my apartment), a long and narrow room with old-fashioned yellow tiles and a small breakfast nook at one end. I stood in the center and stared at the stove as if it would solve all my problems. "I'm going to have some cocoa," I announced finally. "Want some?"

"Sure." Gavin sat himself in one of the two rung-back chairs at the small pine table under the window as if he were a friend come over for a cozy chat, and watched me measure hot chocolate mix into two mugs. "How are you do—"

I set the pot of water and milk on the stove with a clang. "Don't ask me that."

"All right." He shifted the chair a little bit so he could stretch his long legs out toward the center of the kitchen, and helped himself to a chocolate chip cookie from the plate I slapped down in the middle of the table.

I busied myself with unnecessary kitchen chores until the cocoa was ready, then brought the mugs to the table and sat across from him.

"So," I prompted, stirring my cocoa with the spoon and sipping from it.

"So." He sighed wearily and stirred his own cocoa in unconscious mimicry. He took a meditative sip, wincing slightly as the boiling hot liquid scalded his mouth. As he put the cup down, he glanced at me, and something in my face must have communicated my mounting impatience for he dropped the kid gloves treatment and began to talk in what I thought of as his cop voice. "The EMTs noticed the odd wound on Bob's neck. When the captain learned of it, he arranged for an immediate autopsy and then sent for me."

I reached for a cookie and broke off a piece, scattering crumbs across the sunflower print tablecloth. "Will says he didn't do it."

Gavin's face froze for a split second but quickly—so quickly, I thought I must have imagined that look—his features resumed their usual appearance of benign professional curiosity. "Oh?" he said.

I told him about Natasha's visit and, leaving out the kissing part, how Will had cornered me in the parking lot when I was leaving. As I spoke, a dark flush of anger began to spread over Gavin's face, and I hurried through the rest of my story. "He said he wouldn't have—'recruited' is how he put it, I think—any man, much less Bob. Apparently the female vampires recruit males."

"How quaint."

I ignored the comment as if he hadn't spoken. Gavin had a nasty habit of baiting me and this time I was going to make sure he heard me out. I pulled the cookie plate away from him to get his attention. "I think Natasha killed Bob. He saw her as she was leaving my classroom, and thought she was gorgeous. And I promise you, she's not one to miss that look in a man's eye. I wouldn't be surprised if she came back after I left and cornered him in my classroom."

"Sexual attraction is how they reel in their victims," Gavin said. His attention shifted from his cocoa mug to my face.

I flushed.

His eyes rested curiously on my neck. He said thoughtfully, almost to himself, "You Will said found you alone in the parking lot tonight. Why didn't he bite you again?"

"I—I don't know," I admitted. I was rather curious about that myself. "I think he was being considerate, nice." I stared at the tablecloth and corralled my cookie crumbs into a neat pile.

"Nice? A vampire? Are you sure he didn't bite you again?" His hand reached for my bandage. I slapped it away.

"Stop doing that! It hurts!"

"Sorry." The apology was automatic, mechanical. His thoughts had already moved elsewhere. We sat there for a moment, sipping our cocoa in silence until he spoke again. "Where was the security guard while you were having your little chat with the vampires in the parking lot?"

Fred! A horrifying image rose before me clear as day— sweet, portly, old Fred lying on the quad, navy uniform rumpled, thick glasses askew, one wrinkled hand clutching ineffectually at his neck as blood seeped through and drained away. "Oh my God. I forgot to make sure he was okay!" I stood up. "We have to go back and check! Will said he didn't hurt him but—"

Gavin motioned me to sit back down and reached into his jacket pocket for his phone. He contacted one of the officers who was still at the school and instructed him to look for the guard. I stared intently at Gavin's phone until the officer reported back that Fred was fine if a little confused that the police were asking after him.

I sank down into my seat and put my head in my hands. I was the lowliest of worms. What was wrong with me these days? I had the attention span of a gnat! If anything had happened to Fred...

"Jo? Are you okay?"

"No, I'm not." I let out a breath of air in a long sigh and moved my hands away from my face. "At least Will was telling the truth about Fred. I guess that's something."

"Will was telling the truth about Bob, too. He didn't do it. No vampire did." Gavin spoke reluctantly, as if hating to give Will credit for anything decent. "The teeth marks were faked. No one actually bit Bob's neck—no saliva."

"What? Why?"

"That's what I'd like to know," Gavin said sharply.

"You think I know something about this?"

"No. As I understand it, you had an alibi—unless a parent and the middle school principal were in it with you, which I'm inclined to doubt."

Thank you, Gavin, for that vote of confidence.

"As I was saying, the 'teeth marks' seem to have been made with something sharp, like glass."

I thought back to my ruin of a classroom. "There was a lot of broken glass around, you know. Maybe some of the glass shards nicked his neck."

Gavin shook his head. "No. Someone deliberately made those marks, Jo. Someone tried to make Bob's death look like it had been done by a vampire. One in particular, I'd guess—you."

"But I'm not a vampire! You said so yourself. Besides, no one knows."

"Are you sure about that? Someone could have seen or overheard us at the bar the other night. We weren't exactly keeping our voices down."

"Surely we would have noticed…" My voice petered out uncertainly as I realized the fallacy of this statement. Godzilla could have been behind me roaring and spewing fire and I wouldn't have noticed. "The place was so empty, I guess I assumed we were alone—except of course for the dead people coming back to life, and all the vampires popping in and out."

"If someone *had* overheard us, they would know that I would suspect you when I found the bite marks on Bob's neck." Gavin's voice grew harsh. "That we would assume Bob was your first victim."

"But you don't think that."

He sat back in his chair and crossed his arms across his chest. "You have an alibi."

I scowled at him. "Whose side are you on anyway?"

"Bob's."

"Sometimes you're just a big jerk, you know that?" I snatched the cookie plate away from him and brought it to the sink. I didn't feed jerks.

Gavin watched me rinse the plate. "Bob was murdered at 8:40. According to the schedule posted outside your door, you had another conference at 8:45." He held up a hand as I began to correct him. "Yes, I'm aware it had been canceled, but someone looking at your schedule wouldn't have known that. *You* were supposed to have been found hovering over Bob's body."

I waited for the rest of the explanation, but Gavin had finished. "*That*'s your theory? That someone—a teacher or a

Bayshore parent—snuck unseen to my classroom, killed Bob and arranged things so I would get the blame? Shouldn't they have at least planned for contingencies, like the fact that I was in Maxine's office when the glass broke?"

"Even so, you would have gotten there first had, er—" he glanced down at his notebook, "Alan not happened to have been on his way there, purely by chance. And if you *had* been the one to find the body, how could the police have been sure that Bob was really dead when you got there? That he hadn't merely slipped, knocking the glassware as he fell? That you had discovered him unconscious and bleeding, and had taken advantage of his weakened state to get your first kill."

My mouth hung open for a moment in pure outrage and I shut it with a snap. "That's the lamest thing I've ever heard! Not to mention insulting. I don't even know why you're spending time devising such a crazy scenario when it's so obvious Natasha did it."

"No, she didn't—I told you, the teeth marks were faked."

I dismissed his theory with a curt wave of my hand. "Don't you see? It must have been her. No one else could have done it. Every teacher in my department had an alibi, and the only parents in our wing of the building were in conferences."

"All the logical suspects have an alibi so *of course* it *must have* been a vampire." He rolled his eyes. "A vampire who killed Bob the traditional way. It's brilliant, really. No one would suspect her. But does she leave behind a perfect murder? No, she makes fake bite marks on his neck to draw attention to herself and all others of her kind, despite their collective efforts to remain hidden. Have I got that right?"

I glared at him.

"Let me ask you, how did she get by everyone without being seen?"

"I don't know. Maybe she turned into a bat."

"I see. And why, may I ask, did she go to all this trouble?"

I shifted uncomfortably against the counter. "I don't know. She hates me for some reason."

"I thought you'd never met her before tonight."

"I haven't!" I shivered. "You should have seen the way she looked at me."

"Well then. If she *looked* at you…"

I went back to glaring at him in silence.

Gavin could mock me all he wanted about my sensitivity to atmosphere, but it didn't mean I wasn't right. He'd never met her. I had. And faking the teeth marks clearly wasn't as stupid as Gavin had suggested—hadn't he summarily ruled out vampire involvement because of it? She was plenty devious to have planned it that way.

No, I was not so ready to rule Natasha out, even if I couldn't explain how she'd gotten up to my room and back down again unseen. If Gavin wasn't letting that technicality hinder his theories, I didn't see why I had to let it interfere with mine.

Of course, if I could allow that Natasha could get around undetected, I really should put Will back in the suspect pool. But he was another story. He could've had his way with me in the parking lot tonight (take that any way you wish and you're probably right, drat it). There was really no reason for him to have thought up such a convoluted way of getting at me. Besides, as much as I hated to admit it and as screwy as it may seem, I believed he had more integrity than that.

Gavin interrupted my thoughts. "If we can put aside Natasha for the moment… Can you tell me anyone else who may have had a problem with Bob? I don't mean murderous intent, necessarily. It's quite possible his death was unplanned, an argument that got out of control—"

"An argument with silent yelling?"

His eyes narrowed. "Not silent, but surely you can believe they would have made an effort to keep their voices down."

He had a point. I gave it some thought but didn't come up with much. "As far as I know, Bob was pretty universally liked. The only person I know of who has—" I gulped, "had—an issue with Bob is one of the middle school parents, Mrs. Farryll. She was upset that Bob wouldn't let her son play on the high school soccer team. But I have a hard time imagining her killing him over it, especially since Bob was just following school rules and the season's almost over. Besides, she was booked solid in conferences on the other side of campus. I saw her schedule."

Gavin didn't seem very interested in Mrs. Farryll. "What about the other teachers?"

"What does it matter? They all have alibis."

"All the same, any issues there?"

I shrugged. "Not that I know of, but I'm still pretty new there—I'm usually too busy trying to keep my head above water to keep track of all the gossip. I do know that Roger, our department head, would have been happy if Bob had decided to leave so he could teach biology, but that is not the sort of thing people get killed over or we wouldn't have a teacher left standing. Anyway, Roger never would have talked to Bob about it or even argued with Bob about it. Roger's more of the 'stab you in the back' type."

"What about Alan?"

"Because he found the body? I haven't heard anything, and besides, I can't believe he had anything to do with it. The man looked like a ghost and I don't know that you can fake shock like that."

Thinking about Alan brought back images of Bob's body. I saw myself bend down to check for a pulse, finding his torn and bloody neck instead. "You didn't tell Maxine or the headmaster or anyone about me—"

"No, you needn't worry about that. No one at Bayshore even knows about the teeth marks, except the person who made them and you. We don't plan to broadcast the alleged vampire angle. Only a couple people at the station are aware of that situation anyway, and they won't say anything—most of my colleagues think I'm with Internal Affairs. As for the paramedics, they think it was nothing more than a mildly humorous coincidence, a view we've taken pains to encourage. With all the weird stuff they see, it probably won't even rate a casual mention."

"What now?" I said, suppressing a yawn. "I suppose you want me to see if I can dig up a little more gossip on Bob?"

"No. You do nothing. You let the police handle this." Gavin stood, collected the mugs and brought them to the sink.

I felt like he had slapped me. "It's a little late to begin patronizing me now."

He put the mugs down with a clatter and turned to loom over me. "What do you want to do, play amateur sleuth at school tomorrow? Your friend is dead, Jo. Someone at Bayshore—one of the teachers, parents, or students—murdered him. Do you get that?"

I got to my feet and closed the distance between us. "Yes! But I also get that they killed him in my room and they tried to implicate me."

"Exactly. Someone capable of murder has you on their radar for some reason, and we don't know who it is, or why they did it, or what they'll do next." He clenched his fists and looked up at the ceiling. "I'm trying to protect you and you want to go flush murderers out of the bushes."

I poked him in the chest. "Well in case you haven't noticed, I'm just this side of being dead as it is. Frankly I'd rather be pushed over the edge trying to clear my name and avenge Bob's death than hang around wringing my hands on the sidelines and waiting for Will to come finish me off."

Gavin's eyes were dark with barely suppressed anger. "No one's going to kill you as long as you take some basic safety precautions. Stick to public places, even at work, don't go out by yourself at night, and don't play chicken with a killer."

"You want me to sit there and do nothing when my job, my reputation, even my life is at stake?"

"Yes, dammit!"

We stood a few inches apart, glaring at each other. Gavin's jaw was clenched so tightly the tips of his nostrils turned white.

Gavin broke first. He turned and headed for the front door. "It's late," he said, pulling it open and stepping through. "Try to get some sleep."

The soft click of the door closing behind him was somehow louder than if he had slammed it.

Chapter Twelve

ๆ๑

I was not quite sure how to begin my sleuthing. You don't just sidle up to someone who's mourning a murdered colleague and ask if they might possibly have had a reason to have killed him. I had to be subtle and tactical, and by that I mean I had to ditch my very sound, very sane silent pledge to stay out of the grapevine. My days of pleasantly burying my head in the sand were over. I would have to keep my eyes and ears open, I would have to start watching the soap opera that is The Bayshore Academy.

In hindsight, I know that was a stupid plan. It can't be done. You either gossip or you don't. There are no half measures—if you don't gossip back, offer up tidbits of your own, no one will tell you anything (anything good, that is), and if you don't make an effort to listen to what people are saying, you won't be able to correct rumors about yourself.

An even bigger misjudgment on my part was the idea that I would sort of sneak my way into the gossip pool, wade in gently, if you will. I hadn't realized that the fact that Bob had died in my classroom had put me smack in the middle of things. The headmaster's little tête-à-tête the night before took on new meaning as I realized he had been warning me not so much against the murderer who had killed Bob but the dangerous swell of public opinion.

From the moment I got on campus the next morning, I noticed people were treating me differently. The all-school assembly was brief and more We Will Soldier On than informative about Bob's sudden demise. People filed out quietly, instinctively bunching into small groups and talking in subdued tones or not at all. I was alone in the crowd. I went with the tide as far as the administration building and broke off to collect my mail. Conversation abruptly ceased when I stepped into the faculty lounge. Some teachers who hitherto hadn't wasted more than a polite smile on me in the four months I'd been teaching there stopped to ask me how I was.

Just as I was naïvely answering that deceptively simple question, Carol came in, took one look at all the ears swiveled in my direction and got me out of there.

"God, you're a babe in the woods, aren't you?" she said under her breath as she pulled me along to the science building. As we mounted the stairs to the second floor at a brisk pace, she warned quietly, "Tell your students you'll be teaching in Bob's room today, but that they can't come in yet because you have to do some prep work."

I stopped by the group of students huddled a small distance from my classroom door and did as instructed. Under the watchful eye of a uniformed police officer charged with guarding my classroom door against the possible entrance of an intrepid student with a filched master key carefully passed down and hoarded for just such an occasion, the kids shuffled quietly down the hall to regroup in front of Bob's classroom. As I automatically began to search for a key I didn't have, Carol pulled out her own master key from a pocket of her lab coat and let me in. She shut the door behind us.

"Roger has a key to Bob's room for you. He should have been here with it by now, but as long as you have one before you have to close up for lunch, I guess it's okay." Both her tone and her frown indicated her personal views on that matter, but she had more pressing concerns than Roger's sloppy handling of the keys. She turned worried brown eyes to me and pushed her glasses up to a more secure position on her nose.

"How are you doing? No, don't answer that. No time." She gave my arm a sympathetic pat in case the answer had been something less than "fine" and continued talking. "Jo, I understand the headmaster talked with you last night, but I'm not sure you appreciate how difficult this may be for you."

I didn't. "Geez, Carol. You're acting as if I'm the one who got hurt last night. Aside from being sad and a little tired, *I'm* fine. It's going to be a little weird teaching in here, and I'm sure my students are going to react in new and horrible ways, but I'm used to my students acting out."

She shook her head and regarded me earnestly. "You don't get it, Jo. Bob died in *your* classroom. It doesn't matter that you weren't there, or that you couldn't possibly have had anything to do with it. A lot of people are going to think you did, and those who don't think it are going to wonder it."

"But—that's absurd!"

"Of course it is. Nonetheless, you have to be prepared for a lot of uncomfortable questions. People who barely know you are going to ask you seemingly innocent questions, and read all sorts of things into your answers. I can see you don't really believe me, but please, be careful what you say—oh, darn it, that's the bell. I've got to go. Just try not to talk to anyone, as much as possible." With that last bit of advice, she gave my arm a squeeze. "Hang in there, kiddo."

She left, moving adeptly from years of practice against the chaotic tide of students pushing into the classroom.

I directed them to take a seat and pull out their homework. "Ms. Gartner?" One of my students raised her hand and kept on talking, as if the gesture alone gave her the floor. "Is it true Mr. Bob died in your classroom last night and the policeman's there to guard his dead body?"

A chorus of *eews* and a couple dramatic squeaks and shudders met the idea that there was a dead body next-door in their science classroom. A couple of boys immediately took advantage of a popular girl's distress by making creepy crawly fingers on her back, causing her squeaks to escalate into shrieks, and her posse immediately joined in the chorus. Into this melee, Roger arrived, looking down his nose at me in the best way a man two inches shorter can, and held out a set of keys.

My day went downhill from there.

By lunchtime, I felt like a wrung out dishrag and I was seriously debating whether or not I should leave Bayshore. Not for the rest of the day, permanently. Carol had been right, as always, and while her warning had probably saved me a great deal of unnecessary angst, there was plenty more to take its place.

I collected some food on a tray and headed for my usual table, but stopped before I'd gotten halfway. Not only was my usual seat taken, extra chairs had been pulled up to accommodate all the extra bodies eager to hear the latest straight from the mouths of the science teachers they had trapped there. I stood uncertainly, not sure where I should go, until I spied Roger and Alan sitting alone at a table in the corner.

"Mind if I join you?" I sat down before they had a chance to tell me to go away.

Alan, who looked as haggard as I felt, told me to suit myself. Roger was too busy bragging about how well his parent conferences had gone to pay me any attention. With a sigh I was too weary to let out, I kept my head down and ate my hotdog in silence. Eventually, Roger finished the story about how wonderful he was and packed up his dishes and left. Alan and I exchanged glances.

"Too bad he didn't get it instead of Bob," Alan said.

Twenty-four hours ago, Alan never would have said something like that to me. But the fact that *he* had found Bob dead, and that Bob had died in *my* classroom had forged some sort of bond between us. We were fellow pariahs. The fact that I understood his pain probably meant that I should have felt sorry for him, but I didn't. I was glad—no, thrilled—to have someone in the pit with me.

I leaned across the table. "I know. I'd settle for seeing the police throw him in jail, but I'm not sure they'd buy my theory that Roger irritated Bob to death."

Alan's wry half smile turned into a wide grin. "I would. I'm sure people have killed for less. I've got a better theory than that though." He lowered his voice and leaned in a little further. "Bob was going to give him a bad teaching review." He opened his eyes wide, as if he'd told me the world's dirtiest little secret, which in a way he had. Teaching was Roger's life, Bayshore, his world. The idea that Roger would have a black mark on his record was almost heretical.

"You're kidding me," I said, delighted.

"Nope. I'm the alternate on the faculty review committee so I have his notes."

"Real-ly."

Alan just grinned. It was the first time I'd seen him so animated. "Yup. And I don't think my review's going to help the average." He put down his hotdog in disgust. "The man teaches from ten-year-old overheads he keeps filed in a drawer."

"I know. He's supposed to be my mentor."

A look of horror crossed Alan's face.

"It's okay," I assured him. "He's too busy to do more than stop by occasionally and point out what I'm doing wrong, and even then I run it by Carol before I change what I'm doing."

"Good girl. We'll make a teacher of you yet."

We finished lunch and as I walked slowly back to the science building, I thought over what Alan had told me, and began to wonder if Roger could have killed Bob.

Roger had been in the downstairs men's restroom when Bob died. I wondered how quickly he had come out after hearing the commotion upstairs, and whether there was another way in. Determined to satisfy my curiosity, I took a detour around the side of the science building and pretended to tie my shoe as I scanned the part of the building that housed the restrooms. There were, as I had suspected, a line of windows high along the outer wall of the men's room, but they were small and dusty, more for light than ventilation.

Unreasonably disappointed, I made my way back up to Bob's classroom and braced myself for my afternoon classes.

* * * * *

The memorial service Friday afternoon had to be held in the auditorium, the school's pretty Chapel too small to hold all the students, teachers and parents who'd come to pay their respects. It was long and weepy and rather awful. Every time someone got up and shared a bittersweet anecdote, I clenched my hands as a terrible anger flowed through me. Someone, maybe even one of the people who eulogized him so generously, had killed this beloved teacher and coach.

After the service I let myself be herded with everyone else to the reception in the cafeteria but avoided the trays of hard little cookies and punch bowls of overly concentrated pink lemonade that were Bayshore's signature "occasion" fare. I knew better than to partake of the refreshments, particularly the lemonade that no amount of ice hogging could make palatable. Besides, the science department was going out for a memorial dinner as soon as we could decently get away.

The crowd had separated me from Becky and Carol. I was looking rather anxiously for them, lest I get waylaid by yet another curious student or parent who realized I had been "on the scene", when a police officer tapped me lightly on the shoulder, breaking my reverie, and asked if I were Miss Jo Gartner.

I nodded and let him pull me aside. He informed me politely that they—he didn't specify who "they" were—were done with my room, and that I was free to begin using it again. I had a good half-hour at least before anyone would think of leaving for dinner. No one would notice if I snuck away for a quick look around my classroom. The last time I'd seen it, it had been a disaster, and it could only have gotten worse after the crime scene unit or whatever had gone through it. If I needed to spend a chunk of Saturday cleaning up after them, I wanted to know now. I dodged the gossipy librarian heading my way and slipped out and over to the upstairs science wing.

The door to my classroom looked rather barren without the yellow crime scene tape. I unlocked the door, flicked on a light and stared at my room in surprise. It was clean. Someone had swept up all the glass, whether through kindness or because it was evidence, I didn't know. It was tidy, too. The sloppy piles of paper that habitually adorned the counter near the door (my little shrine to entropy) had been neatened, and the dioramas that covered the rest of the counter had been tucked neatly under the upper cabinets. Even the set of old textbooks I kept for reference at the back near the sink had been restacked neatly. Usually I kept them in three sloppy piles. Now, two short stacks had been flip-flopped so their spines touched, a third stack placed perpendicular to them so their spines all formed a T. The remaining books were piled on top, covering the T. One of the CSI people must have been very, very bored.

I wandered slowly around the room, making small adjustment to things, approaching the far end of my classroom reluctantly, gingerly, finally halting near the place where we had found Bob. The back lab bench was still askew from when Bob had crashed into it. My eyes went immediately to the corner that had been coated with Bob's blood. It had been cleaned too.

I grasped the opposite edge of the lab bench, intending to push it back into alignment with the rest of the tables, when I noticed a faint outline on the floor that marked where Bob's body had lain. I released the table as if it were contaminated.

I pulled a large bottle of rubbing alcohol from the back cabinet and grabbed a wad of paper towels from the holder above the sink, pausing in a rare fit of cleanliness to remove a piece of string that a student had wound around the faucet and to put away a lone glass beaker that had survived by dint of having been left in the sink. I knelt down near the outline, poured out a stream of liquid and began to scrub. Rubbing alcohol can get permanent marker off a whiteboard, and it got up whatever they had used on the floor pretty easily, but I continued to scrub long after all traces were gone. I poured a good quarter bottle of the stuff over the lab bench. When I was done, I washed my hands and face and blew my nose and sat down heavily on one of the lab stools.

After a while, I became aware of the ticking of the classroom clock and realized I had been in my classroom for almost an hour. "Oh, no," I cried. "Dinner!"

Chapter Thirteen

৪১

As if realizing our usual seating order would be too harsh a reminder that Bob would never again sit in "his" chair, my colleagues sat at random around the rectangular table at the Italian restaurant. Becky had saved me a seat between her and Kendra.

It was a somber table. Everyone wore navy or black, out of deference to Bob's memory. Even Becky was dressed conservatively in dark slacks and a black turtleneck sweater. "Where have you been?" Becky whispered as I sat down. She kept her voice low, in keeping with the funereal atmosphere around the table.

I just shook my head and Kendra touched my arm and said in a low voice, "We ordered for you."

"Yeah, the scampi. Your favorite."

"Thanks," I said, though these days I would've preferred a very rare steak. "I'm starved."

"Have some bread." Becky grabbed the basket at Roger's elbow and held it out to me.

"No, thanks." Normally, I could have eaten the entire basket of warm, fragrant rolls, but now they looked unappetizing. I silently cursed Will for destroying my appetite for pretty much everything that wasn't rare beef, coffee or chocolate. I hoped it wasn't permanent, or I would die an early death anyway, from scurvy.

"You're not on that Atkins diet or anything are you?" Kendra said.

"No, just holding out for the entrée." The waiter arrived with our dinners just then, thankfully forestalling the inevitable discussion (scientific treatise, more like) on what those diets did to a body.

Everybody dug in hungrily and I forced myself to ignore the enticing aroma of Alan's juicy, rare T-bone and speared a plump garlicky shrimp and popped it in my mouth. Almost immediately, my mouth caught on fire and I gulped down half the contents of my water glass.

"You okay there?" Becky said, laughing as I gasped and blotted my eyes with my napkin.

"I'm fine. What's in this stuff? It's really spicy."

"It's just scampi," she said. "The same thing you always get. I don't think there're any chili peppers in it. You could have gotten a stray one though."

"You're probably right."

I examined the next shrimp carefully before eating it, but it, too, burned like a mouthful of Scotch bonnets. I felt nauseated, and for a moment I thought I was going to hurl then and there, in front of all my colleagues. I excused myself and managed, just, to make it to the ladies' room before I threw up.

When I came out, Becky was waiting for me.

"Did you just get sick?"

"Yeah." I grimaced. "I think the shrimp's bad."

Becky put a comforting hand on my back. "You poor thing. Do you want to go home? I can make your excuses for you, if you want."

Kendra joined us. "Are you okay?"

"Bad shrimp," Becky said, answering for me. "She's going to go home."

"That's terrible," Kendra said. "I'll go back and tell everyone so the rest of the department doesn't come in here?" she said it as a question.

"Thanks," I said gratefully. Becky went out ahead of me, collected my purse, and saw me to my car before I shooed her back to the table so she could finish her dinner.

* * * * *

I'd felt fine ever since the shrimp had come back out, and as the experience didn't seem to have squelched my hunger pangs, I found myself pulling up to a drive-through window on the way home for one of those obscenely large burgers. I ordered it rare, E. coli be damned.

As I scarfed it down in my car in the parking lot—the fast food maneuver of shame—I faced what happened at the restaurant. I wondered darkly who had suggested ordering the scampi for me, and whether it had really been done out of altruism. The shrimp had been fine. I'd put money on it. However, when you order scampi, with the shrimp comes a lot of garlic.

It was the garlic that had been the problem. Or rather, I had been the problem for the garlic.

I had seen horror movies where the vampire backs off cringing and hissing whenever someone shoves a garland of garlic in his direction. I had always thought the vampire's response a little excessive, but now I totally understood. If a tiny bite of garlicky pasta sent me, only part vampire, reeling to the ladies' room, I can only imagine what it did to someone like Will.

It got me to wondering about vampires. I pretty much knew from experience the disgusting things were true. The problems with sunlight? True. My skin was a freaking nightmare. The taste for blood? My sudden interest in licking the raw juice off the steak packaging when I came up from the supermarket was close—and gross—enough for me to buy into that one. And as for the reflection in the mirror, well, mine had gotten so dim I had long since resorted to rubbing gunk on every reflective surface in the science wing, including the glass display cabinets that lined the hallway, so everyone's reflection would look blurry.

But what about the cool things? I mean, when did I get to turn into a bat?

I thought about Will. He seemed so normal—aside from the fascination with my neck and wanting to kill me and all, of course. But was he alive or was he really dead? I understood now why someone had coined the term *undead*—they really did need another category for someone like him—but that's all it was, another category. It didn't tell me what Will *was*.

What did he do when he wasn't trying to recruit new members or harassing me? I tried to remember if I had seen him drink anything at the club that first night but drew a blank. Do vampires ever eat regular food? I wondered. Do they have to shower? Brush their teeth? Do they get colds? Surely they don't sleep in coffins like they do in the movies, I thought with a shudder.

I was getting close to my apartment, and as I looked for a parking space, I wondered where Will lived. Somehow I couldn't picture him in the moldy old castle traditionally associated with vampires. He seemed too modern for that, and on a practical note, there weren't any moldy old castles to be had in Long Beach. I could picture him living somewhere cool, like a chrome and glass house right on the beach, if all that light wasn't such an issue. Actually, the light would be an issue wherever he lived. How in the world did he get around *that* problem?

I wouldn't have to wonder for long. I could just ask him. He was standing on my front porch talking to my mother.

With all that had gone on, I had forgotten that I was supposed to meet her for our monthly movie night.

With a skill I didn't know I possessed, I crammed my car into a tiny parking spot a half block away and ran full-out down the street toward my apartment. I couldn't hear what Will was saying to my mother, but whatever it was, he had definitely captured her interest.

As I ran up the path from the sidewalk to my building, Will leaned toward her and my heart leaped in my throat. If anything happened to her…

I put forth an additional spurt of speed. But I wasn't in time to stop him.

"I adore your daughter." Will's low voice carried clearly through the night air. He was speaking in that confessional way that drove mothers to plan their daughter's wedding—or get rid of the boyfriend.

My mother clasped her chest in delight. And why wouldn't she be thrilled? He was handsome, charming and well-spoken.

"I think I fell in love with her the first night we met," he said. "I noticed her right away—she has the loveliest hair, like a sunrise…"

"She *does* have pretty hair."

I flew past my mailbox and took the stairs two at a time.

Will drew closer to my mother. "I find her intriguing. She's the sort of woman a man wouldn't get tired of, even if he spent an eternity with her."

My mother looked ready to propose *for* me.

"Oh, God," I said between gasps of air. I took the last two stairs in one flying leap.

The sound of my voice—or my heavy breathing—alerted Will to my arrival. He sent a startled look in my direction, kissed my mother's hand, and managed to slip away before I could get to him and kill him. My mother was too enthralled by what she'd heard and the fact that I'd finally brought home a man with lovely old-fashioned manners to notice he hadn't really said a proper goodbye—or that he'd seemed to have gone the wrong way. The walkway dead-ended around the corner. I was a little curious to know how he planned to get down, but hustled my mother inside before we could find out.

"Jo, dear," she breathed excitedly. "I've met your Will!"

"Why don't you sit down and relax, Mom." Damage control. I needed damage control. I didn't know what Will was up to, but this couldn't be good. For her own safety, my mother needed to avoid him like the plague. But by the look on her face she'd already welcomed him into the bosom of the family and was imagining her beautiful grandchildren.

"He's very handsome." My mother sat genteelly on the sofa. "You'd have gorgeous children." Yep. Right on schedule. "You didn't even tell me you were dating anyone. And here I was so worried that you were all alone."

I let the unfeminist remark go. I had bigger problems. I racked my brains. Will was gorgeous, polished, charming and seemed to dote on me. How could I convince my mother he wasn't perfect when he was—except for that tiny personality flaw of wanting me dead, and for all I knew, her too. It was a mark of how desperate I was to keep her away from him that I considered telling her the truth.

"What does he do?" she asked, tipping her head to one side to look up at me.

And there it was. My opening. "I'm so glad you like him," I gushed. "He's an assistant manager at the coffee shop around the corner. That's how we met!"

Her face fell. "Assistant manager?" she said falteringly.

"Oh, yes! He just got promoted. After five years!" I knew for fact our neighbor's teenage son got promoted in a similar job after only eight months and he was the dumbest kid I'd ever met. "I'm so proud of him."

The little hiccup of joy in my voice clinched it.

My mother quickly changed the subject.

Jo one, Will zero.

Chapter Fourteen
ℰ

To my great delight, Saturday morning dawned gray and drizzly, which meant I could go watch the Bayshore boys varsity soccer team play our biggest rival without turning into a patty melt. I slathered on sunscreen with an SPF in the stratosphere, donned a waterproof jacket with an oversized hood that shadowed my face and wound a scarf in Bayshore's colors around the small part of my face and neck that still showed. Dr. Ngata would probably say that my precautions weren't enough and I should wear the mask, but I figured why not live on the edge? I was half dead anyway.

As soon as the coffee pot had discharged enough liquid to fill my industrial-sized travel mug, I drove over to the soccer stadium.

Both sides of the stadium were packed with fans whose colorful, team-inspired attire, waving team pennants, and homemade banners made the institutional gray stands as bright and festive as a parade route during Mardi Gras. A cheerful path of damp and drooping maroon and gold streamers and balloons that nodded and ducked in the wind directed me down a soggy path to the Bayshore side, where a loud, energetic crowd waited for the game to begin. Soccer was a big draw at Bayshore, commanding the sort of frenzied following usually reserved for football, and attendance was even higher than usual. From the snatches of conversation that blew my way as I stood in the aisle looking for a seat, I gathered the game had become something in the way of an Irish wake for Bob. Without the alcohol. Mostly.

About the time I was ready to give up looking for her, Becky appeared out of nowhere, waving her arms and yelling my name. It took me a moment to recognize her—her petite figure was wound so many times with an extra-long, extra-wide Bayshore scarf she looked like a maroon-and-gold-striped barber's pole. Becky never ceased to amaze me. I had never met anyone who could pull off hip punk rocker one day and ardent high school sports fan the next.

She pointed behind her to an alcove near the team bench where enterprising rays of sun would have to get through three feet of concrete if they wanted to touch my fair skin, and I clambered down the bleachers and squeezed in next to her just as the ref blew the whistle to start the game.

"Whew!" I stamped my feet in a vain attempt to knock off some of the water before it soaked in. I cupped my hands around my giant stainless steel coffee mug, glad for the warmth and wished I had thought to bring a seat cushion to protect my hindquarters from the cold bench that seemed to drain the warmth from my body. The ugly weather might be good for my skin, but the rest of me still preferred it warm and sunny.

Down on the field, the difficulty of controlling a wet ball made for conservative playing. After a few minutes of watching the two teams pass the ball back and forth in the middle of the field, Becky's rapt attention began to wane. She kept one eye on the game but turned slightly toward me so we could chat. She pointed to my coffee mug. "I see you're subjecting your stomach to its usual morning acid bath. You must be feeling better. Want some?" She proffered a cardboard container of lukewarm tortilla chips and orange liquid cheese masquerading as nachos.

I shivered and pushed it away. "I was feeling better until you put those in my face. How can you eat those things? The smell alone nauseates me."

She grinned, loaded up a chip with plastic cheese and several pale green rings of hot jalapeno, and chomped down ecstatically. "Mmm. These are great. You don't know what you're missing."

"Ugh. Talk about setting your insides on fire! Isn't a little early the morning to be eating such spicy food?"

"Are you kidding? You should see what my mom eats for breakfast. She makes a tofu chi-gae that'll knock your socks off."

"What's chee gay?"

"A spicy soup—lots of garlic and hot Korean chili paste. Trust me, a couple jalapenos is nothing." She grabbed the Bayshore pennant off her lap and jumped to her feet, yelling as our sweeper stole the ball from the other team and booted it down to our forward line. I got to my feet, too, as Bayshore scored the first goal of the game.

By the end of the half, I had unwrapped my scarf from around my face and was waving it energetically as a makeshift pom-pom. Our boys had continued to dominate the field and were beating the snot out of the competition. Our left wing scored his third goal seconds before the ref called the half, sending the Bayshore fans into a frenzy.

"Man, our team is amazing!" I gushed when I caught my breath from yelling.

"I think Bernard just cemented his soccer scholarship." Becky pointed to the left wing who grinned widely as his teammates held up three fingers and chanted *hat trick, hat trick.*

A familiar-looking, stocky woman who had gone down to talk with the players rejoined us in time to hear this remark and affirmed that this was probably true.

Becky introduced me. "Jo, I'm not sure if you know Rachel. She was the assistant boys' varsity coach last year but now she's head coach over at Polytech."

I remembered then where I had seen her. "I think we met once, when you were at the coffee shop with Bob," I said, shaking her hand.

Her face took on a bittersweet look. "Yeah. The place with all the ambience. Bob loved that rat hole."

Her eyes filled with tears and I quickly changed the subject. "Kendra seems to be filling in nicely as coach."

"Oh, she's great," agreed Becky enthusiastically. "In fact, she'll probably be coaching them next year."

"Actually," Rachel said, "I'm pretty sure she turned down the job already."

Becky's eyebrows shot up into her hair. It was still black from her holiday dye job, but she had added a few maroon stripes. "Why would she do that? The boys' team is way more prestigious than the girls' — not that it should be of course."

"I know. Boys' team coaches can make a small fortune coaching summer league. But for some crazy reason, Kendra decided she wanted to keep coaching the girls."

"Good for her," Becky said. "She's worked hard to build her team — they might have a real chance at the league title next year. It's nice to see that she's not going to leave the girls just to chase money."

Rachel nodded. "She really cares about the sport, even helped me get the job over at Polytech."

I couldn't hide my surprise. I felt sure Bob hadn't known. It had been obvious her departure had been a blow to him — and for the team as well. He hadn't found an adequate replacement or Kendra wouldn't be down there now, pitching in. Rachel must have read something of this in my silence, for she hastened to add, "I asked Kendra not to tell Bob — or anyone at Bayshore for that matter. I didn't want her to bear the brunt of my defection when all she was doing was being nice. It can be hard for women to get good coaching jobs."

Understandable. Commendable, even. "How's your new team doing?"

She dimpled. "We're not in the same league as you guys — literally and figuratively — but it's nice being the head coach. "

"Well, if Kendra doesn't want the job, maybe you could come back next year as head coach."

"Oh, I don't think so," she demurred. "I think they'd want someone more experienced."

"You should think about it," urged Becky, warming to the idea. "Bob said you were good, and I know the kids liked you."

Rachel's reply got lost in the roar of the crowd. The game had started up again and we hastened to take our seats. The light misty rain that had been falling on and off all morning had picked up a little during half time, making the second half more mud-ball than soccer, full of unexpected turnovers and dramatic saves. I booed and cheered energetically along with the Bayshore crowd, but in truth I barely saw the game. My mind was back on Bob's murder.

If what Becky had said about Rachel's credentials was true, Rachel had a good shot at getting Bob's coaching position. As she'd said, it was a prestigious and lucrative job—and one Rachel couldn't have hoped to get in a million years had Bob not died. Was it possible she had killed him for it?

I didn't know if she *would* have done it, but I was pretty certain she *could* have. I wouldn't have been surprised if Bob had invited her to join us for a beer after the parent conferences. His last conference had been at eight. What if she'd made plans to meet him in his classroom? She knew her way around campus. It was possible she'd made it upstairs unseen. After killing Bob, she could have ducked into an empty classroom when she'd heard Alan coming up the stairs, and disappeared past him back down the stairs when he went into my classroom to help Bob.

I stole a glance at Rachel. She was cheerfully absorbed in the game and cheering wildly, and my image of her as a stealth killer faded like the wild fantasy it undoubtedly was. It was hard to imagine her killing Bob, over a coaching job of all things, especially when she already had one that she apparently liked. And she had seemed genuinely sad over his death. But then lots of people have done things in the heat of the moment they've regretted afterwards.

I stifled a sigh. I was having a hard time with this sleuthing thing. Thinking the worst of everyone was unexpectedly depressing. I could, of course, unassign myself, but I knew I wouldn't. Bob hadn't deserved to die. And I hadn't forgotten (nor had the Bayshore community) that I had been tacitly implicated in his death.

On a positive note, I could probably scratch Kendra off the list, since she had turned down Bob's coaching job. *And what a shame that was,* I thought as our team scored another goal to seal the win. She really was a good coach.

Chapter Fifteen

ଏ

It was eight o'clock on a Saturday night and I was sitting at home, alone, on my couch, flipping through channels and getting unreasonably irritated that there was never anything even halfway decent on weekend nights. For some reason, the TV network execs always seemed to believe I led a much more exciting life than I did.

I clicked off the TV and threw down the remote in disgust, at a loss of what to do with myself. I refused to grade papers on a Saturday night out of principle. I should be out doing something—figuring out who murdered Bob, for example. But, there wasn't much I could learn outside of school and besides, I couldn't go out at night anymore, now that I was afraid of the dark. Or rather, what lurked in the dark.

Was this what my life was going to be like from now on?

I had gotten rather used to the monastic life of a teacher—the early mornings, early nights, and days spent in the company of preteens doesn't exactly lend itself to a wild social life. But I had been able to accept it as a short-term problem, a brief dry patch that was probably good for me in some wholesome, personal development sort of way, and had consoled myself with promises to make up for it over the summer. But now...

Even if someone were to ask me out, could I even go? What if I ran into Will? Or even another vampire? There *were* more of them out there and from my experience with them, vampires tended to frequent the sort of places people went to on a date.

Yet if I were to be honest with myself, it wasn't really the vampires *out there* that I was worried about. I was worried about *me*, what *I* might do. What if, some time between the appetizer and entrée, my vampness suddenly took over and I bit my date? Could I even do it? I ran my tongue worriedly over my incisors. Were they growing longer? They seemed normal, but maybe I was just used to my new fangs.

I reminded myself that Will's teeth had looked perfectly normal when I had met him, and felt a moment of relief. Maybe that whole pointy incisor thing was just a myth. Nonetheless, just to be sure, I forced myself to recall what Will's teeth had looked like after he had bitten my neck, and for a moment, I was transported. I remembered the fear, felt the terror that held me captive as I watched his teeth descend again toward my throat. I made a noise like a gargled scream and snapped myself out of it. A cold sweat beaded my brow and I wiped it away with a shaking hand.

It wasn't a pleasant memory, but I had gotten the information I'd wanted. Will's incisors had been wolfishly long, much longer than he wore them normally, if that's the right way to put it. I leaned back on the couch, taking deep yoga breaths—with my eyes open—until the memory had faded, and soon my native curiosity reasserted itself. How *did* vampires get their teeth to work?

There must be some sort of trick to it, some way to get them to grow on cue. Unfortunately, if there was a trigger I didn't know how it worked. What if I set off my fangs by accident? Worse, what if I couldn't get them to retract? What did I tell my date? "Sorry, gotta go, dental emergency. Could you be a doll and call 1-800-DENTIST for me? Tell them to send a van."

I paced frantically around my small apartment for a while before ending up, as I always do in times of great stress, in front of the fridge. I opened it, but instead of taking out butter and eggs for cookies, I found myself reaching for an apple. I stared at it for a long moment.

Then I tilted my head and sank my front teeth into it.

"Ow!" I cried, fingering my aching teeth in dismay. They hadn't penetrated more than a couple millimeters into the cold, hard fruit. I probed my aching incisors curiously with my tongue. Nothing. Undeterred, I plucked a large tomato from the fruit bowl on the counter.

This time, I was more successful, at least insofar as my teeth made definite headway into the fruit, but it was a *very* ripe tomato and it squirted everywhere. Okay, I reasoned, wiping seeds off my forehead, the first one was too hard, this one was too soft. But that was about as far as I got with the logic part, as I refused to admit to myself that what I was really looking for was something approximating a person's neck.

I began trying things pretty much at random, biting them in the order I found them. In short order, a bell pepper, a cucumber, an orange, and a head of lettuce joined the growing reject pile on the counter. In growing frustration, I routed around in the fridge for more things to try. I had high hopes for the cheddar cheese, but it, too, was a bust. Finally I tried what I should have started with—a raw steak. I pulled tomorrow night's dinner from the fridge and removed the butcher paper. I held it firmly between my hands, thought vampire-ish thoughts, took a bite and...nothing happened.

I conceded defeat. I hadn't succeeded in getting even the tiniest of fangs with anything I had tried. I must have been going about this the wrong way. Maybe it wasn't a physical trigger. Maybe it was something more...bloody.

Unfortunately, most of the ways I could test that theory were disgusting, immoral, and impractical, unless I wanted to bite my own arm, which was just plain gross.

After some consideration, I pulled the blender out of the cabinet and threw in a cup of water and the steak. Once I had puréed it into a fairly homogenous red mash, I poured it through a sieve into a glass. Tiny specks of red floated around randomly like dust motes. I took a cautious sniff. It smelled, not surprisingly, like raw beef. I closed my eyes, tried to imagine it was blood and I was a vampire, and took a large drink.

I don't know which was worse, the taste or the texture. The blending had warmed it a little which made it, if possible, even nastier. I spat it out into the sink and rinsed my mouth under the tap for good long time.

I was so absorbed in getting every last speck out of my mouth that I didn't hear the doorbell ring. I did hear the pounding on my door. It was Gavin.

"Oh good, you're home. I thought you might be."

"What's that supposed to mean?" It was one thing for Gavin to find me home alone and dateless on a Saturday night and quite another for him to expect it.

He checked his automatic progress toward my kitchen and the cookie jar to look at me in surprise. "Your car was out front and the lights were on in your apartment."

Oh. "Well, I'm busy." I placed myself squarely between him and the kitchen. He regarded me suspiciously for a moment and then moved past me. He stopped just inside the kitchen doorway and stared open-mouthed at the mess.

The various items I had mangled and discarded lay on the counter in haphazard piles, and the meat purée, which had oxidized to a sickening brownish grey, coated it all like a foul slime.

But that wasn't the worst part. Even from where I stood, I could see teeth marks in several of the fruits and vegetables. The tooth imprints in the red apple, in particular, were clearly demarcated, like a picture in a Snow White storybook. It didn't take a brain surgeon to guess what I had been doing.

"Had a little trouble deciding what to have for dinner?"

I pushed past him and began shoving the ruined food into the trash. I could feel the red flush of embarrassment spreading from my burning cheeks to the tips of my ears. Gavin didn't say anything as I tossed and wiped and cleaned. When I was done, the entire counter area by the sink was sparkling, in conspicuous contrast to the rest of the kitchen.

I dried my hands on a clean kitchen towel and turned around slowly to face him. I didn't know what to say. He stared at me for along moment with unreadable silver eyes and then slowly reached forward and brushed a finger against my cheek. When he pulled his hand back, there was a tomato seed clinging to his finger.

"Come on." He spoke roughly. "You need to get out." He led the way back outside and after a brief hesitation, I grabbed my coat, tucked my driver's license, a credit card and two twenties into the back pocket of my jeans, and followed him. It wasn't as if I had anything better to do.

"I thought I had to stay indoors at night," I said as he beeped open the Jetta.

"You should," he agreed. He stretched the seat belt across his broad chest in one quick, efficient movement and pulled away from the curb.

"I thought you were supposed to encourage me to do what I 'should' do."

"I'm supposed to keep an eye on you. I can do that from the batting cages. Just be sure to choose a wooden bat, just in case. That's a joke, Jo."

"Uh huh."

Twenty minutes later we pulled up to a well lit urban amusement park I never knew existed. The place pulsed with light and sound. "You were serious about the batting cages," I said, trying to take it all in. In addition to the batting cages, there was a mini-golf course, a speedway where you could race miniature roaring Formula One cars on a winding track, and a giant arcade with glittering, jangling machines of all types. In the middle of it all, a large, multicolored outdoor carousel piped out old-fashioned music that wove through all the discordant sounds like a cooling breeze.

Two hours later, after I had knocked many, many balls senseless, Gavin steered me into the food court and bought me a large hot fudge sundae. I felt like a little kid, happy and tired after a healthy dose of good clean fun. Vampires and murderers seemed as distant and remote as fairy tales, and for once, Gavin didn't bring them up. I couldn't help but wonder why he had done this for me, and how he knew this was just what I needed. Maybe he hadn't been lying when he told me I reminded him of his little sister.

Despite having taken great pains to eat my sundae like a lady, I managed, as I somehow always do, to get hot fudge on myself and had to go to the bathroom to de-sticky.

It was the first time I'd gone into a public restroom without first doctoring the mirrors, and I entered warily, not sure what I'd do if someone noticed that I didn't reflect as well as everybody else. Thankfully, I had it all to myself.

I wet a wad of flimsy brown paper towels and dabbed gently at my chin, but I couldn't see myself well enough in the mirror for such a genteel cleanup to have much effect so I bent down and washed my face in the sink. As I was rinsing off the soap, I heard the door open and stole a glance at the mirror, trying to assess whether it was mounted high enough over the sinks for me to stay out of range. Fortunately, it didn't matter. No one had come in. I breathed a sigh of relief. Really, this whole vampire thing was ridiculously hard to live with.

I reached for more paper towels to dry my face when suddenly I felt the hairs on the back of my neck stand up.

"Hello, Jo," said a voice behind me as a blast of musky perfume hit me like a wall.

I jumped about a foot in the air and turned to find Natasha standing behind me. She was calmly applying lipstick—by feel, I assume, since her lovely heart-shaped face didn't reflect one whit in the mirror. "Jesus," I said, clasping a hand to my chest. My heart was beating so fast I wondered if I was having a heart attack. "You scared the crap out of me!"

Her smile made my flesh crawl. "Oh, did I? Poor Jo. I'm so sorry."

"What are you doing here?" I tried to keep the nervousness out of my voice, though I knew Natasha was well aware of her impact. "Are you following me?"

"Now, why would I do that?" She drifted closer, blocking my path to the door. I resisted the impulse to move backward, surreptitiously bending my knees instead, in case she attacked.

She pouted prettily. "Really, Jo. I don't know why you act so hostile toward me."

"Maybe it's because you killed my friend." Truth be told, my fear of her had little to do with whether or not she had killed Bob.

This gave her pause. "Did I?" she said delightedly, "Which one was he? Oh wait, you don't mean that teacher, do you?" She tilted back her head and laughed. "Really, honey, that's not my style." Her smile faded and her lovely face took on an unbecoming hardness. "You know as well as I that I didn't harm a hair on his head. Will told you he'd put him off limits."

She stepped closer, eyes glittering dangerously. "You're off limits too." She reached out a hand tipped with long, red nails and stroked my hair. I cringed. "You're his new pet. None of us can touch you. He wants to turn you himself. You should be flattered. He hasn't troubled himself over a new recruit in a long time."

I shoved her hand away from me. "How interesting. Wait, don't tell me. The last person he recruited, it you wasn't it?"

Her eyes narrowed dangerously as she managed, barely, to keep herself in check. "Don't act so smug, you little bitch. He would never think to blame me if you bled to death from slashed wrists in a public bathroom, would he?"

I realized I'd made a mistake and had pushed her too far. I was pretty sure she didn't have a knife on her—her tiny purse wouldn't hold one, and the bulging curves in her formfitting clothes were all her—but that didn't mean she wasn't dangerous. I glanced wildly around the room, looking for something I could use as a weapon or a shield, but even the trashcan was nailed securely to the wall.

Natasha smiled excitedly, a singularly unpleasant look, and began to circle me, like a cat playing with a mouse. I was about to scream for Gavin, when a group of girls came storming into the bathroom, giggling and rushing for the stalls. I pushed past Natasha and ran out of the bathroom toward the food court. I took the last corner at a full sprint and ran smack into Gavin.

"Aaargh!"

He grabbed my shoulders to steady me. "Are you all right? Did something happen in there? What took you so long?"

I took a gulping breath. "Natasha."

A single word was enough. Gavin headed for the ladies' restroom at a run. I followed, and when he would have gone in after her, I grabbed his arm and held him back.

"What are you doing? You can't go in there!"

"What?" He strained against my hold.

"There's half a dozen high school girls in there."

"Then I definitely need to get Natasha out of there."

I shook my head. "She's long gone. She was right behind me when I left." Besides, if I read Natasha right, the last thing she'd want was a bunch of nubile sixteen-year-olds hanging around the love nest back at the castle, or wherever it was they called home.

Gavin led me back to our table in the food court and we both wordlessly turned our chairs so our backs were fully against the wall. I sat down with a thump. My knees were still shaking. The carnival music that had so charmed me earlier jarred my ears with its frivolity.

The food court was in the middle of everything and had floor-to-ceiling windows. It was an ideal location to hunt for someone—wayward children, potential dates, vampires—and had probably been designed with just that attribute in mind. "What did she want?" asked Gavin.

"Oh, I don't know, to kill me?"

"She won't hurt you."

I made a noise of disbelief. "Says you."

Gavin stopped scanning the room for a moment to focus impatient gray eyes on me. "I told you. She can't. Not unless Will allows her, and he won't. He won't let another vampire finish off his work, especially a lower ranked one. It would make him look bad. She's just trying to scare you."

Natasha had said as much, but she'd also suggested an easy way around such restrictions. "Know that for a fact, do you? Well, you're free to believe what you want, but I don't think she's harmless. Besides, Will probably doesn't even know she's here. She could have knocked me over the head in the ladies' room and no one would ever have known it was her. You wouldn't have, would you? You'd probably think it was just some gang banger. You are ridiculously closed minded when it comes to vampires killing people the regular way."

"Back on that again, are you? I told you, they don't work like that."

"And I told you, however much you believed in your theory, it's just that. A theory. Pardon me if I choose not to believe Natasha's filled with good intentions when it comes to me."

Gavin reached for his phone.

"Who are you calling?"

"Backup. If she's still here, there's a good chance she hasn't killed yet, and I'm tired of finding bodies." He broke off to speak with the person at the other end of the line.

When he was done, he turned back to me. "I'll have another officer take you home. In the meantime, why don't you give me as detailed a description as you can. I think I have a pretty good idea of her physical description from the last time you saw her. So why don't you start with what she was wearing."

As little as possible. "A dark blue miniskirt and a lighter blue camisole. Trust me. You'll know her when you see her. She's every man's fantasy."

"Not every man's." His phone beeped. "They're here." He stood up. "C'mon."

Chapter Sixteen

&

I balanced my jumbo cup of coffee atop a thick stack of handouts that were still warm from the copy machine, pushed my classroom door open with my shoulder and stopped dead on the threshold. "What the hell?"

Every surface gleamed. There wasn't a paper out of place or a book out of line. Even the glue gun gone wild dioramas were as tidy and well-behaved as a row of altar boys on a Sunday morning. The headmaster must have ordered the janitorial staff to give the room an extra scrub over the weekend, and boy had they. The room was clean. Too clean.

The place looked like a morgue.

But if there's one thing I'm equal to, it's a clean room. In no time at all I had the room messed back up to my usual level of casual housekeeping. I re-cluttered the counters with handouts and papers I'd graded over the weekend, dragged the dioramas back to their usual spots and hid as much of the gleaming desktops as I could with dusty trays of soil samples that probably hadn't seen the light of day since 1965. When I was satisfied my room looked its usual lived-in self, I popped down to the faculty lounge to check my mail, leaving my classroom open for the early birds as had been my habit. I wanted things to be as normal as possible for my students.

In the faculty lounge, Roger was holding court near the coffee maker. By his side was a small mousy woman I judged to be in her mid-thirties. Roger beckoned me over to meet her.

"This is Mrs. O'Neill. She will be taking over for Bob." His voice rang out as if introducing royalty and then dropped to just above a whisper as he introduced me like I was the poor stepcousin. "Jo teaches eighth-grade earth science, and is new to the profession. I'm sure she'll appreciate any tips you can give her."

His words had me seeing red but she held out her hand in a friendly gesture and I forced my tight lips into a smile.

"Hi Jo, I'm Leah." She spoke quickly, in a cheerful rush. "It's a pleasure to meet you, and I hope you'll be the one to teach *me* things. As it stands, I can barely find my way to my classroom. And it's *Ms*. O'Neal," she corrected Roger nicely. "I'm a single parent."

Roger frowned at this unexpected broaching of what he considered an indelicate subject and steered her firmly away from me—as if I were poisoning her—toward a group of English teachers. I left to the sound of Roger reciting Leah's credentials (they were impressive) in a pompous voice and puffing out his chest at their nods of respect, as if *he* was the one with the master's degree from Harvard.

I had been away from my classroom longer than I had planned and hurried back, taking the upper hallway at a run when I heard all the noise coming from my classroom. I arrived wheezing for breath at my doorway to find two of my more "challenging" homeroom kids having a sword fight. And not just any sword fight—one of the boys was lunging at the other with a giant six-foot lance made from two meter sticks stuck together with duct tape.

"Knock it off!" I grabbed hold of the "sword" just in time to prevent a decapitation. "Take the tape back off the meter sticks and put them away."

"Aww!"

"But we found them this way!"

"Right. And the meter sticks just pulled themselves out from under the sink and tied themselves together." I raised my eyebrows and made an untying gesture with my hands and they sullenly began pulling off the duct tape. I didn't kid myself that they heeded me out of any respect for my authority. I'd spent the past five months establishing a useful system of bribes or punishment, and they knew better than to be the reason no one got doughnuts on Friday.

The bell rang, cutting off the rest of their complaints as they shuffled off to their classes. My first period students arrived on the heels of their departure and I instructed them to get out the homework I'd assigned over the weekend. Lots of grumbling and whining about the workload accompanied the zipping of backpacks, sounds of shuffling paper, and loud thunks of earth science texts being dropped onto desktops. As I made the rounds, I overheard a lot of gossipy speculation about where exactly in the classroom Bob had died, but the urgency about Bob's death had clearly faded over the weekend.

It was a little sad, how quickly he was becoming a memory. But it had been almost a week since his death — and they still thought Bob had died by accident.

And that wouldn't change unless the police arrested someone, but they were no closer to finding his killer. Nor was I, for that matter. Maybe it was time to step up my efforts? I would, I promised myself, but later. I pushed all thoughts of Bob's murder to the back of my mind and forced myself to focus on my students.

I finished my rounds, put my grade book on my desk and went to the whiteboard in the front of the room. "All right," I said, uncapping a blue marker. "Now." I looked out at my students and saw…complete and utter disinterest. These were good students. They'd read the chapter on minerals and answered the questions at the end of it — or at least taken the trouble to copy someone else's — and knew what was in store for them. Unit 3: Rocks and Minerals. They didn't like it. Neither did I. I don't know what brilliant minds decided eighth graders were the proper recipients for long chapters on ore deposits and glaciers, but they should be hauled out back and shot.

I'd be happy to hold them down, and by the looks of it, quite a few of my students would volunteer as well. I turned to face my class and projected as much enthusiasm as I could muster into my voice. "Minerals," I said. I wrote it on the board in big blue letters and examined my handiwork. Maybe I should have chosen a more lively color. Didn't blue put people to sleep? I held up a rocket-shaped rose crystal; a thin, flaky sheet of pale gold; and a shiny, metallic cube made up of hundreds of smaller cubes. "Rose quartz, mica muscovite, and galena." I passed them around. "All minerals, all different. Can anyone tell me what they have in common?"

A hand shot up. "Ms. Gardner?"

"Yes?" I tried to keep the sound of desperation out of my voice.

"Do we get to set anything on fire today?"

I sighed quietly. "No." They sighed quietly. It was a long class. When three girls in the front row started passing notes back and forth, I could hardly blame them.

* * * * *

Now that the third quarter had begun, I lost my second period prep to second-period study hall. *Yippee.* Thankfully, the group was so small I was able to hold it in my classroom instead of the cavernous room off the library that had lots of pillars for students to hide behind and doodle on. I had a reasonable chance of controlling them. Even so, Maxine had arranged for me to have an aide, a nice Junior boy who needed some charity work to buff out his college applications. He made all the difference in the world.

I might lack that essential gravitas seasoned teachers have — that ability to walk into a room and command attention with The Teacher's Look. But my aide had something nearly as good — it worked effectively on half my charges, the female half. Christopher was a decent-looking young man, and one who would need a prom date in a couple months. If you thought that state of affairs would escape the notice of twelve- and thirteen-year-old girls, due to something so trivial as age difference, school rules or gross unattainability, you have thought wrong.

With Christopher's help—he leaned against a counter and smiled—I got my study hall relatively under control and went to the back to set up the mineral trays. Christopher followed me back and volunteered to help. I took him up on his offer before he could change his mind.

"What's this?" Christopher held up a nondescript brownish gray mineral.

How the hell did I know? "The names of all the minerals are on the container lids." I may not have mastered The Teacher's Look, but I had gotten very good at temporizing.

He held up a chunk of quartz about the size of his fist. "That one's huge. You don't want it in the trays do you?"

"No, that's a demo specimen. It belongs on the counter there, next to the amethyst—that big purple one."

Our conversation—or rather the proximity of Christopher—had not gone unnoticed by the girls seated near the back. They hadn't done a lick of homework since Christopher had entered the room. One of the braver girls spoke, pitching her voice just above a whisper to match ours. "Oooh, I like that one. It's pretty." She flipped her hair and pointed to a golden knob of pyrite.

Chris was immune to the hair flip but responded to her comment. He really was a nice boy. I don't know how he'd made it to eleventh grade. He held up a rather nondescript hunk of rock that looked as if it had had rusted on one side. "This one's ugly."

I frowned and leaned forward for a closer look. It hadn't had that stain last week. And it hadn't been hidden away in a cupboard. It had been out in the open, on my desk.

I stared at it for a long second before I pulled myself together. "Can you put that down on the counter for a second, Christopher? I just remembered I need to contact the middle school principal about something. If you wouldn't mind taking a note for me?"

"Sure."

I refocused the girls' attention back on their homework and went to my desk in the front of the room to write a note to Maxine. I stuck it in an envelope and sealed it. He was probably too nice a kid to read the note, but under the circumstances I wanted to make darn sure.

Three minutes later, Christopher returned with a note from Maxine requesting that I come to her office during the morning break. I was to leave the rock for the police. As soon as the bell rang, I shooed out the students, carefully locked the door behind me and headed for the administration building. As I rounded the corner toward Maxine's office, Becky flew by me at a run.

"What's the rush?"

She spoke over her shoulder. "Gotta finish prepping for my double lab. See you at lunch." She barreled through the door and disappeared around the corner toward her classroom.

I knocked on Maxine's door. It was open and she was waiting for me, but something about the administration building brought out my polite gene. "Hey Maxine, it's Jo. I got your note—" I stopped on the threshold in surprise. In Maxine's brown leather chair, sitting behind the large, well-polished cherry desk as if he belonged there, was Gavin.

He glanced up briefly from the notes he was making and spoke rather formally, as if to a stranger. "Come in, please, and shut the door behind you."

Surprise made me do exactly as bid, and I took a seat in one of the cushy blue chairs opposite him. "How did you get here so quickly?" It had been a scant ten minutes since I'd sent the message.

"Never mind that." Gavin dismissed me in a gesture and bent to his notes.

I regarded his neat, down-turned head in confusion. Why the sudden cold shoulder treatment? After all we been through surely we were…maybe not friends, exactly, but something!

"Were you already here for some reason?" I asked.

His only response was the scratching of his pen across paper. *Fine. Be that way.* "You must have been," I mused aloud. I recalled my run-in with Becky, who wouldn't normally have left the prep for her double period chem lab to the last minute. "Ah, I have it. The timing of finding that rock in my classroom was mere coincidence. You're here on an official visit, something to do with Bob's death? Re-questioning everyone, are we?"

I plucked a tiny Krackle from the dish of mini candy bars Maxine kept on the corner of her desk and relaxed back against the plush fabric of the chair. It crossed my mind that ten-thirty might be a little too early to start eating chocolate, like drinking before noon, but I decided I didn't care. It seemed a little like closing the barn doors after the horse had gone to try to hide an embarrassing chocolate habit from a man who'd seen me lick the juice off raw hamburger packaging.

Gavin ignored me so studiously I knew I was right, and I couldn't resist needling him. "Poor Detective Raines. Did his boss send him to the principal's office? Are we in twou-ble?"

Gavin's mouth stretched taut in a grim line, and somehow, despite the fact that his square jaw was cleanly shaven and his button-down shirt still crisp across his large, trim frame, he looked as if he already had put in a long day. "I'd like to ask you a few questions…"

"I'm right, aren't I?" I said, leaning forward. "A few concerned, well-connected parents called your boss and complained that no one had been arraigned for Bob's murder yet, so he told you to get over here ASAP before they started complaining to *his* boss. Hah! Welcome to my life, puppet!" I sat back in my chair and grinned widely.

"Are you quite through, Ms. Gartner?"

"Please," I said graciously, with a small elegant wave of my hand, "call me Jo." I popped another Krackle bar in my mouth and chewed happily.

"Dammit, Jo!"

I decided I liked him better when he was acting like a big brother and buying me sundaes. "Okay, okay. I'll behave. I assume you want to know about the rock Christopher found in my room." Thinking about it had a sobering effect, and I put down the next Krackle only partly unwrapped. I explained briefly how we'd come across the rock.

Gavin continued scribbling a few moments after I finished. When he was done, he regarded me from across Maxine's desk, a frown darkening his face. "Show me."

I led the way back to my empty classroom. Here." I pushed aside a glitter- encrusted foam comet and pointed to the rusty-looking specimen I'd stowed behind it. "Christopher found it, in a box of quartz, on the shelf up there but it's feldspar." I realized I was starting to babble and forced myself to focus. "The night Bob died, it was on my desk. I used it as a paperweight."

"Looks like we found the murder weapon." Gavin turned to face me. "I'm afraid I'm going to have to kick you out of your room again." He didn't even try to sound sorry.

Chapter Seventeen

ɕɔ

The next morning before work I hesitated like a coward in the administration building's elegant parquet hallway before slinking through the back door into the faculty lounge to get my mail. I didn't think I could handle more of the ostracism I'd experienced after Bob died.

Fortunately, I didn't have to. My colleagues just went about their business as usual, yawning, bustling, filling coffee cups, reading mail, and generally ignoring me, for which I was truly and ridiculously grateful. I never thought I'd be so delighted to be ignored! It was so much better than being *avoided,* and had Gavin been in the room I would have thrown my arms around him in gratitude. He had managed the impossible and kept my discovery of the murder weapon quiet. It was just as well he was back at the station—he probably would have hurt himself trying to get away from me, and my reputation as a treacherous fiend would have been cemented for good.

In my mail cubby, under a pink phone message and a still warm recycled-paper copy of the daily announcements, lay a creamy white envelope with the Bayshore Academy insignia in the upper left-hand corner and my name in perfectly slanted script across the front. It was from Maxine. She was the only one I knew who still used a fountain pen. I could never get the things to work, myself. My words always came out as invisible dry scratches framed by vast puddles of ink that got smeared across the paper when I wrote the next line.

I ripped open the envelope and pulled out a matching correspondence card embossed with the Bayshore crest.

Maxine was happy to inform me the police had finished with my classroom and I was free to begin using it again.

My shoulders sagged in relief and I offered up a silent prayer of thanks. I'd been forced to show a movie yesterday and I didn't think I'd survive another day of it. My students were even harder to control than usual when the only diversion was a flickering twenty-inch image of badly dressed scientists with hair at least twenty years out of date and a tendency to talk in sleep-inducing monotones. I know I'm promoting an unfair stereotype, but even *I* had trouble focusing on what the eminent scientists were saying under the runaway eyebrows. I kept waiting for the Queer Eye guys to rush in and do a group makeover. You can imagine my disappointment when they failed to show up, four times in a row.

Shortly after the bell rang for morning break, Becky and Carol appeared at my door, bearing coffee. "Hey, guys. What's up? Ooh, Starbucks! What's the occasion?"

My happy smile faded a little as Becky, looking unusually somber, reached back to shut and lock the door behind her.

"Uh, oh. What's up? Am I in trouble or something?"

Becky's eyes opened wide. "In a matter of speaking," she choked.

Carol looked appalled. "Becky!"

I looked from one to the other. "What's going on?"

Carol opened her mouth to speak, but Becky got there first. "Well, the good news is, you're not bulimic."

Huh?

"Really, Becky, that's enough!" Carol said. I was really worried now. Carol never spoke sharply. Never to one of us, anyway. She put a comforting hand on my arm and regarded me earnestly through her gold-rimmed glasses. "Jo, you were seen throwing up in the bathroom the other night at the restaurant, after Bob's memorial service. We weren't the only people from Bayshore there, you know. In fact, quite a number of Bayshore families stopped in after the service."

"Didn't I warn you that you became a public figure the second you signed that teaching contract?" Becky demanded.

"So what?" Frustration crept into my voice. I didn't understand what the fuss was all about. "I had some bad shrimp and threw up. People do that sometimes."

Carol shook her head. "Not so quickly after ingesting the item — unless you have a seafood allergy, which you clearly didn't show signs of — at least according to Dr. Gossip at the next table. And," she added gently, "people who have food poisoning, or the flu, don't stop for a burger on the way home."

"You shouldn't have spurned the nachos at the game on Saturday," Becky chided.

"At least I have some standards," I said. Becky made a face at me but Carol just looked worried. "Look, am I missing something here? I feel as if we're having two different conversations. I mean, who gives a rat's ass what the hell I eat?"

Becky and Carol exchanged an uncomfortable glance.

"What?"

"Jo, people are saying you're pregnant," Carol said quietly.

"It's not true, is it?" asked Becky.

"No! Of course not. What? I — " I was so flabbergasted I couldn't get the words out.

"It gets worse," Becky said. "They're saying it's Bob's."

I opened my mouth to respond but this time not even a sound came out.

The bell rang signaling the end of break. Amid a flurry of sympathetic pats on the back and admonitions not to worry, they rushed off to teach their classes and my students began pouring back in. I just stood there, leaning against my desk for support, staring helplessly down at my cardboard coffee container.

When I noticed the barista's order notes, in thick black ink down the side of the cup, I closed my eyes in defeat. They'd gotten me decaf.

* * * * *

A couple hours later when I stepped into the cafeteria for lunch, two hundred pairs of eyes swiveled instantly in my direction, killing any remaining hope that Becky and Carol had exaggerated the pregnancy rumor. I wanted to crawl in a hole and die, or at least take a tray up to my room and hide out there for a while, but the way things were going, if I left now people would probably think I was rushing off to the bathroom to take care of my new prenatal body functions.

I stiffened my spine, sat at my usual table and I pretended I didn't notice everyone watching what I ate, said and did, just as I ignored the huddled heads and lowered voices as people speculated whether or not the rumor was true. I ate mechanically, forcing every scrap on my plate down my throat, though I was almost defeated by the carrot sticks. They had a funny bitter taste that made me want to gag and a last two went down through sheer willpower alone. On the plus side, it was probably the healthiest meal I'd had in weeks. I resisted the impulse to flee the second I was done eating, and sat laughing and joking with Becky and Carol and Alan until the bell rang. I should have won an Emmy Award for my performance.

By the time the school day was over, I was exhausted from pretending the gossip didn't bother me. Getting drunk had definite appeal, but I was tired of dealing with people and really wanted nothing more than to hole up in my apartment with some books and a *lot* of junk food. Unfortunately, I was all out of books—I seemed to be going through them rather faster than usual of late—so I made a quick detour over to the library on the way home.

I lucked out at once, finding several out-of-print mysteries on the For Sale rack, perfect for restocking my Shitty Day Drawer since I wouldn't have to return them. I tucked them under my arm and then wandered through the stacks, looking for something strong enough to assuage today's indignities. I picked up a couple of science fiction books and then headed to the classics rack to look for a copy of anything by Jane Austen. I picked up three for good measure, and then found myself fingering a paperback copy of *Dracula*. After a moment's hesitation, I added it to my pile.

For some reason, that small decision opened some sort of floodgate. By the time I got to the checkout counter, I had collected a half-dozen more vampire books from the shelves, including two from the Young Adult section. I felt oddly guilty, as if I were checking out self-help books or porn, and was ridiculously relieved when the librarian, oblivious to my inner turmoil or just well trained not to raise so much as an eyebrow over anyone's reading choices, merely look bored.

When I got home, I unplugged the phone and settled on the couch with a giant mug of hot chocolate and the rest of the chocolate chip cookies. Then I pulled all the vampire books out of my bag and spread them on the table. After careful deliberation, I picked up *Dracula* and began to read eagerly, curious to learn something about Will. Not that I suddenly believed *Dracula* was some sort of Vampires for Dummies. But it did seem reasonable that there might be *some* truth among the fiction. After all, the common perceptions about vampires had held up pretty well against the reality. So far.

I got through about half the first paragraph of the introduction before I snapped the book shut. Feeling a little numb, I replaced it with one of the vampire novels I had gotten from the regular fiction section. I made it a whole ten pages in that one before hurling it away from me. In desperation, I picked one advertised as a "fun, breezy read". It had flowers on the cover. I lasted only two chapters before tossing it on the floor and pushing the remaining vampire books off the table with it in disgust. What were these people trying to do? Scare me?

The whole idea was stupid anyhow. Even if there were facts to be found amid the fiction, how the hell was I supposed to identify them? I couldn't tell a legitimate horror from a trumped-up bit of dramatic license and wouldn't be able to, no matter how many vampire books I read, until it actually happened. And from the little bits I had just read, *that* was going to be bad enough. I didn't see any point in scaring myself needlessly in the meantime. If I really wanted to know something, I probably could just ask Gavin. I didn't know how much he knew about vampires, but what he did know, I was sure I could rely on him to tell me straight, without any embellishments. I could call him right now.

But I didn't want to. What I wanted, what I needed, was to enjoy some purely human entertainment. I upended the cookie jar onto a large napkin I'd spread over my lap and settled back into the couch cushions with *Emma*.

* * * * *

At six-thirty the next morning I should have been on my way to work, but I was sitting cross-legged on my bedroom floor in my jammies. Around me, rejected outfits lay crumpled and worthless on the floor. I stared in hopeless desperation at my half-emptied closet, willing new, better clothes to appear, but though the clock ticked inexorably on, none did.

Becky had been right about my stupid, frumpy, old lady cruise-wear wardrobe! Everything I owned made me look pregnant or as if I were trying to hide that I was.

At ten minutes to the hour, I couldn't stall any longer. I threw on a turtleneck sweater over some dark gray pants and hit the road. The sweater was probably baggy enough to house a pregnancy well into the second trimester, but I didn't care anymore. People could think what they wanted—they would anyway. Besides, how long could the humiliation last? I worked at a *school* for crying out loud. It was only a matter of time before someone did something outrageous or embarrassing enough to draw the gossip mongers' attention away from me, and then the stupid pregnancy rumor would die on its own. And if it didn't, I thought grimly, I'd just have to kill it myself. Drinking gin in the hallways between classes and carrying around jumbo boxes of tampons should do the trick.

* * * * *

After school had let out and the last of my students needing extra help had gone home, I popped next door to see how Leah, Bob's long-term sub, was holding up. She was the one person who didn't seem to be in on the pregnancy rumor, which made her an invaluable companion. She was sitting in front of a computer, peering nearsightedly at the screen. I knocked lightly on the open door to get her attention and she looked up with relief.

"Oh good, someone's here to distract me."

"Yup. How're things going so far? Okay?"

"Oh, that's fine," she said dismissively. "Just a little review to make sure the kids are where they should be." She hunched back over the keyboard and frowned at the screen. "Now if only I were as good at these things."

"I'm no expert, but if I can help I will."

"Well what are you waiting for? Pull up a stool and help me find Bob's old lesson plans."

After a half-hour of hunting, we managed to find a couple of promising files. Leah gave an exasperated sigh. "Surely it shouldn't be this hard."

"Normally it isn't. But Bob was a popular guy who taught a popular but difficult subject. He had students in his room all the time. If he hadn't been cryptic about this sort of thing, a determined student could have downloaded his tests in a heartbeat."

Leah moved to the printer tray and began flipping doubtfully through the meager stack of printouts. "This is a start, but I'm still missing a lot of stuff."

I drummed my fingers thoughtfully. "You know, Bob was in the habit of doing a lot of his prep work in coffee shops. I'm pretty sure he brought along his laptop, and it's a good bet he sent copies of things to himself. If you're lucky, you might find some of the stuff you're missing in his e-mail."

"And if I'm not lucky?"

"It's all on a tiny memory stick somewhere. Good luck finding that."

She groaned but rallied. "I think they gave me his e-mail password…" She rooted around the desk and triumphantly held up a bright green Post-it. "I used to think it was a horrible invasion of privacy when I read that employers could monitor their employees' e-mail, but right now, I'm all for it."

I looked away as she carefully typed in Bob's password and hoped such nobility wouldn't cost me later.

Her cell phone rang. "I've got to take this," she said, glancing at the screen. "It's my sitter."

"Want me to keep poking around?"

"Would you?"

As she stepped over to the window where the reception was better, I clicked around in Bob's e-mail, trying to find something that would help Leah out. Bingo. He'd archived his e-mails from last year. I scanned last February's messages, finding a couple labs and the test in short order.

I began opening e-mails at random. I lucked upon lecture notes, which I added to the print queue. As I panned down to the next screen of e-mails I saw one that made me hesitate. The subject line read, "Hey there, sexy thang!"

I vacillated briefly between curiosity and respect for Bob's privacy before going with the former. Gavin had Bob said most likely had been killed in a moment of extreme anger or passion.

If he was right, this letter could be important. I printed out a copy, tucked it in my pocket and deleted it. It was bad enough I'd read it. Moving quickly, I scanned the rest of Bob's e-mails for similarly personal letters, but didn't find any.

By the time Leah finished her phone call, I had February's test back up on screen and was organizing the printouts. She was thrilled and thanked me effusively.

The e-mail was burning a hole in my pocket, but I didn't look at it again 'til I was safely home. I sat down heavily at the kitchen table, smoothed it flat, and read it again. "Hey Sexy," it began. It didn't say much, just thanked Bob for a good time—a "rockin' good" time actually—and ended with the suggestion that they should do it again soon. I read it several times over, trying to determine precisely how close the relationship was, hoping desperately the answer was "not very".

I thrust the note away from me. I should have followed Gavin's advice and stayed out of it.

The e-mail had been sent by "Ag1410". The first part was easy enough to decipher. Ag is the atomic symbol for silver. A quick check in a chemistry text told me 1410 was its melting point. Only one person I knew would have that e-mail tag. A person who had dyed her spiky hair back to a silvery-blonde just that day. Becky.

Chapter Eighteen

ഗ

Early the next morning, I headed for Becky's classroom armed with two cups of Peet's coffee and a bag of cinnamon buns I'd stress-baked around midnight the night before. After much soul-searching, I'd decided to confront Becky about her relationship with Bob before handing the e-mail over to the police, and now I was on my way to do it. Maybe I was being stupid or foolhardy, but Becky was my friend. She wouldn't have thrown me to the wolves, and I couldn't do it to her.

Her classroom was unlocked. Guided by the strains of an old Hendrix tune, I headed past a giant periodic table and a wall of The Far Side cartoons to the chemical storage room in the back. Becky was mixing a batch of dilute sulfuric acid and singing along in a passable voice to *The Wind Cries Mary*.

She shifted her attention away from the large triangular beaker she was filling with distilled water long enough to greet me brightly. "Hey, Jo. You're here early. What's shaking? Give me a sec to finish this up, will ya?"

Her cheerfulness made me feel even more tired than I was. Becky was one of those lucky people who only needed a few hours of sleep at night and could burn the candle at both ends. I, on the other hand, was no Queen of the Night (however hard Will might try to change that), and started in on my coffee while I waited for her to finish.

When she was done, she divested herself of lab coat, gloves, and protective goggles in a fashionable lime green and black that flattered her dramatic coloring. Becky had her own personal supply of lab goggles, "because if you have to wear them all the time, you might as well look good in 'em."

She led the way back to the front of the classroom. "It doesn't smell so bad over here." She accepted the coffee I handed her and tore into a cinnamon bun with a look of rapture.

"God, these are so good. If teaching those little soul-sucking monsters of yours doesn't work out, you should go into the baking business. I swear, just set up a little cart at the front gate before school and at breaks and you'd make a fortune!"

She caught sight of my face, and the dreamy, slightly mercenary light faded from her dark eyes. I had a sudden appreciation for how awkward it must have been for her and Carol to tell me about the pregnancy rumor.

She waved her paper towel napkin in the air like a white flag. "Whatever they're saying, I didn't do it."

I felt a cowardly urge to lie, tell her it was nothing, stop myself from saying something that could irreparably harm our friendship before it was too late. I didn't have to be the one to show her the e-mail. She need never know that I'd seen it. I could just hand it over to the police and Gavin could ask the awkward questions, bear the burden of her response.

But then I'd always wonder, wouldn't I? And if they didn't find the killer, which seemed increasingly likely, that ugly fissure of doubt would grow into an unbreachable chasm, and I would lose my friend just the same.

I pulled the printout out of my pocket and handed it to her before I changed my mind. "Are you sure about that?"

She gave me a brief, quizzical look, unfolded the e-mail, and began to read. "Good Lord! Where did you get *this*?" She giggled.

I hesitated. It was not the reaction I had expected.

"Jeez, Jo, get your mind out of the gutter," she scowled. "What, did you think Bob and I slept together or something?"

"Honestly, I didn't know what to think."

Becky's dark eyes met mine, clear and straight. The only flicker in their depths was one of self-deprecating humor. "Well, I suppose it is suggestive, though *I* wasn't the one lusting after him at the *Dead* concert, or the one who started calling him 'sexy thang'. A group of college girls from somewhere in the South—at least they *said* they were in college, I put them at about sixteen—followed him around all day giggling and sighing." She wiped away a mirthful tear that had collected at the corner of her eye. "Poor thing." She flipped the e-mail over. "Where did you get this anyway?"

"It was in Bob's e-mail files."

"Bob's e-mail? What were you doing rummaging through Bob's e-mail?"

I explained how I'd come across the letter while helping Leah the night before.

"You didn't see any other messages from me, did you?"

"How many more were there?"

"Hell if I remember. We probably e-mailed back and forth a few times before and after the concert. A *Grateful Dead* concert isn't exactly the type of thing Headmaster Huntington wants us to broadcast." She leaned forward and said in a dramatic whisper, "People smoke the evil weed at those things!" She sat back up and said disgustedly, "He gets enough flack from parents about my *hair* for Christ's sake."

"This is the only e-mail I saw, and don't worry, I deleted it for you."

She grinned. "Thanks. I owe you one."

I didn't respond. I felt undeserving of her gratitude. The copy I'd made for Gavin burned a hole in my pocket.

Becky didn't notice my silence; she was re-reading the e-mail and chuckling reminiscently to herself. "Typical," she muttered. "He would save the one with 'sexy' in it."

The early bell rang shrilly, bringing us back to the present with a start. We both glanced reflexively at the clock, even though we already knew it was five minutes past seven and time to let our homeroom students in. Becky leapt to her feet, popped the last bit of cinnamon bun in her mouth, and threw the napkin in the trash. "Thanks for breakfast, and for showing me this." She waved the e-mail and gave me a conspiratorial grin. "I needed a good laugh."

I'm lucky she doesn't hate me, I thought miserably as I fought my way through the chattering upperclassmen outside her door. I had been too quick to suspect a friend on pitiful little evidence. Wasn't it precisely to *prevent* such circumstantial, knee-jerk detecting that I had gotten myself involved in solving Bob's murder in the first place? The police were the ones who were supposed to be ignorant of people and their relationships. *They* were the ones who were supposed to make ridiculous accusations and suspect people who couldn't possibly have done it, not me! I was an idiot and a fool! If I had learned anything from all this, it was to leave the detective work to the professionals.

Gavin would have his way after all. I was off the case.

* * * * *

"Do you think you'll stay on next year?" I chose a golden delicious from the box set out for the teachers during the morning break.

A few feet away, Becky was talking animatedly with Carol. She seemed to bear no scars from our talk that morning, but I was too consumed with my own guilt to join them. I turned back to Leah and pretended I was interested in the answer to my question.

"It depends on a lot of things, most importantly whether Dick Huntington asks me back," Leah replied. She seemed to think twice about the apples when I put mine down with a moue of distaste. The apples were fine, it was just that I had caught myself trying to pretend it was the rare juices of a burger that cascaded over my tongue.

Leah glanced behind me and added, "Speak of the devil... Hello, Dick, Roger, care to join us for a cup of coffee?"

"Certainly." The headmaster's rich voice boomed as he took the short flight of steps up to the covered terrace. Schedule permitting, he liked to join the teachers at coffee break. "Do I understand that my ears should be burning?"

Roger followed in his wake like a runty dog, looking peeved at having lost the headmaster's attention.

"Oh, it was nothing," said Leah. "I was just telling Jo how much I'm enjoying teaching here."

"And we were glad to have you here. I understand the students are adjusting satisfactorily." He looked to Roger for confirmation, but Roger had feigned a sudden and convenient deafness. What should have been a compliment suddenly turned into a subtle questioning of her ability, even though she had been working her tail off and by all reports was doing a great job.

"According to my study hall aide, she's doing a good job filling Bob's shoes. Word is, she's tough, but the kids all seem to like her..." I stopped abruptly when I caught a glimpse of Roger's face. The look in his small, dark eyes was so venomous it sent shivers down my spine. I don't think I had realized how badly Roger wanted that biology position until just then.

Apparently I was the only one aware of Roger's real feelings. Leah pinked slightly at the praise and modestly tried to change the subject, and Headmaster Huntington looked pleased and clapped a hand to Roger's shoulder. "Well Roger, maybe if we're lucky we can get Leah to stay on next year."

Roger managed to say something noncommittal and the headmaster favored us with a wide parting smile and moved on to work the room. Leah suggested a trip to the faculty lounge to check our mailboxes and I went with her. As we walked away, I felt Roger's glare digging between my shoulder blades like a knife.

* * * * *

I thought I had overdramatized Roger's reaction until he showed up in my classroom that afternoon for an impromptu evaluation. There was only one reason why he would have wasted a free period on me when he was about to be swamped with department-wide evaluations in a couple of weeks—to put some black marks on my record. He would probably get what he came for. Today was the day I was starting the dreaded mineral lab, or as I liked to call it, Caveman Weapon Appreciation Day.

So there I was, handing out trays of would-be projectiles, along with bottles of dilute hydrochloric acid and steel files, to a room full of jaded squirrelly tweens. Roger sat on a stool in the back of the room, watching with the benevolence of an orc.

Usually the presence of another teacher turned the students into quiet little angels, so that one tended to get dinged for weak class participation. But my sixth period students seemed to be spurred on to more craziness than usual. I had to take the steel file away from one group of boys who would not be otherwise deterred from drilling a hole through everything they could get their hands on. Mindful of their audience, they responded with loud, crocodile cries of, "But however are we going to learn, Ms. Gartner?" I took away their hydrochloric acid, too.

Roger took it all in with mean little raisin eyes. His face was fixed in a deep frown of disgust, except in those moments when he would note a transgression in his notebook. Then he would smirk. After only twenty minutes, he left patting his notebook and grinning from ear to ear.

When the bell rang, Carol appeared at my door and pulled me aside, taking care to smile benignly at my departing students as if she had just popped in for a chat. She also took pains to hide the fact that she had sprinted from the administration building, which made conversation difficult. "Roger...notes...administration," she wheezed in low tones.

I felt as if someone had punched me in the stomach. "He went straight to Maxine, didn't he?" I said furiously. "He's such a rat..."

"No. Dick Huntington." Her eyes were pools of regret.

"Bastard," I amended in a horrified whisper. Roger was supposed to go over his notes with me and then file a record of our discussion with Maxine, and frankly, that would have been bad enough. Going to the headmaster was worse than tattling, it was selling me out. I knew why he'd done it, of course. My credibility needed to be put into question immediately, lest Dick forget who had praised Leah that morning. A nice ironic twist on the spirit of "consider the source".

Carol glanced at the clock and said hurriedly, "Sally said Huntington will stop by for a visit in about a half-hour." Sally was the headmaster's secretary, and if she said the headmaster was coming to audit my class, he was coming to audit my class. "You'll be fine." Carol patted me on the shoulder and hustled out to get to her next class.

I felt my career slipping away from me. All that hard work I'd put in, all the progress I'd made, had come to nothing. *This* moment, *one* singularly out-of-control class, was what would be remembered when it came time for contract renewal.

My seventh period students had bounced in with their usual high energy, and instead of taking their seats when the bell rang, they stood chatting in groups, fingering the specimens in the mineral trays. They were being curious rather than disrespectful, but after all that had just happened, I snapped. I gave them a talking-to that went down in the history of talking-tos, followed by a good three minutes of righteous glaring. The classroom was so quiet I could hear the clock tick through the minutes. In truth, the students were probably more scared I'd gone off the deep end than sitting in respectful silence, but I didn't care.

When the headmaster "happened by" later that period, my students were models of good behavior.

Hah! Feeling victorious, I headed out of the middle school semester grade review meeting.

* * * * *

Despite the close air of the staff meeting room, I was wide awake and slack-jawed with horror at the gossip coming out of some of my colleagues' mouths. Did we really need to know that Jon Edgecome's algebra grades had taken a dive after his father had gotten remarried—to a twenty-one-year-old Norwegian supermodel?

I wrenched my attention away from an eye-popping picture of the new Mrs. Edgecome in time to answer Maxine's query about the low grade I'd given Chucky Farryll.

Before Maxine could respond, Chucky's French teacher chimed in with a sour look. "I don't believe the Farrylls really care about the boy's education. All they talked about was how much Chucky wanted to play varsity soccer."

His math teacher nodded. "I have to wonder about them as well, Maxine. His mother didn't even show up for her parent conference and I waited in my classroom until 8:45!"

"She was probably collecting her son," Roger said. "I caught the boy roaming the halls around eight and told him to find his mother and go home. Students are not supposed to be on campus during parent-teacher night."

"That's a silly rule." The chair of the English department's scraggly salt and pepper bun quivered with righteousness. "I find I often get better results when the students are present. None of that *he said, she said* nonsense."

Maxine held up a hand to regain control before the meeting dissolved into a free-for-all. "I will talk to Mr. and Mrs. Farryll to see if we can't resolve Chucky's little sit-in before we begin the extra tutoring. Now, let's move on. Sarah Chen. B-student everywhere, D+ in social studies. Jeff, what's the story there?"

"Sarah spends the entire time staring at Erik Evans, no matter where I seat her. Frankly, I'm surprised she managed the D."

Maxine's reply must have been a good one, as it elicited a round of laughter, but I didn't hear it. Had no one but me noticed that the soccer-obsessed Mrs. Farryll had been on campus and unaccounted for during the time when Coach Bob had been killed?

I let out a sigh. My plan to sit quietly on the sidelines and let the police handle Bob's murder investigation hadn't lasted even a day.

Chapter Nineteen

ဢ

By the time the middle school grade meeting ended and I made it to the police station, Gavin had already left for the day.

"Is there any way I could reach Detective Raines tonight?" I asked the desk sergeant. "I really need to talk to him."

"I'm sorry, Miss. I can take a message, if you'd like, or perhaps you'd like to talk to another officer?"

"No, that's all right," I said. I added wryly to myself, "He'll probably be by later anyway."

"What was that, Miss?"

"Oh, nothing, just talking myself." His pale blue eyes regarded me narrowly as I thanked him for his help and left.

When I got home, I fixed myself something to eat and perched outside on the top step to wait for Gavin or one of his lackeys to cruise by. They weren't pulling all-night watches anymore, but someone, usually Gavin, made a drive-by at least a couple times a night. At eight-thirty, when Gavin finally showed, I was still sitting outside, comfortably warm in a sweater in the mild night, grading papers under the surprisingly adequate outdoor lights.

He came up the walk at a rapid pace and took the stairs up toward me two at a time. The yelling started before he'd gotten halfway.

"What the hell are you doing out here? They could come by and pull you off the stairs before you even knew what had happened."

I frankly doubted *that*—I always knew when Will was nearby from the hormone fluctuations.

Gavin pushed me inside and then came in after me. After making a big ceremony of locking the door behind him, he stomped into the kitchen and sat down at the table. He got up almost immediately to pull the fat yellow seat cushion out from behind his back, and lobbed it onto the table where it slid onto the floor. I picked it up, placed it neatly back on the table and sat down across from him.

His anger hadn't cooled one whit, but I ignored the irritable fidgeting, tapping fingers and angry glare. "I waited outside because I wanted to talk to you. I tried to reach you at the station, but you'd already gone. If you'd bothered to give me your cell phone number…"

"You have my work extension and there's always 9-1-1."

"You never answer your extension and do you really want me calling 9-1-1 to discuss vampires with the dispatcher? This is stupid. Why won't you give me your cell phone number?"

He glared at me with eyes like silver balls. "What do you want, Jo?"

"The reason I've invited you here," I began, enjoying myself a little too much as his mouth got white at the corners from clenching his jaw tightly in irritation, "is because I have a new suspect."

"I thought we agreed you were not to go hunting for suspects."

"*We* didn't agree to anything. But that's beside the point. I didn't hunt for this one, it came to me." I explained what I had learned about Chucky being on campus and his mother missing her 8:30 conference the night of Bob's death. "They had opportunity and motive, which is more than I can say about anyone else at Bayshore."

The last part came out before I could stop myself, but to my surprise, Gavin didn't respond to my implied admission of sleuthing with his usual lecture. Instead, he stood up and headed for the door. "Fine. I'll look into it. Thanks so much. Do you think you can stay inside now?"

Boy, someone was cranky. I decided to let Becky's e-mail wait until he was in a better frame of mind. I was quite sure it was a dead-end, and I didn't want his anger at me to prejudice him against her.

* * * * *

"Excuse me, are you the teacher?"

A man wearing blue chinos and a blue and white shirt that screamed uniform was standing by my classroom door, looking back and forth between me and my departing students.

No, I'm 13. "Yes, what can I do for you?" I spoke briskly, hoping he'd make it fast. I wanted to make it to the cafeteria before all the gravy was gone. It was French Dip Friday, one of the few meals I liked at Bayshore these days. It hadn't always been a favorite. That high honor went to the cafeteria's fabulous homemade macaroni and cheese. It was rich and velvety, with lots of melted cheese and crunchy breadcrumbs on top. They served it with steamed broccoli and cauliflower so you could pretend it was a healthy meal. Now it made me gag. Will had ruined it for me and in my opinion this spoke of the fundamental problem with vampires. They couldn't enjoy a good old-fashioned plate of macaroni and cheese. A little comfort food would probably go a long way to resolving all that dark, scary, Lord of the Night stuff.

"I'm Rudy. I'm here about the gas leak." He stepped into my classroom and the heavy leather tool belt strung low on his hips clinked and jingled as he moved.

"Gas leak?" Sure enough, the blue and white patch on his shirt identified him as an employee of the gas company.

Roger came in and eyed Rudy with satisfaction. "Ah, good, you're here. Now, these classrooms are outfitted with air and gas valves." Roger pointed to the paired nozzles that emanated from the walls above the countertops at regular intervals. "The leak could be coming from any one of them, though I suspect more than one is defective since the students in the back seemed equally as affected as the ones in the front."

Rudy nodded and aimed a long narrow instrument near the tip of the first gas valve. It made a slow ticking noise like a Geiger counter.

"What's going on?" I asked Roger.

"I believe there's a gas leak in this room," Roger said. He hovered over Rudy, who was doing a capable job of ignoring him.

"I gathered that. *Why* do you think there's a leak?"

"Your classes have been unusually quiet lately."

I gritted my teeth. "Roger, may I talk to you outside, please?"

He gave Rudy unnecessary instructions to keep working and followed me out into the hallway.

"What's going on, Roger?"

Roger regarded me with distaste. He didn't approve of emotion, especially in women. "After observing the abrupt change in your students' behavior this week, I became concerned. They were very quiet and still. They're usually quite rowdy."

I gripped my hands together to keep them from going around his neck, and told myself to count to ten. I only made it to five. This time he'd gone too far. "I have been working with them on their classroom behavior, Roger. After your first visit, I reviewed the classroom rules with each of my classes. What you saw was my students responding to that lecture, *not* a gas leak!" Despite efforts to speak calmly, my anger vented a bit at the last part.

"Please, Jo, calm yourself."

I wanted to kick him. There's nothing more infuriating than the person who's just riled you up telling you to calm down.

"I'm only concerned about the health of your students," Roger said.

That was it. "And I'm not, Roger? This is insulting, even for you. There is no gas leak. Don't you think *I* would have been affected as well, especially as I spend all day in that room?" *You stupid, pompous…*

Rudy came out just then, saving me from committing career suicide or homicide, or both. He paused awkwardly in the doorway. "Sorry to interrupt, but I've checked the room thoroughly and found no sign of a gas leak, or any pooling of bad air. Did you want me to check out another room while I'm here?"

Rudy and I both looked inquiringly at Roger. His face was a little flushed from arguing with me. "No, that's fine."

Rudy sketched a wave and ambled out, clunking and jingling. As Roger turned to follow him out, I stopped him.

"When my performance review comes out, I expect to receive full marks for classroom control. Right now, I'll settle for an apology."

Roger drew himself up to his full five-foot-seven. "There's no need to apologize for being concerned about our students here at Bayshore, even if a teacher's ego may get a little bruised in the process. You'll be a better teacher once you learn that. Now if you don't mind, I'd like to get my lunch." He turned on his heel and marched out.

Once my temper had subsided, I followed more slowly, lost in thought. Despite what I'd said, it was hard even for me to believe how well-behaved my students had suddenly become. If Roger hadn't gone about it so insultingly, I would have asked Rudy to check all the rooms on the hall and the one underneath me, just in case.

* * * * *

After lunch I looked for signs of surreptitious text messaging or good old-fashioned note passing. Better I find it than Roger.

But I didn't find a thing, and believe me, I know where to look. That was the good news. The bad news was that I'd been so focused on what my students were doing, I neglected to pay attention to what *I* was doing, and had royally screwed up the diagram I'd been drawing on the board. "Er, let me redraw that."

I had my back to the class for a full two minutes trying to fix it before I heard the telltale sounds of someone blowing a bubble. Chewing gum is outlawed at Bayshore. It's practically a criminal offense. Nonetheless, I considered it a good sign. Only a week ago, something would have been set on fire by now, or some poor schmuck would be dangling out the window. Heartened, I decided to give my classroom control a little test.

Not turning around, I said, "Whoever is chewing gum, please put it in the trash can immediately."

I waited expectantly for the sounds of someone dutifully pushing back their stool and walking to the trash can in the front of the room, but heard only another loud pop and a few giggles.

It was enough. I knew exactly who it was, Carlos, one of my students with too much personality—the kind you can't help but like, but rather wish was in someone else's class. I turned around and leveled my new Teacher's Look at him. "Throw it away," I directed softly.

"Yes, Ms. Gartner."

He and those seated around him looked petrified. Like victims in a horror movie just before the crazy monster puts an ax through their heads.

I stared back just as horrified as realization finally dawned. *Oh. My. God.* I was the monster! I hadn't mastered The Teacher's Look! I had been using my Vampire Stare on them.

I forced a smile on my face and said something, I don't remember what, that got the frightened look off their faces, and muddled through the rest of class, avoiding eye contact with my students, lest I scar them for life.

I left the moment the bell rang, telling the students who'd come for extra after-school help that I had a doctor's appointment. Somehow, I got myself home. Bundled against the bright late afternoon sunshine like a crazy street person, I ran from my car to my apartment and let myself in with shaky hands. Just inside the door, I ripped off the excesses of outerwear and stood in front of the hall mirror. I looked desperately for signs I hadn't turned into a shriveled nearly hairless creepy thing with long fingernails and Yoda ears—a female Nosferatu—but I couldn't see my own reflection well enough to tell one way or another, and I could feel tears of frustration course down my cheeks.

All along, I'd treated the "almost vamp" thing as a sort of sick joke. Yes, it was awful and sometimes the side effects had sent me on a crying jag, but it was also rather exciting and a little glamorous—like being the heroine in a movie. A girl couldn't help but be a little flattered when a man so knee-meltingly handsome as Will was doing the chasing.

But now, as I blinked and squinted furiously, trying to force my blurry, faded reflection into the clarity I'd once taken for granted, all I felt was the horror of my situation. Gavin had described it as being balanced on a knife edge between human and vampire. But I no longer felt poised equally between the two. I was slipping irrefutably into a world I didn't understand, into an existence that horrified me.

Half blinded by tears, I ran into my bedroom and jumped under the covers, pulling my comforter over my head. There, I huddled clutching an old ratty teddy bear like a frightened child for minutes or hours, I didn't know which, until blissfully, unconsciousness claimed me.

Chapter Twenty
 හ

A creature with sharp talons and a flaming head was screeching gibberish at me. I was sure I was dreaming, until those sharp talons gripped my shoulder and shook me hard enough to convince me I was awake. I blinked the sleep out of my eyes and the harridan resolved back into a familiar figure. Not a dream then, but maybe a déjà vu.

"Mom?" I croaked.

"Really, Jo!" My mother's forehead was creased in concern. "What is wrong with you? I've been shaking you for ages to get you awake. Did you take sleeping pills? I know sometimes a person *needs* them, but you should know better than to take so *many*."

I opened my mouth to correct her, but closed it instead. What was I going to say? Better for her to think I was abusing legal drugs than becoming a creature she, like any normal person, thought was a work of fiction. Sleeping pills might be far off from reality, but at least it was something she could deal with.

Her beautifully manicured fingers moved fretfully across my chest and shoulders as she tucked the comforter tighter and tighter around me until I began to feel a little claustrophobic. "I don't know what is wrong with you these days, Jo. First you nearly miss Christmas with the family, you never answer your phone, your skin's still a mess, and you've stopped attending Mass."

She waited for a response, but I didn't know where to begin. It was all absurd, ridiculously twisted or in the last case true, but for a reason that was twisted.

"What time is it?" I asked.

"It's seven."

"In the morning?" Forget that I had slept for something like fifteen hours. What was she doing in my apartment, much less waking me up, at dawn on a Saturday morning?

"Mom, why are you here?"

She sniffed and looked away.

I pushed myself up to a sitting position. "Is it Dad? Is something wrong?"

She turned back, and didn't even comment on the fact that I had slept in my work shirt. She regarded me steadily. "Your father is fine, Jo. It's *you* I'm worried about."

I was too horrified to speak. Oh, God, she'd figured it out. She knew her only daughter was turning into an evil bloodsucking parasite. What do you say to that?

She cupped my cheek lightly, sniffed again and blinked back a tear, and I realized that no matter how disgusting I got, she would always love me. I thought I had cried out all the water in my body the night before, but my eyelashes got damp again.

My mother abruptly interrupted my sweet Hallmark moment with a *sniff!* I knew that sniff. It was not a sound of pain but of martyrdom. It never boded well. She dropped my chin and shot me a hurt look. "Raphael told me about your *situation*." Hurt infused her voice. She sat ramrod stiff on the edge of my bed, with the perfect posture she had tried with lesser success to instill in me. She was all of two feet away, but it felt like ten.

"Who?" I had no idea what she was talking about.

"*Raphael!*" she repeated, as if that cleared things right up. "I had to hear that you were *pregnant* from my hairdresser!" She clasped a dusty pink manicured hand to her chest. "My own daughter!"

"What? No! Mom, I am not pregnant."

She gave me a quick look up and down. "Of course you're not. But I didn't even know you were dating this Bob—I thought you were involved with that coffee shop busboy, Will. And now he's dead!"

"Assistant manager," I corrected automatically, even though I'd made it up. "And Bob's dead, not Will." Technically, anyway.

She flicked her hand in annoyance. "That's what I said. The point is, Jo, this," she paused ever so slightly, "*Bob* was obviously important to you, a man I've never met! You never even told me about him, and all of *Raphael's* is *buzzing* with it. *Mrs. Dallas* knew about it before I did!"

"Oh, dear God," I said rolling my eyes. This was it. My mother had finally lost it. The chemicals in the hair dye (Raphael had recently transmogrified her hair from *sultry magenta* to *flame*) had finally eaten away a critical number of brain cells.

"Don't take the Lord's name in vain," she snapped automatically.

"Mom," I said, forcing myself to be patient. "This is ridiculous. Bob was little more than an acquaintance. I was never pregnant with his or anyone else's child. I never slept with him. I never dated him. I never wanted to. There was, for a very brief period, a rumor around school that I was pregnant, because some gossipy fool misinterpreted a brief bout of food poisoning as morning sickness, and proceeded to share that delusion with everyone in hearing distance. I never bothered to tell you about it because it was so absurd, I never imagined you'd hear it, much less break into my apartment at 7 a.m. on a Saturday morning because you believed it."

"Well what was I supposed to do? I tried calling you several times last night, but there was no answer. Your answer machine didn't even pick up."

Hmm. I vaguely remembered yanking the phone cord out of the wall sometime in the night. I stopped being defensive, and as I let my mother vent, I thought about what had happened. In the bright light of day, my meltdown over the vampire glare seemed a trifle excessive. It was just another symptom, like my extreme sensitivity to sunlight or my fading reflection. At least this one had the potential to be useful!

What was I saying? I couldn't use it on people! It was wrong, deceitful. Worse, it was pure vampire—what if using it was what finally pushed me over the edge?

When my mother was done venting—and had received apologies to her satisfaction—she hustled me into the shower, picked out "a nice outfit" for me, and before I knew it we were tucking into breakfast at a ritzy little restaurant down the coast on a cliff overlooking the ocean. She demanded, and got (of course), one of the highly coveted inside tables on a platform, where diners could get the unimpeded ocean view without the wind-mussed hair (or, my case, the tiniest bit of sun exposure). We were getting along so well, Mom didn't even vocalize her horror when I ordered the steak tartare—I didn't even have to use *the look*.

Well, not much, anyway, and surely a *tiny* glare wouldn't do me in. Besides, she had her own tools of persuasion and she didn't hesitate to use *them* on me, which is how I found myself, much against my better judgment, promising to go to church with her the following morning.

I spent the rest of the day in a state of anxiety. Weren't churches toxic to vampires? Wouldn't I explode or melt or something? Or get flung backward, propelled by an invisible force field? On the plus side, maybe Father Stevens could perform an exorcism and de-vamp me, but on the whole, I rather doubted it.

No, I definitely couldn't risk it. That is, I couldn't risk embarrassing my mother. I took the coward's way out and left her a message later that evening, when I knew my parents would be out for their usual Saturday night dinner, telling her not to pick me up as I'd meet her there.

* * * * *

My plan was to meet her under the archway after Mass and tell her I had been a little late and had sat in the back. It was a good plan. Everyone knew Father Stevens didn't like people in the aisles after Mass had begun, and he was too nearsighted to be able to identify people in the outer pews.

It was genius and it worked like a charm. I caught up with my mother after Mass just outside the church's ornately carved double doors as she moved to greet Father Stevens. He was resplendent in vestments that hid his slight paunch and made his receding gray hair, thick wire-rimmed glasses, and heavy jowls look majestic. Father Stevens greeted me like a long-lost child, as he always did after even the smallest lapse in attendance.

His cry of, "Josephine! How lovely to see you at Mass today!" squelched my mother's suspicions, just as she'd leaned over to whisper them in my ear.

I was quietly celebrating my victory when it happened. I had just turned to head down the wide, well-worn pale marble steps when my mother grabbed my sleeve and pulled me back. "Where do you think you're going?" She dipped her index finger in the gilded bowl of holy water set in an alcove near a delicate statue of the Virgin Mary and reverently made the sign of the cross on herself. Before I could move, she dipped again and reached for my forehead like she had when I was a little girl. I panicked and ducked.

"Josephine Gartner!" she hissed in an angry whisper. "What is wrong with you?" She held my arm in an iron grip and stabbed at my forehead, my chest and both shoulders. I felt burning on my forehead where the holy water touched my skin and quickly arranged my hair to cover it.

On the way to the parking lot, my mother let loose a steady stream of sotto voce outrage over my behavior, while managing to nod, smile, and exchange pleasantries with friends and acquaintances as we passed.

"We are not done here, young lady! You're lucky your father expects me home or…" The rest of the threat was lost to the wind as she turned to beep open her Lexus.

When she finally drove off, I climbed into my car and pulled back the oversized hood that covered my face and studied my forehead anxiously in the rearview mirror. I couldn't see myself well enough to assess the damage.

I sat there, gripping the wheel in silent frustration, until a child's happy yell shook me out of my black study. A little girl I recognized from the bi-monthly post-Mass coffee and doughnuts mixers had won the race to the family sedan parked next to me. She called excitedly for her parents to follow, but they were deep in conversation with another couple a few cars down. I got back out of the car. Opportunity had knocked.

I bent down a little so as not to intimidate her and smiled brightly. "Hi there," I fought for the memory and emerged triumphant, "Debbie." She smiled back in shy recognition and squirmed shyly against the car. Her parents glanced over. We did the polite, "Hi, how ya doin'" head nod exchange, and they went back to their conversation.

I told Debbie, "I'm meeting my boyfriend in a few minutes and can't seem to find my compact. Can you be my makeup advisor today?"

Her china blue eyes lit with interest and she nodded eagerly. I had gone from slightly intimidating grown-up to Barbie doll. She was in her element now. I pushed back my hood, brushed the hair away from my face, and bent down so she could get a good look at my forehead. "How does it look?" I asked. "Is my make-up even? Did I miss a spot anywhere?"

"Well," she said shyly, "I think you should fix it."

"Where? Here?" I pointed at my forehead where I could still feel a residual tingle from the holy water.

"Noooo, that part's okay." She was gaining confidence with every word. I was creating an Estee Lauder here. "But the rest of it's too red. Your blush got everywhere."

I thanked her solemnly for her expertise and left, not to get back in my car, but to go back to the church. By now, Father Stevens had gone back inside and most everyone else had left. I approached the little outdoor alcove where the holy water resided and tentatively dipped in a finger. It stung. I quickly wiped the liquid on the back of my hand and as I watched, the angry, red skin turned pale. I shoved my hand in my pocket, turned and left.

Chapter Twenty-One

∞

I don't know whose brilliant idea it was to schedule department meetings on Monday afternoons. Having us cap off the longest teaching day of the week with a couple hours of Roger was cruel and unusual punishment and should have been outlawed. We all had developed a strategy for enduring them. Mine was to tune out, occasionally tuning back in to make sure we hadn't gotten to anything interesting or that required an actual response. The technique generally served me well, and if I mistakenly tuned out too long, Carol would nudge me. She always paid attention, lest Roger one day realize he was preaching to a roomful of zombies and start rubber stamping his own agenda unchecked.

During today's meeting, I was so absorbed in my own thoughts that Carol had to nudge me three times before I realized Roger had asked me a question and was waiting for a response.

"What?" I said, subtly hiding my inattention.

He repeated the question slowly, as if to an imbecile. "I was saying we needed someone to take over the Science Olympiad, now that Bob's...er..."

He hadn't stopped out of delicacy. I had trained *the look* on him.

"I don't think I'm the best candidate, Roger. Why don't you ask someone else?" I suggested gently. I felt like Obi-Wan Kenobi in the original *Star Wars*, when he did that mind trick on the Stormtroopers outside the cantina.

Roger turned to Kendra. "Jo's right. It's too important for her to handle alone. Kendra, why don't you assist her. You've done it several times before."

Kendra shot me a dirty look and I groaned inwardly. That was *not* how I had wanted it to go. Either I had little control over the look or Roger was such a fiend he was immune. Probably both. The meeting adjourned shortly thereafter. Kendra and I stayed after to discuss the Science Olympiad.

It was a short discussion. She handed me a list of five of the ten categories.

"Here." She spoke briskly, as if she wanted to get this over as quickly as possible because she couldn't stand to be in the room with me. "You take these, I'll take the rest. We'll have the first meeting with the students later this week. Thursday okay?"

I nodded. Saying sorry was so inadequate as to have been insulting. The best thing I could do was not slow her down.

"They can sign up for their three activities then. We'll take alternate weeks coaching them in our respective areas. I'll take the first week. You'd better sit in on it, to see how I balance the training among the five areas. Since you're such a weak candidate for the job."

I sat there for a moment after she left, adding a little well-deserved self-flagellation to the mild upbraiding Kendra had delivered. What had I been thinking, trying to use a vampire's trick on a coworker? I'd seen what it had done to my students, and had been rightfully horrified. How had I concluded it was okay to try it on adults? What about my plan to avoid using it, lest it pull me closer to the dark side?

* * * * *

That night on the way home from work I did something terrible. That doesn't mean I can't justify what I did. I can—and believe me I did a snow job on myself while on the way to do it—but the fact remains that I stole from a church. My church. I stole from work, too—a beaker and a rubber stopper. But compared to the other, that hardly bears mentioning, even if Bayshore is a parochial school.

Too ashamed to park in the church's lot, I left my car on a little-used side street and skulked over to the front of the church where I ducked into the shadow of a stone column. I stayed there for ten minutes, wanting to make sure the place was deserted before I made my move. (I was sure after five minutes, but by then I had to talk myself into it all over again.) Then, moving casually as if I had legitimate business there — in front of a locked church, after dark — I made my way to the little alcove near the wide double doors of the church, where a small bowl of holy water was always kept filled.

In one smooth motion, I dipped the test tube into the bowl, filled it with holy water and plugged it tight with the stopper. Muttering a quick prayer of apology, the contents of which are between me and my maker, I tucked the vial into my pocket and strode quickly back toward my car.

The moon was high, the evening bright, and my conscience busy. If I noticed the wide gaps between the streetlights on the narrow road, they didn't trouble me. My right hand hadn't left my pocket after depositing its burden, and my fingers worried the stopper while my actions worried my conscience. So absorbed was I in my own dark thoughts that I didn't realize I had come upon my car until I had nearly passed it.

Or maybe I didn't realize it was my car because someone else was standing possessively by the driver's door.

"Will." I felt my mouth go dry and my legs turn to rubber. This was it. I couldn't fight him off if he was determined. The first time I'd surprised him. The second time, Gavin had been there to intercede for me. I knew very well the reason I was alive and pilfering today was that Will hadn't yet tried a third time. That last time I'd seen him didn't count — he had held back out of an odd nobility that I didn't like to think about.

He came toward me, moving smoothly on his long powerful legs, almost as if he were gliding. I stood there, unmoving, taking in his starkly handsome face as if I were having a dream. The moonlight threw his sculpted face into relief. His long, wavy hair fell in a blue-black curtain past his broad shoulders and his eyes were dark pools of shadow. When he got within a few feet of me, I stopped staring like a lovesick teen and ran.

I hadn't gone more than a few yards before I realized the street dead-ended up ahead. I veered between two cars and doubled back to my own, circling it twice while I scrabbled for my keys. Will followed, gaining on me. Holding out the door key with both hands, I made a wild dive for the driver's side door lock, and missed. Will closed the distance, coming so near he made the little hairs on the back of my neck stand up. My breath came in frantic shallow gasps and tears streamed down my face. I panicked completely and tried to burrow in through the metal.

"Jo," he said, touching my shoulder gently. I flinched as if he had shocked me and cried harder. There was no one to help me.

"Turn around."

"No," I said in a cracking voice I hardly recognized as my own.

He touched a hand lightly to my hair. "Please don't cry. Everything will be all right." He ran a finger caressingly down my cheek, wiping away the tears that soaked it. It was the tender, romantic gesture of a lover, only it was all wrong.

I pushed his hand away. "Stop that!" I turned to face him, and now the quaver in my voice was one of fury. "If you're going to kill me, do it. But stop," I sputtered angrily, "toying with me. Don't pretend you care about me. It's insulting!"

Will was taken aback. "I do care about you!"

His apparent sincerity made me even angrier. "No, you don't! If you did, you'd notice you're scaring the crap out of me. I don't want to be a vampire! Do I look willing, Will? Do I? Well, I'm not!"

I pulled the test tube out of my pocket and held it up. He took a step back.

"Do you see this?" I demanded, tears of anger streaming down my face. "This is holy water I stole from my church. Stole! Why? Because I met a handsome man whom against my better judgment I kissed because he charmed me with a witty intelligent discussion about *books*. And I woke up the next morning like *this*." I gestured down at myself and Will took another step back, wary of the test tube I was swinging wildly about. "I can no longer run or hike because the sun burns my skin, my complexion scares children, and I can't enjoy a single stinking bite of shrimp scampi without people concluding I'm pregnant with a dead colleague's love child!"

He held out his hands in a supplicating gesture. "Jo, I — "

"I'm not done! Do you know why I stole this?" I asked in a deceptively calm voice.

"You want to pour it on me?"

"No. Because it will heal my skin. At least I think it will. I've never stolen a thing in my life — except a pack of gum from the supermarket when I was four, and I felt so bad I gave it back the next day — but tonight I stole from a church to clear up my complexion. My complexion! What kind of person does that? My values are in the toilet and now I'm going to hell all because you randomly picked me out of a crowd one night and tried to turn me into a vampire."

"It wasn't random, Jo."

"What's that supposed to mean? Is that supposed to make it better? You denied killing Bob because you said he wasn't someone you would have wanted to spend eternity with. Did you bother to wonder what it'd be like to be stuck for all eternity with me? Don't you least want a girl who's willing?"

His temper flared and he yanked me away from the car. I stumbled but he caught me up against him and captured my lips in a bruising kiss. I felt a familiar warmth course through me as the kiss began to change subtly into another kind altogether.

Will thrust me away and took a step back. I fell back against the car, feeling the cool night breeze where his body had been pressed against mine. His deep blue eyes burned down into my own.

"Are you quite sure you're not willing?" He didn't wait for an answer but turned angrily on his heel and walked away.

* * * * *

I got home, somehow; I couldn't remember the drive.

Once again, Will could have bitten me, could have completed my transformation, but he hadn't. I didn't know why and my speculations weren't good company.

I tried not to think about Will, but I couldn't think of anything else. It was true, what he'd said. Part of me did want him, and it wasn't just the vampire part. And, though I didn't care to admit it, there was a part of me that liked him, even respected him.

I forced the thought away, horrified and scared about what it might mean, but it kept eating at me until I faced it. Maybe he was right. Maybe I did want to be with him. Wanted to let go of my resistance. Wanted, in fact, to complete the transformation, to stop living this half-life, to become, in full, a vampire.

No. I couldn't let it happen. I wouldn't. With shaking hands, I pulled the vial of holy water out of my pocket, wrested out the cork, and splashed some of the liquid onto my face. I gasped sharply at the pain, nearly dropping the vial. But I continued ruthlessly, almost welcoming the pain, my hot jagged tears mingling with the holy water as it burned into my cheeks, my chin, my neck. I rubbed what liquid remained onto my hands and arms, rousting him out with each of turn of my hand.

Chapter Twenty-Two

ɞ

The next morning I woke abruptly before dawn. I felt funny, somehow. Different. It took me a moment to get the sleep fuzz off my brain, but when I did, I remembered my experiment with appalling clarity. Oh God! What had I done to myself? I reached a shaky hand up to touch my face, but the skin felt smooth and cool. I flicked on my bedside lamp and anxiously examined my hands.

For a moment I was too scared to believe what I saw, unwilling to accept the evidence before me lest I suddenly wake up to find it had been only a cruel dream. But the longer I sat there, the more I believed it was true. The scaly patches on my hands were gone, the redness had dissipated, and they were no longer painful.

I threw back the covers, heedless of the goose bumps that sprang up as the cold night air hit my sleep warmed skin, and rushed to the bathroom. I turned on the bright overhead lights and examined my face again, this time with the help of a mirror. Tears filled my eyes and spilled down my pale, dewy cheeks. I looked…like *me*, as I had before all this had happened, down to the light scattering of freckles across my nose. It took me a moment to realize the best part—I could *see* my skin in the mirror. Not perfectly mind you, I was still a little blurry, but now, if I went in the haunted house at Disneyland, I would at least cast a better reflection than the ghostly hitchhikers at the end of the ride.

I felt as if a great weight had been lifted from my shoulders and to celebrate, I did something I had wanted to do for weeks. I kicked the face mask into a dark corner of my closet and went for a long run on the beach, chasing waves with the long legged sandpipers and their avian mini-me's, the tiny sanderlings. By the time I got back, tired and happy, the sun was up and a familiar figure was sitting on my steps waiting for me.

"Hello, Gavin," I greeted the detective amiably as he wordlessly unfurled himself into a standing position at my approach. Disapproval radiated from him like heat from a fire. His eyes were like hard silver balls and his well-shaped mouth was compressed into a tight little line, but I didn't care. I'd have greeted Jack the Ripper amiably just then, I was in such a good mood.

"Good morning, Jo." He spoke like a parent whose child had just rolled in, drunk and oblivious, from a night of unauthorized partying.

Ignoring the censure implicit in his greeting, I knelt down and ripped open the key holder I wore attached to my right running shoe and pulled out my door key. Gavin followed me in and sat himself down at the kitchen table, arms crossed and frowning, while I gulped down a cool glass of tap water at the sink.

"You're looking well." His eyes raked me coldly from head to toe.

"You make that sound like a bad thing."

"Is it?"

"Don't burst my bubble, Gavin." I kept my tone light, but there was steel underneath.

He made a small conciliatory gesture. "I didn't intend to. I was just wondering why a girl who couldn't go outside for two minutes during the day without incurring a nasty burn is out running," he looked pointedly at my face, "without incident on a Saturday morning."

"The sun rose about five minutes ago and I'm wearing a bottle of blackout sunscreen, long sleeves, gloves, running tights, and a hat. I'm in far greater danger of heat exhaustion than sunburn."

He just looked at me.

"I found a new skin treatment, okay? Something the dermatologist recommended but they don't sell here. My mother bought it for me in London. Do you want their numbers?"

He searched me probingly for a second or two and then the invisible string that had wound him so tightly gave a little. "That's all right," he grunted, but his eyes lingered speculatively on my pale, dewy skin until it turned red for a different reason. "My sergeant said you weren't home when he drove by at eight last night." Gavin rested his elbows lightly on the kitchen table. I wasn't taken in by the seeming idleness of the question; his gray eyes were fixed on me like a tracking device.

I didn't like where this was going. I wasn't about to admit where I had been or what I had been doing there. I certainly didn't want to discuss my latest run-in with Will—I didn't really understand it myself. And, I didn't need a lecture from Gavin on the stupidity of parking in out-of-the-way places at night. His couldn't begin to compete with the one I'd given myself.

"I was working late." I changed the subject. "How's the investigation going?"

It was his turn to look uncomfortable. "It's stalled. We have no suspects to speak of. Everyone in your department had an alibi and no one has more than the most specious of motives."

It wasn't a new position. The police had started with that premise after questioning us the night of the murder. But it was one thing to conjecture an impossible situation, another to know it. "I know. Everyone seems to be in the clear. I couldn't find out a darn thing."

"What do you mean *you know*? I thought you were staying out of this."

Oops. I had *got* to learn to think before I spoke. "I am staying out of it. But people do talk, and sometimes they say suspicious things."

"What sort of suspicious things?"

The phrase *sexy thang* seemed to hang like a storm cloud over the room, but I pushed it out of my mind. I knew that Becky hadn't done anything to Bob, but some of my initial discomfort over that e-mail lingered, like a rotten grape leaves a bitter taste even after you spit it out.

"Take Roger for instance, our department chair. His reputation is everything to him. *He* thinks he's God's gift to teaching, but Bob was going to give him a scathing review. Bayshore is Roger's world. If that review had been made public, especially by someone so universally liked and respected as Bob was..." I held up my hands. "I don't know what he would have done."

"Who told you this?"

"Alan. He's replaced Bob on the review committee, and has Bob's notes."

"Alan. The same guy who found the body? Might he by chance have noticed that you were poking around, looking for motives?"

I had wondered the same thing myself, but somehow it sounded insulting when Gavin said it. "I have not been *poking around.* Alan brought it up one day at lunch after Roger had said something particularly condescending. If you don't want to hear this, say so."

Gavin leaned back in his chair, but I didn't deceive myself he was calm or relaxed. His severe gray eyes and bent nose made him look like one of the scarier voodoo idols. The sort the weary explorer finds when he is too deep in the jungle for running away to make sense, and yet he runs anyway. Gavin's jaw was clenched so tightly the words came out funny when he spoke. "Go on."

"Then there's Kendra, the ninth grade science teacher."

"She has a rock-solid alibi," Gavin said. "She was talking with the older woman—Mary Mudget?—who teaches seventh grade, when they heard the glass break."

"I know. They *all* have rock-solid alibis. That's why I'm focusing on motive. I don't know how it was done, but it *was* done, and I find it highly unlikely that a total outsider could have gone all the way up to the science wing without having been noticed. Between the security guards, administrators, teachers and parents, someone would have noticed a person who didn't belong."

"You mean someone like Natasha?"

I ignored the sarcasm. "Exactly. She didn't fit in, and I brought her up. And while you may have written her off, she still on my list."

"That is not what I meant, and you know it. Natasha looks nothing like a Bayshore parent. Too young, too flamboyant. And yet, not only did she have the run of the campus, but she successfully spent ten minutes in a one-on-one teacher's conference. With you. And, you wouldn't have thought to mention her if Will hadn't identified her as a vampire for you later that night."

That was low. I crossed my arms and glared at Gavin.

"All right. Fine. You've made your point. So. Where *are* all these strangers who had it in for Bob?"

Gavin didn't respond, unless you count more jaw clenching.

"Perhaps, since your theory isn't yielding any suspects, you'd like to hear what I have to say," I said with a fake smile.

"Absolutely," Gavin said with equally fake solicitude. "I believe you were telling me about Kendra."

Drat. I didn't have much on her—she had been my weak middle example, and now she had to be my strong lead-in. I beefed up the story a little. "I'm not sure if you're aware how big a deal soccer is at Bayshore, but it's the biggest sport on campus."

Gavin looked unimpressed.

"Bob was the boys' varsity soccer coach. Kendra got stuck with the girls' team. Even with Title IX, there's a big difference between the two, especially in the money you can earn on the side coaching summer league and giving private lessons. Bob probably doubled his income that way."

"That's fascinating, but what does it have to do with Bob's murder?"

"Kendra got Bob's assistant coach a job at another school. With her out of the way, the plum coaching job was offered to Kendra."

"And did she take it?"

"No. But that doesn't mean she won't change her mind later. She'll be put on the search committee for sure, and it wouldn't be too hard to engineer things so that we can't find a suitable coach, and she has to step in to save the day after all." I was beginning to warm to my own hyperbole. Maybe I was on to something!

"So you're suggesting Kendra killed Bob for a coaching job she's already turned down? Have I got that right? Hold on, let me write that one down." He wrote laboriously in a small wire notebook.

"Got any more insights for me?" He tilted his head to one side and looked eager.

"No."

"You sure?"

"Have you gotten anywhere with the Farrylls?"

He replied matter-of-factly. "Mrs. Farryll says she caught up with her son soon after your department head demanded she go fetch him. Then they went home."

"And you believe them?"

He shrugged. "I have no reason not to. There's nothing to connect them to the murder scene."

I made a noise of protest.

"We can't just up and arrest people on a flimsy *maybe*, Jo, but that doesn't mean we're not keeping an eye on them."

Maybe I had watched too many detective shows, but I really had expected the police would have figured out who had killed Bob by now, or at least would have had some good leads, but Gavin seemed to have gotten nowhere.

Could I blame him? I mean, was there anywhere to get? Maybe it was the perfect murder after all. But I didn't believe it. Something niggled at the back of my brain. I was sure I had learned something important, if I only remembered what it was. I thought over everything that had happened in the past few weeks since Bob's death, but nothing stood out. Everything remotely odd had a logical explanation.

"So what now?"

His response came out like one long, tired sigh. "We go over the information we have, we ask more questions, follow any loose ends."

"It doesn't sound very promising."

Gavin looked weary. He was probably no more than thirty, but looked ten years older. "It isn't. If you want the truth, chances are we won't solve this. I'm sure you've heard that the likelihood of catching a murderer drops substantially after the first couple of days. It's true. Frankly, the only reason we're still devoting substantial manpower to this is because he was killed at a school."

I bristled. "That's a terrible thing to say! Bob was a human being, a good and decent man. You should be working hard to bring his murderer to justice because of *that*."

"I agree wholeheartedly with you, Jo, but the reality is that we have other cases, more than we can handle, and we get more every day. If you want that to change, tell the taxpayers to fork out more money so we can hire more cops!

"Oh hell, never mind. Ignore what I just said. I assure you, Jo, we're doing the best we can." He stood and headed for the door. When he reached it, he put his hand on the doorknob but didn't turn it right away. Instead, he turned to face me. "I want to find whoever killed him as badly as you do, but I don't want to find Bob's murderer because he or she is standing over *your* dead body with a bloody glass shard." His mouth formed a grim line and his eyes were unreadable. "You've already got a price on your head, Jo. You don't need to go asking for trouble, you've already got it."

He opened the door and stepped out. As he turned to close the door behind him, he added grimly, "I've worked hard to keep you alive. Try to keep yourself that way."

* * * * *

Student interest in the Science Olympiad was greater than I thought it would be. I'd had to add a second page to the sign up sheet Monday before the end of morning break. As I taped it to the wall outside my classroom, I gave the original sheet a once-over and discovered the reason—Chucky Farryll, our little would-be Pele. Chucky had signed up no doubt because his mother had made him, no doubt because Maxine had made *her*. Our middle school principal was a big believer in getting slackers refocused on their schoolwork by getting them involved in something only peripherally academic, rather like sneaking vegetables into the meatloaf.

Evidently, Chucky had made some of his friends eat the veggies with him. And since he was a popular boy, the girls had followed. The Science Olympiad had thus gone from low-key geeky pastime to high-profile cool person social event.

I decided I had better get my butt onto the Internet to prepare for my role as club co-advisor, and when school was over for the day and the kids needing extra help had all gone home, I headed for the computer room. I visited all the weird sites first. Surprisingly, or perhaps not so surprisingly given the Olympiad's typical participant, most of the sites were hosted by geeky kids. I learned a lot of interesting tips about each of the events, and bookmarked the better sites for my students to look at. After a while, I decided I needed some structure to my research and went to the event's official website. As I had expected, there wasn't much more to it than dates, rules and regulations, information we already had. They had a rather dry history section; out of curiosity, I ran a search on Bayshore. We had done surprisingly well over the years, given that most of our students did only the barest of prep work (several of the competing schools had serious, year-long classes devoted to the Olympiad). I scanned the photographs posted on the site and was pleased to see that most of the kids looked like they were having fun.

I did a double take on one of the photos. It looked like Roger, only younger and with more hair, and it was. Sure enough, Roger had been listed as Bayshore's faculty adviser for a four-year stint before he had passed it off to Bob. Roger had even won an award for training the kids, and for two years in a row, his students had won the big kahuna of the Olympiad, the Rube Goldberg experiment, where as far as I understood it, kids had to create an absurd machine that would get a ping-pong ball from one end of a room to the other in the most indirect way possible. If you can remember Dick Van Dyke's breakfast making contraption in *Chitty Chitty Bang Bang*, you've got the general idea. Kendra, thankfully, was taking on that one this year.

I admit I was relieved to see that Bayshore had never placed better than fifth in the paper airplane toss or the egg drop, the two semi-plum categories on my list. Low expectations were good.

I spent several more hours poking around the various sites, until a particularly vicious growl from my stomach reminded me how late it was. I grabbed my printouts to read at home over dinner. The sun had long since gone down. Prompted by an unnerving combination of Gavin's dire warnings and my own heightened fear since my recent run-in with Will, I pulled out my car keys as I walked to the exit and listened and looked both ways before leaving the building. In a welcome piece of luck, I spied Fred out doing his rounds, and called out to him in greeting. He seemed happy to have a bit a company and offered to walk me to my car.

I slowed my pace to match his stiffer gait. "You shouldn't stay so late," he scolded, rubbing his knuckles against a grizzled cheek. "It's not healthy."

"I know. I had to get some stuff done."

"You should take a lesson from the older teachers. You don't see them here. They know better than to be here all the time. You get burned out easy, doing this job." His watery blue eyes searched mine to make sure the warning had sunk in, and I assured him I didn't plan to make a habit of it. Especially as I had several hours of grading and prep work waiting for me at home.

As I got in my car, Fred ambled back over to the guard box to open the gate for me. When I pulled up to the gate, he held up a hand for me to stop.

"That lady ever find you tonight?" he asked. "I have a note here from Carter that a Mrs. Beckworth was here to see you."

I froze. That was the name Natasha had used on parent night. "Um, no."

"She a blonde lady? Stylish?"

Stylish was a reasonable Fred substitute for *young, hot, and scantily clad*. I nodded.

"She came by last night, too, oh, 'round eight o'clock. Said she hated to make an appointment, as her schedule was unpredictable and she would like as not have to cancel last minute-like. Said she'd keep trying, and would catch you one of these nights. Oh well, serves her right for not making an appointment. Now you go straight home, have something to eat, and get an early night, you hear? Yer looking a little peaked."

Peaked was not the word for how I felt. "Thanks, Fred, I will."

As I drove home, curiosity slowly encroached upon the fear that had frozen my brain. Why had Natasha been looking for me? It was one thing for her to have harassed me when I practically fell into her lap at the amusement park, but another for her to *come looking* for me. Hadn't Will told her to leave me alone at work?

Had I misunderstood? Perhaps even deliberately, preferring to believe Will had a chivalrous streak when it came to me? No, I didn't think I *had* misunderstood, and that left me with one of two disturbing conclusions—either Will had changed his mind and it was now open season on turning me, in which case I should expect more vampires coming my way, or Natasha had decided to follow through with her threat of getting rid of me the old-fashioned way.

Chapter Twenty-Three

ॐ

"Miss Gartner, may we have a party in your classroom?"

It was lunchtime. Becky was sitting across from me out of the girls' view and rolled her eyes in a way that said as clearly as if she had spoken out loud, *Middle schoolers and their cupcake parties!*

I finished my mouthful of the cafeteria offering for Cheeseburger Wednesday and politely took a sip of my drink, pretending I was considering their request.

"No."

"Please?" they begged in unison.

"I'm sorry, girls, but it's out of the question. We can't spend class time having parties."

Becky blew her drink back through her straw with what sounded suspiciously like a snort.

The girls weren't giving up that easily. "It doesn't have to be during class."

This gave me pause. The whole point of a party at school was to get out of doing schoolwork.

"We can do it after school. Whenever's convenient for you."

I thought I caught a slight inflection on the word *you*. "What's the party for?"

They exchanged glances. "It's a surprise."

"You're going to have to give me more than that. I can't just blindly authorize an activity in my classroom."

"Why don't you tell me," Becky offered unexpectedly in a sweet voice.

I gave her a narrow look. She seemed to be enjoying this a little too much.

The girls hesitated, but ultimately decided it was easier to confide in her.

Becky's eyebrows shot up and she flicked a glance at me. "That's very sweet of you girls, but it's not true." She spoke sternly, without a trace of softness to mitigate the impact. "None of it. Someone made it up. You girls should know better than to listen to gossip, or to repeat it."

Both girls turned red with embarrassment. They were young and innocent enough for her censure to weigh heavily on them. As they turned to leave, the quieter one mustered up the courage to say softly to me, "Mr. Bob seemed pretty nice. I'm sorry for your loss."

I watched her go with open mouth.

"Oh my God," I said.

Becky was trying her damnedest not to laugh but lost the battle once the girls had gone round a corner. She burst out laughing, wheezing for air. When she could breathe again, she wiped a tear from her eye and said, "You might have to switch schools," before losing it again.

Alan and Kendra put their trays down on the table and joined us.

"What's so funny?" asked Alan.

Becky pulled herself together with an effort and told them an abridged version of the story.

"You poor thing," Alan said, chuckling.

"The whole thing's ridiculous," Kendra said.

"Of course it is," Alan said, "but some rumors are just too juicy to be squelched. No offense, Jo."

"None taken," I replied truthfully. It was so obvious that no one at the table thought the rumor the least bit credible that I just couldn't get worked up about it anymore. And really, it *was* funny.

I took up my cheeseburger again and regarded it unenthusiastically. It had gone from tolerably lukewarm to stone-cold, and the yellow square of cheese, never a high point for me even before I'd gone All Meat All the Time, had turned to rubber.

Becky examined my lunch disapprovingly over a forkful of salad. "What is it with you and hamburgers these days? Are you sure you're not pregnant without your knowledge? You'd better find out—you're going to need to eat a more balanced diet if you want your secret love child to come out healthy."

"Oh, shut up, Becky. You're just jealous because Bob secretly loved me more than he secretly loved you," I said, scraping off the offending cheese and taking a bite of my now naked burger.

"*You're* just jealous because he secretly, secretly loved me," she retorted.

"That doesn't even make sense," I said.

"Shut up, both of you," Kendra said.

"What she said," Alan said. "I'm trying to eat here. You know biology makes me nauseous."

"Is that why you went into physics? I always thought it was because you were too geeky for any of the other sciences," Becky said.

"That's interesting," he said. "I always thought *you* were too geeky for a secret, secret love affair."

"Man, don't you guys ever shut up?" Kendra slammed her plate onto her tray and went to sit a few tables away with Roger.

Becky and I looked chagrined.

"What's with her?" Alan asked, folding a fry into his mouth.

I rolled my eyes in disgust. At least *we* had the good grace to feel remorse after joking tastelessly about Bob in front of his best friend at Bayshore. "Men!" I said.

"Yeah," Becky said. "Can't live with them, can't have a secret love child without them."

I pushed my tray away, put my head down on my arms, and laughed so hard I wet my shirt sleeves.

* * * * *

The first Science Olympiad meeting was a little crazy. We had forty kids packed into my classroom and a good half dozen more who told me they were interested but couldn't attend the first meeting. Kendra did a double take when she came in.

"What the hell?" She dropped a short stack of handouts on my desk and unslung a heavy bag full of notes and handouts from her shoulder. "Do these kids know they're here for the *Science* Olympiad?" She eyed a rather chatty group of girls whose uniform skirts, rolled at the waist to make them into minis so short their trendy boxer shorts peeked out from underneath, identified them as popular. Kendra rolled her eyes and turned to address the group.

They quieted down for her depressingly fast, and for a moment I reconsidered my decision not to use my vampire-esque powers on the kids. I chastised myself for my own weakness in trying to find the easy way out, and forced myself to pay attention.

Kendra spent the next several minutes explaining the activities in this year's Olympiad and then invited the kids to sign up for as many events as interested them, cautioning that we would hold some sort of competition later on to determine who would go on to represent Bayshore in the county event. To keep them entertained while the sign-up sheet was being passed around, she organized an impromptu paper airplane flying contest. I helped out several of the kids with some of the tips I picked up in my web research, and we had a pretty good time.

After the meeting was over, Kendra rushed off to coach soccer practice and I sat down with Chucky Farryll, who had stayed after for his private tutoring. Having had Kendra there was a cruel reminder that he wasn't allowed to play on the varsity team and he was even more antsy and unfocused than usual. After a futile half-hour trying to drill some science into his head, I let him go.

I could have left after that, but my room was a mess, even for me. The Olympiad kids had tidied a little before they left, but that wasn't saying a lot. There were still dozens of unclaimed paper airplanes littering the room (some of them, admittedly, my own) and I sorely needed to reorganize the mineral trays lest my first period think quartz was a boxy, silver-colored mineral and pyrite was a six-sided hunk of hard brown dullness. By the time I finished organizing everything, it was well after six again. I really needed to stop these twelve-hour days, not so much because I still had to prep for tomorrow's classes and thin the ever-growing stack of papers to grade, but because the idea of being on campus at night with Natasha out there looking for me gave me the shakes.

After a quick peek outside, I left the second floor of the science building and headed downstairs, car keys at the ready, knees bent for immediate flight. After I passed Maxine plugging away in her office and ran into Roger in the mailroom, I made myself stop edging around corners as if I expected the boogie man to grab me and headed out into the parking lot.

As I reached my car, I heard a single soft *click* somewhere behind me. I turned around. The parking lot was empty, except for me. I chided myself for jumping at every last noise, but as I bent to fit my key to the lock, my hands were shaking so much I dropped the keys. They ricocheted off my heavy canvas book bag and landed somewhere under my car. Typical. With a heartfelt curse, I stretched out on the ground and fished them out from behind the wheel.

As I clambered back to my feet, I heard a gunshot and something whistled by me and slammed into the car door. I yelped and dropped to the ground, banging my chin painfully on the asphalt.

I lay there waiting for the next shot, my hands laced uselessly over my head like they teach you in an earthquake drill. Seconds, maybe minutes, ticked by in absolute silence. I had almost convinced myself the shooter had gone when I heard someone moving at the other end of the parking lot, by the doors to the administration wing.

The footsteps echoed eerily in the half empty lot and then stopped, as if someone was listening, searching. They headed in my direction. I rolled under the SUV parked next to me and forgot to breathe.

The footsteps stopped short as someone came running from the gym. "Hey," they called, "is everyone okay over there?" *Kendra.*

A voice replied from where I'd last heard the footsteps. "I don't know. Did you see anything?" *Maxine. It was just Maxine and Kendra.* Relief flooded me. The shooter was long gone and rescue had arrived.

Kendra slowed to a walk as she joined Maxine by the administration building. "I was just putting the soccer balls away when I heard the noise. It sounded like a gunshot. I thought maybe it was just someone's car backfiring, but then I thought I heard someone scream, and I ran over in case someone needed help." She took a few steps out into the parking lot. "Is anyone here?"

"Don't!" Maxine said. "Wait here with me. I called 9-1-1, they should be here any second."

"But what if someone's hurt?"

"Someone has a gun. It's not safe."

The sound of sirens prevented me from hearing Kendra's reply. A police car, followed by an ambulance and a second police car, pulled into the parking lot at high speed. The officers got out of their cars and crouched behind the open doors. One of them called for anyone in the parking lot to show themselves immediately.

I stayed where I was. If I suddenly popped out from under the SUV, I was afraid they might take a shot at me, and I wasn't counting on two misses in the same evening. Besides, it seemed I was stuck.

Three of the officers silently peeled off and began moving quietly through the parking lot, guns and flashlights out, searching.

I always park at the far end of the lot. I tell myself it's because I can use the extra exercise, but it's really because I usually get to work too late for any of the good spots. It took a while for the officers to get to me. By the time they had me pinned under their flashlights, and had ordered me to put my hands were they could see them, Gavin had arrived.

He hurried over and crouched down to peer under the car. "Jo?" His face looked drawn. "Are you all right? Shit, you're bleeding."

"I'm fine," I said, as coolly as I could under the circumstances. "I think someone took a shot at me, but they missed."

"How did you get under—never mind. Can you get up?"

"I don't think so," I admitted.

Gavin's head disappeared before I could finish. He briskly addressed one of the officers. "Chris, get an EMT over here. Now. She's hurt."

The EMTs duly hustled over. Gavin backed away to give them room and ordered the officers to go on with their search.

"I'm fine, really," I told the man and woman who bent down to assist me. "I'm just stuck," I said miserably.

They gently pulled me out and insisted upon wrapping me in a blanket against shock and tending to the bloody scrape on my chin. They made sure I wasn't hurt anywhere else before they pronounced me good to go.

Gavin escorted me to one of the police cars and guided me gently into the front seat. Then, he crouched down in the doorway, blocking out some of the light and noise, and asked me what had happened. I gave him a quick summary.

"Did you see anyone in the parking lot when you came out?"

They had left the car running and the heater felt warm on my feet, but my teeth had begun to chatter a little and I huddled in the protective warmth of the blanket and shook my head.

"So you dropped your keys, you bent down to get them, and someone shot at you. Then what?"

"I hit the ground and banged my chin."

Gavin's eyes flicked quickly to my bandaged chin and then back to me. "And then?"

"I stayed there. I wasn't sure what had happened—I mean, I thought it was a bullet, but it's not like I've ever been shot at before and it seemed so, well, surreal."

"Did you see anyone? Someone running away?"

"No. I didn't feel it was prudent to get up and take a look."

"Did you hear anything? Anything at all?"

I thought back. "Noooo, nothing for a while, but then I heard Maxine come out of the administration building, and then Kendra came running over from the gym." I explained the conversation I had overheard. "And then the cavalry came," I summed up with a wave to all the emergency vehicles.

Gavin asked a few more questions, pressing for details, which I answered as best I could.

He went silent a moment, staring at a point past my left ear. "What I still don't understand," he said slowly, "is how you got stuck under the SUV." His gaze flicked to me.

I didn't deign the question with a response.

One of the officers came over to the car and said in a low voice to Gavin, "I have a few people for you to talk to, sir, when you're ready."

"I'll be right over." Gavin turned back to me. "Stay here. I'll be right back." He tucked a trailing end of my blanket into the car, patted me on the shoulder and left.

He had locked me in, and there I sat for a very long, boring time. I watched as Gavin spoke first with Maxine, and to Kendra, and then to Roger who had come out only after the police had arrived, though he must have heard the shot. Typical. Roger would always think first about saving his own skin. A few other teachers and students, and even a parent or two, trickled over to see what the excitement was all about, but an officer, assisted by a suddenly officious Fred, kept them back.

It wasn't very interesting to watch conversations I couldn't hear, so I turned my attention to the other officers. I couldn't see much from my vantage point, but from the activity over by my car, I guess I they had managed to dig the bullet out of my door.

I had memorized every button and light on the dashboard and was beginning to nod off when the door opened. The fresh air made me blink.

"Jo? Come on, I'll take you home in my car." Gavin said. He helped me out of the panda car and into his Jetta.

"How come I only ride in your car after something bad has happened?" I said querulously as we left the parking lot. "And what took you so long? I'm starving."

Wordlessly, he pulled up to a fast food window. When the disembodied voice asked what we wanted he turned to me with his eyebrows raised in silent question.

"I want your largest hamburger, very rare, with nothing on it." I'd never liked mayo on hamburgers, and for obvious reasons, ketchup now gave me the creeps. "Wait, make that two."

Gavin ordered a grilled chicken sandwich and a side salad for himself. He paid at the window, and handed me the bag when the food was ready, but I didn't bother opening it. To my way of thinking, there is no point to eating in the car when you're less than three minutes from home, except to snitch some fries, and Gavin hadn't ordered any.

"You must never date," I said.

"What?"

"You didn't order fries."

"I didn't want any."

"Everybody wants fries."

He stopped the car at the edge of the fast food lot and turned toward me. "I didn't. If you wanted fries, why didn't you order them?"

"I didn't—Oh, never mind."

"Do you want to go back? We can get some fries."

"You can't get fries now," I protested. "That's just wrong."

He looked confused.

I took pity on him. "Really, Gavin. It's okay. We can go."

He hesitated, to make sure I was serious, and then pulled back into traffic.

"Gavin?"

"What."

"If you do go on a date, get the fries."

"I thought you didn't want the fries." He gripped the steering wheel as if he wanted to strangle someone.

"Never mind, Gavin."

Chapter Twenty-Four

ℬ

I ate the first burger in record time and managed half the second before Gavin cut me off.

"I need to talk to you, and I'll need you awake and functioning for that."

"What for? I already told you what happened." Despite my protest, I put the burger down and wiped my hands and face on a couple of paper napkins as I had pretty much reached my burger limit anyway. I got up to throw the whole mess into the trash and brought the cookie jar back with me. I had been well trained by my mother to use plates for everything, lest I drift inexcusably into heathen territory, but that night I didn't bother. This had not been a one or two cookie evening.

Gavin helped himself to the cookie jar and went over my statement again with me. When he was finished we sat in silence.

I pushed the cookie jar away and wound a corner of the tablecloth around my index finger. I unwound it and started winding again on the next finger. I glanced at Gavin. He was staring at the wall, his mouth drawn down in a thoughtful frown.

"So, did this have something to do with Bob's death, or is one of my students a little too bitter about his or her grade on the last test? I'll admit I set the curve a little lower than normal this time, but I wanted to give them a little push. Because you know once spring hits they're going to want to slack off—"

"Someone shot at you with a silver bullet," Gavin said.

"What?"

"A silver bullet. Not silver colored, silver-*plated*."

"Cheap bastards. They could have at least sprung for gold if they were only going to plate the damn thing."

"Jo." Gavin turned to face me. His chair squeaked on the linoleum. "Do you understand what that means?"

"Someone thinks I'm a werewolf?"

The corner of his mouth curved up briefly in response as if he couldn't help it, but his eyes remained grave. "No. Aside from a stake to the heart, a silver bullet is the only way to really kill a vampire, according to some authorities."

"But I'm not a vampire. Dammit, Gavin, why do I have to keep saying that?"

"Someone thinks you are, or wants us to think it."

"That again? Don't you think you're rushing to conclusions? For all you know someone could have been fooling around with an antique pistol with an old silver bullet in the chamber. The fact that I'm part vampire, or whatever, could be completely coincidental."

"No. The bullet wasn't new, but the plating was."

There went that theory. I scraped cookie crumbs into a little pile and began forming it into a small snake with the side of my index finger. "Still, it could have been an accident."

Gavin shook his head. "They don't exactly sell silver bullets at the corner drugstore, Jo."

I wanted to make another joke, but nothing came. I left off my snake and stared blankly at the tablecloth until the sunflowers became disarticulated blurs of yellow, green and white. The implications of Gavin's words sunk in slowly, coating my brain in a thick fog that limited all thoughts but one: *Someone really wanted me dead. Someone had planned it.*

"Hey," Gavin said, "you didn't get bitten by a zombie, too, did you?"

I didn't say anything. My teeth began to chatter.

Gavin got instantly to his feet. "Oh, no. C'mon, Jo, it's all right. You're safe now." He pulled me up, steered me to the couch and gently tucked the afghan around my shoulders. He turned on the TV to the *M*A*S*H* reruns I liked and made me drink some tea that was very hot, very sweet, and very liberally laced with alcohol. When I was warm enough to have pushed off the afghan and had begun to laugh in the right places, Gavin quietly saw himself out.

* * * * *

I had just fallen asleep on the couch wrapped in the Afghan when someone knocked on the door. I pulled one of the throw pillows down over my ears and buried my head in the corner of the couch like a mole burrowing back into its nest, and tried to go back to sleep, but whoever was at the door was too persistent for me to ignore. I hauled myself up off the couch, pushed my feet into the pink bunny slippers my mother had gotten me at Christmas and shuffled sleepily to the door.

"Who is it?" I had to raise my voice to be heard over the sound of the neighbor's yappy dog.

"It is I, Jo, open the door. I need to talk to you."

"Geez, Gavin. Now what? Can't it wait 'til morning?" I undid the deadbolt and pulled open the door. But it wasn't Gavin on my doorstep. It was Will, all six foot plus of him, long, lean and gorgeous in black Armani. I stood there, staring at him, until another round of barking from the neighbor's dog snapped me out of my stupor.

"Oh shit!" I pushed the door shut again. I should have known better than to open it—Gavin wasn't nearly so particular about his grammar.

"Jo, please. I won't hurt you." Will spoke as if the idea were repugnant to him. He hadn't tried to prevent me from closing the door but remained a foot or two away, proud and unruffled.

"That's what they all say." But I hesitated, undone by his calm. I was curious to know why he had come. He didn't seem dangerous. No, I take that back, a man who could send frissons down my spine from three feet away would always be dangerous, but I just didn't believe he had come there to kill me. I eased the door back open, taking the precaution of containing my gaze to his feet. If my wimpy vampire stare could keep my sixth period class in line, his could do just about anything.

We stood there, wrapped in a thick silence save for the continued yapping of the neighbor's dog.

"That dog," Will said abruptly in a clipped voice that emphasized his faint accent, "needs to go to obedience school."

It wasn't what I had expected him to say. It was so…*normal*. I glanced up in surprise. "I know. I try not to make noise past nine o'clock—once you wake him up, he'll go on like that for hours."

Will's answering smile was conspiratorial and brimming with humor, and for a moment, I remembered why I had been so attracted to him in the first place. With it came the uncomfortable realization that he wasn't as one-dimensional as I wanted him to be. I couldn't just categorize him as terrible and evil, put on my white hat and ride off into the sunset. He wasn't so easily labeled or so easily dismissed. I *liked* him, the quickness of his mind, the ready wit, the intellectual bent of his humor. I had grown to respect his queer sense of honor, so unexpected and so at odds with who he was, or more precisely, what I had labeled him as.

All that could have been meaningless—vampires are by nature charming, it is part of their allure—if it weren't for his *awareness*, his appreciation for the irony of our situation. It was almost as if he was giving me a choice, or perhaps that he was giving himself one. I shook these dangerous thoughts out of my head and reminded myself I was standing at my door in the middle of the night talking to a vampire.

"What you want, Will?"

"What do I want?" he repeated slowly. His mouth quirked up wryly in unspoken answer, and for moment I thought his blue eyes looked wistful, almost sad, as if something he yearned for had touched him just long enough for him to taste its intangible sweetness before moving out of reach. The impression of melancholy was fleeting, gone so quickly I would have been sure I had imagined it had I not seen it before, that night we met. I didn't flatter myself that it had anything to do with me, except perhaps peripherally. It was too deep-rooted, too woven into the fabric of who he had become to have been awakened so recently.

Will didn't answer his own question but he did address mine. In a voice that grew harsh with fury, he informed me he had come after learning of the commotion at school that night. "I heard someone shot at you. Is that true?"

"Yes, in the parking lot as I was leaving."

Will look outraged, as of he wanted desperately to find the person who had had the temerity to shoot at me and beat the pulp out of them. I felt an inner rush of satisfaction. Whether I liked to admit it or not, every girl secretly wants her own personal champion, someone who'll rush in and beat the crap out of anyone who looks at her sideways. The kicker, of course, is there's a fine line between a knight in shining armor and a chauvinistic jerk. I want someone who will go to bat for me, not take away my bat and tell me to sit nicely on the bench where I won't get dirty, if you know what I mean.

I reminded myself again that Will was a vampire, not a prospective boyfriend.

"How did you find out so quickly?"

He moved closer to me and I had to force myself to ignore how his proximity made my pulse race.

"Natasha."

For some reason, that scared me more than the bullet had. "She was there?"

"I asked her to keep an eye on you."

It was my turn to look outraged. "Who gave you the right to that?"

He looked surprised at my reaction. "I was concerned about your safety."

And you sent her? "Concerned!" I sputtered. "*You* want me *dead*, remember?"

Will took a deep breath. "You're wrong. I don't want you to die. Quite the opposite, in fact." He slowly reached out a hand as if to reassure me, but abruptly stopped short of the door frame.

I looked in surprise at his hand, which had been rebuffed as if by a force field. I spoke slowly, disbelievingly, though I couldn't hide a small note of triumph and relief. "It's true, isn't it? If I don't invite you in, you can't come in. Not even a part of you."

He shrugged indifferently, but I could feel frustration radiating from him. His eyes glittered. "Why don't you come outside and find out?"

I caught my breath. I felt an almost physical pull, so intense was my desire to step forward out of the safety of the doorway.

"I don't understand," I said gripping the doorway to keep myself back, my voice barely above a whisper. "Why didn't you — take me — the other day? You had the chance."

Will looked offended. "I am a man of honor. I'm not a mindless slave to my desire."

I couldn't believe him. "How can you say that after what you did to me the first time that we met?"

Will regarded me silently for a long while, but his face was closed and his eyes gave nothing away. "That was different," he said finally.

What was that supposed to mean?

"Do they know who shot at you?"

"No. I'm hoping they can trace the bullet."

The dog had started barking again. Will stared pensively in its direction, though I didn't think he really heard it. "It's not always that easy," he said, unwittingly echoing Gavin.

"It should be this time. How many people buy silver bullets?" Will's blue eyes jerked up to meet mine. He looked stunned. And angry. He turned and left without a word.

* * * * *

Maxine gave me the day off after the shooting incident, or rather, banned me from the premises, lest she lose what control of the students—and parents—she still had. This gave me an entire three-day weekend to think over what had happened and come up with the vital clue that would lead me to the identity of my would-be killer. But I didn't want to think about being shot at, or about Bob's murder, or about vampires, or Natasha or the confusion I felt about Will. What I wanted to do was forget about it all, which I did with a fair amount of success, at least at first.

I spent the first day and a half curled up in the fetal position, occasionally unfurling myself when nature called or the hunger pangs got too strong to ignore. That wasn't often— I'd just replenished the cookie jar with a quadruple batch of chocolate chocolate chip, and I still had a few bags of the mini candy bars I'd bought for classroom prizes.

I can eat a lot of chocolate when I'm upset, even in the fetal position. If I thought about it—which I didn't because the whole point of drowning one's sorrows in chocolate is to avoid exactly such unpleasantness—it was just typical that being part vampire had killed my ability to enjoy just about anything healthy while my taste for chocolate had, if anything, mushroomed.

Gavin showed up Saturday afternoon and banged on the door until I let him in. He was dressed more casually than I was used to seeing him. He wore jeans that molded nicely over his long, muscular legs and a yellow short-sleeved shirt that revealed well-defined arms and showed off the slight tan that my mother would have called a *healthy glow*. His short brown hair was damp from the shower and he looked tired but calm, with the sort of relaxed energy that comes after a long, hard workout. I remembered he had told me he was in training for a biathlon, and I wondered with a stab of pure envy if it had been today.

While I was trying to control my jealousy, he took in my baggy sweat pants, faded orange Beaker t-shirt, and hair that hadn't seen a comb in two days and probably more than resembled Beaker's broom-like coif. His face showed no emotion, though a muscle jerked in his cheek as he asked, "Have you even left the house since Thursday night?"

I couldn't tell if he was judging me or not, and decided I didn't care. "What do you want, Gavin?" I left him to lock up or not, and flopped on the couch. I noticed that I had the little tip of a Hershey's kiss stuck to the front of my shirt, which was a little embarrassing as I had finished off those yesterday.

He sat across from me on the edge of the old club chair I had liberated from my parents' garage. It was a deep, overstuffed monstrosity in cracked cherry-brown leather, the sort of thing that could swallow you whole if you let it, which Gavin didn't. "You didn't come by the station yesterday to sign your statement."

"Oh." I rubbed a chocolate stain lightly with a tissue and got hundreds of tiny white balls stuck to the front of my shirt for my efforts. I frowned and tried to brush them away, but they seemed to have melded to the fabric. "I was busy."

"I see that."

I pulled my attention away from my shirt and met his eyes, which were carefully wiped of any expression. "Look. I'm sorry if you're a little behind in your paperwork. I didn't feel like driving over there yesterday, okay? I didn't sleep particularly well Thursday night. I got shot at, remember? By some freak with a silver bullet, who apparently knows my secret and will probably tell everyone, so I'll probably lose my job and my friends. But that's okay I suppose, 'cuz Will stopped by after you left, and invited me to live with him and the rest of the…"

"Will stopped by?" Gavin's Buddha-like inscrutability deserted him completely. "Here? Why?" He spoke accusingly, his eyes searching my face like lasers.

"How the hell do I know?" I crossed my hands over my chest and shrugged them and my shoulders in one large, defiant movement. "He'd heard about the shooting and just showed up."

"He heard about the shooting?" His voice was just short of a yell.

Mine wasn't. "Are you going to repeat everything I say?"

Gavin pursed his lips so tightly they turned white. "How did he know about the shooting?"

"Natasha told him. Apparently she was there."

"I see." Gavin's voice was soft and the shuttered look was back on his face. "Did he try to — recruit you?" He stumbled over the words, as if in self-mockery at employing a euphemism.

"No."

His light gray eyes focused intently on mine. "Why?"

My anger gave way to confusion. "I — I don't know."

He didn't reply. His eyes didn't leave my face. Under such close regard, I shifted uncomfortably in my chair.

"I wonder," he said finally. He looked away, as if he couldn't bear looking at me, and I felt oddly bereft. "Has he given you no indication of his plans? Told you nothing to explain why he hasn't sunk his teeth into your jugular again, given the chance? And he's had plenty of chances, hasn't he?"

"What are you trying to say, Gavin? That it's my fault? Do you think I'm encouraging him somehow?"

"I don't know. Are you?" His eyes met mine again, searching, probing.

My mouth dropped open, but for a moment I was too outraged to reply. Hot tears of righteous anger pricked my eyes, spurred on by a resentful part of me that secretly worried he might be right. "Maybe he just likes me." I threw the words at Gavin. "Some people do, you know."

Gavin leaned forward. He was close enough to touch me, but didn't give me the comfort of a friendly hand on my shoulder. He wanted me to face what he had to say, to feel its cruelty. "No. Vampires aren't 'people', Jo. They're not nice or altruistic. Stop thinking of Will as a person! He's not. He's a vampire. He takes what he wants destroying lives, families…" He abruptly stopped talking and stared fixedly at the floor while he struggled to regain his composure.

"You don't know that," I began.

His head snapped up to look at me. His face was mottled with anger and his eyes were pure silver. "Yes, I do! A vampire killed my sister!" He stood up, as if the seat could no longer hold such raw energy, and turned away.

Silence enveloped the room like a mantle of ice.

After a long while, I spoke. "I'm sorry," I said inadequately. A slight movement of his shoulders indicated he heard me.

"Was it…Will?" I ventured tentatively.

Gavin was silent for so long I wasn't sure he would answer me. "No." He stared unseeingly at the bookshelves, at something only he could see, something he wanted to avoid but couldn't stop his mind from playing out now that it had started. His voice was low and harsh. "A different group. Up near San Francisco."

After a brief silence, he continued in a different voice, as if he'd shoved the image back into the compartment where he kept it locked. "That was several years ago." He turned from the window, sat back down on the chair opposite me, and reached for his briefcase, suddenly all business. He pulled out a thin sheaf of papers and a pen and handed them to me. "Here's your statement from the other night. Why don't you read it over and sign it."

I wanted to say something, but knew anything I could say would be so inadequate as to be insulting. The last person he'd want to hear sympathy from would be someone like me, with ties, however unwanted, to those who had done it. I accepted the papers without comment, gave them a quick read, signed, and handed them back.

"Thank you," Gavin said. He stowed them in his briefcase and walked to the door. I followed him.

He barely looked at me as he stepped out. "I'll step up the surveillance on your home. If Will comes around again, we should be able to protect you. Whatever you do, don't invite him in."

"I won't," I said, stung anew by the implication that I would willingly do something so foolhardy. As before, a little voice deep inside reminded me that, if only for a moment, I had considered doing just that, so intense had my desire been to be with Will.

Gavin's eyes met mine squarely, as if binding me to my promise. "Good."

Chapter Twenty-Five

ɞ

I had thought the pregnancy rumor tough to weather but then I hadn't gambled on the notoriety of getting shot at. My students, for once, were hanging on every word I said, but I didn't kid myself it was my scintillating lecture on rocks that commanded their attention. When, after five minutes or so, I didn't naturally segue into the exciting thrill that is being shot at, they brought it up.

"I am not going to discuss what happened last week. Don't bother asking about it. I'm not going to answer any questions unless they have something to do with this unit."

A hand shot in the air.

"Yes, Carlos?"

"Ms. Gartner, can you make a bullet out of rock?"

I cursed my own stupidity. Had I learned nothing in six months of teaching? "That's hardly—"

Another hand went into the air.

"Er—"

"Can a bullet go through metamorphic rock, like it did your car door?"

After that, it escalated in a free-for-all. They stopped bothering with the hand raising altogether.

"Where does a bullet rank on the Moh's hardness scale?"

"If someone shot you with a bullet made out of rock, would it hurt as bad?"

I closed my eyes. Oh God. Somebody kill me now.

By lunchtime, I had a raging headache and I was off people. I would have preferred to have hidden in my room, but between pilfering from churches, hiding from vampires, and dodging silver bullets, I hadn't got a chance to do something so mundane as go to the supermarket to stock up on snack food, and I was too hungry to skip a meal.

Getting to the cafeteria was one of the queerest experiences of my life. Usually, the high schoolers didn't pay me the slightest bit of attention. But today as I cut through their locker area, a bubble of space and silence seemed to surround me. No one pushed past me to rush to a class across campus, no overloaded backpacks jostled me. The cell phones were quiet, the laughter absent, the conversations muted. I almost pinched myself to make sure I hadn't died without my knowledge and was haunting the hall as a ghost.

All that for fishwiches. I bypassed the hot food line, opting instead for a peanut butter and jelly sandwich and a salad. I wouldn't eat much of the sandwich, just enough to tide me over until I could sneak out for a burger during a free period, and probably none of the salad, but it would give me something to do while everyone else ate.

I sat down at my usual table with Alan, Kendra, and Becky and pretended I didn't notice the abrupt shift in the conversation to sports. I asked Kendra how the boys' soccer team was situated for the finals match later that week.

"Well, my money's on us, of course, but it's not going to be an easy win. The boys are going to have to work for it."

"I hear some middle school kid is working out with the team," Alan said, licking tartar sauce off his fingers.

"No way." I put down my sandwich uneaten. "Maxine caved on Chucky?"

"Huh?" Becky said.

"She didn't really cave," Kendra said. "Rachel—Bob's former assistant coach—put in a good word for him. She's agreed to coach the team next year, and knows Chucky from summer league. He's allowed to practice with the team, but I don't get to play him, which is a shame because he's good."

"Ah, not cave but compromise," Becky said, swishing a limp fry in the pool of ketchup on her plate.

"Is he good enough to start?" asked Alan.

"Yup," Kendra said.

"Against high school seniors?" Becky said.

"Well, you have to keep in mind that he's a wing. He doesn't have to be big. He has to have good ball control and he has to be fast, and he's both."

Becky asked, "How's the team taking it?"

Kendra frowned and gave a little shrug. "Mixed, frankly. Josh, the captain, loves it—Chucky gives the defense someone new to practice against. But Josh will do anything to win, and keep in mind he plays sweeper. The forwards are a little less thrilled."

"I can imagine," I said. "How long has he been practicing with the team?"

"He started the beginning of last week."

"That's funny," I said. "He didn't say anything about it when I tutored him after school last week." *The same night someone shot at me.*

Kendra shrugged again and speared a lettuce leaf with her fork. "Maxine probably advised him not to mention it. You know how some of the teachers are about after school sports—they think kids shouldn't be on the teams if they can't keep their grades up."

"They shouldn't," Alan said.

Kendra responded immediately with some heat. "You're being shortsighted, Alan. Sports are an important outlet for a stressed-out kid, and sometimes it's the only thing they feel they're good at. Taking it away often makes things worse."

"Uh oh, here it comes," Becky said.

"Oh God, not the self-esteem argument again," Alan said, rolling his eyes.

"Gosh, would you look at the time. I have to go prep for my next class." I piled my dishes back on my tray and got up. Becky caught my eye and grinned knowingly, but didn't follow suit. Unlike me, she liked to watch people argue. She followed several of the reality TV shows, espousing them as fascinating sociological experiments.

"We're still on for our Olympiad meeting today, aren't we?" Kendra asked me.

I nodded unenthusiastically and she and Alan went back to arguing. Becky watched avidly, occasionally putting her oar in, probably when it got too close to resolution.

I walked away lost in thought. If Chucky was practicing late with the team, his mother would have had to pick him up and drive him home. That would've put her on campus the night someone shot at me and yet I didn't recall seeing either of them in the crowd that had gathered in the parking lot. Surely that was a conspicuous absence. Almost as conspicuous as the fact that Rachel had taken the coaching job after all.

* * * * *

Kendra entered my classroom soon after the last bell. She slung a thick folder on one of the lab benches and sat down. "I've got Bob's old Olympiad files. We'll need to sort through it sometime, might as well get it over with."

"Right." I sat across from her and she handed me a pile of mismatched papers stacked every which way.

We worked in silence for a while. Kendra was sorting as efficiently as a computer and I tried my best to fight back the boredom and keep up.

"Man, you're fast," I said.

"I've done this a few times. I use to co-chair with Roger back when he did it."

"Really? I saw pictures of him on the website. Barely recognized him with all the hair." I giggled.

Kendra grinned. "I know."

"I'm surprised he stopped doing it. I mean he won a bunch of teaching awards for it."

"Yeah, he was amazing."

I held up a yellowing sheet of paper. "Talk about carryover crap," I said. "I think this is an entry form from 1992."

Kendra stopped me from tossing it into the trash. "Hold on. Let me see that. Nope, we keep it. It lists the events from that year, with good descriptions. We can use them for our practice rounds. Throw it in this end pile here where I've put all the administrative stuff."

"If you say so." I tossed it into the pile and went back to my sorting. In the middle of a brochure on metric estimation, I discovered a nice thank you note to Bob from a parent whose child had placed fifth in the Egg Drop.

I got a little choked up. "Aw, that's so sweet," I said, refolding the note.

"What's sweet?" asked Kendra.

I handed her the note. "Just a thank-you note to Bob."

She read it and got a little teary too. I went back to my pile and unfolded another small note card, this one, with "Blondes have more fun!" printed on the front. It too, was addressed to Bob. But it wasn't from a parent, unless one of them referred to herself as "Pookie," loved him "always and forever," and was "counting the minutes until their next night together."

I must have made a sound, for Kendra looked up and said, "Is that another one? Let me see," she took it out of my hand. Her grin faded as she read it. "Geez."

"Yeah." It was one thing to read a nice little thank-you note about a deceased friend, and quite another to read a rather personal love letter.

"Okay, not a keeper." She ripped it in half and threw it away. "There aren't any more in there, are there?" she asked, hesitating by the trash can.

"God, I hope not. But if I see anything that looks remotely like a letter, I'm checking first to see if it's from *Pookie* before I read any further."

"People do choose silly pet names for themselves when they're in love," Kendra said, returning to her pile.

"It's hard to imagine Bob in love with anyone who would refer to themselves as *Pookie.*" I returned reluctantly to my own pile of papers.

In another half hour, we had finished. Kendra rushed off to soccer practice while I stayed behind to pack up my things.

As I reached to turn off the lights, my eyes dropped down to the love letter Kendra had thrown away. I stooped down, pulled it out of the trash, and tucked it into my back pocket.

I wasn't sure why. It had probably been written by an old girlfriend. There hadn't been a date on it, and since the papers had been arranged so haphazardly, the fact that I had found it next to a letter written last spring was an unreliable guide, at best.

My mind went back to that e-mail Becky had written to Bob.

No, I told myself. No way did Becky write this trite, gushing love letter. I wasn't all that familiar with her handwriting, but I was pretty sure I could rule her out on the basis of the cheesy pet name alone.

And yet…I *had* heard Becky use the phrase, "Blondes have more fun," on more than one occasion when asked why she bleached her hair.

No. I couldn't believe it.

Chapter Twenty-Six

𝕭

As I left campus, I found myself heading for the divey coffee shop across from the police station. There was nothing I had to say that couldn't have been handled in a phone call, but Gavin was annoyingly difficult to get a hold of. The man turned up like a bad penny every time he wanted something from me, but had been noticeably reticent in returning the favor. Frankly, I didn't understand why—in TV shows, the detectives always give the victims a number where they can be reached, day or night, and urge them to use it at the slightest provocation. Not Gavin. No, my detective pulled a full Garbo—he wanted to be left alone.

About the time I had finally settled into my grading, Gavin came out. I shoved the papers back in my bag with silent apologies to the students whose quizzes I'd mangled and ran across the street to the police station parking lot. I intercepted Gavin just as he got to his car.

"I could give you a ticket for jaywalking, you know."

"I thought detectives were above writing tickets," I wheezed, trying to catch my breath.

"Not when you do it in front of the police station."

"Oh, for heaven's sake. I just want to talk to you."

He crossed his arms and leaned back against his car. "All right."

"Can't we go somewhere more private?" It had gotten dark and I was starting to get nervous.

A couple of officers passed by and snickered.

Gavin greeted them with a pained looking smile that faded into a grimace as they passed.

"What's wrong with them?"

"Nothing," Gavin said. "Where's your car?"

"Around the corner, why?"

"Geez, Jo," he said tiredly. "Can't you at least try to practice some basic safety precautions?"

"I do try! It was the only space I could find. What's wrong with you? Did you have a bad day or something?"

He just let out a sigh. "Get in. I'll drive you to your car. We can talk at your place." As he got in the driver's side, he mumbled something under his breath. I directed him to my car. He double parked behind it until I'd pulled away from the curb and followed me home.

When we reached my apartment, Gavin headed straight for the kitchen and sat down in his usual seat at the table. He crossed his arms over his chest. "Well?"

He really was acting oddly, even for him. "Are you hungry?" I asked. "I can make you a hamburger, or I may have some cookies left if you'd rather."

"I'm fine. What did you want to tell me?"

Gavin had never been particularly warm and fuzzy, but I'd never seen him like this. I sat across from him. "Is something wrong? Did I do something to piss you off?"

He just sat there, as responsive as a block of wood. Talk about passive aggressive! He was worse than my mother on of her Martyr-Mom days!

As the moments ticked by in silence, I began to worry. It wasn't like him to be so quiet. Maybe it wasn't me he was mad at. It wasn't as if he was shy about yelling at me. Maybe something bad had happened at work? I remembered that odd treatment he'd received from those other officers in the parking lot tonight and then it hit me.

"You're getting shit back at the station about me, aren't you? Is that why you wouldn't give me your cell phone number? Because the guys might talk?"

His head snapped up and he glared at me. "Of course not."

I didn't believe him. "That's it, isn't it? You said before that pretty much only your captain knows what it is you really do. The other officers have no idea what you're trying to protect people from—they must think you're hanging around me for no reason other than because you want to. And I thought I was working with a bunch of eighth-graders!"

"Shit," Gavin said, rolling his eyes. "If you're going to go on like this, maybe you *should* give me something to eat. These absurd mental leaps of yours are a lot to take on an empty stomach."

I stayed planted in my seat. "Are you sure you want to have dinner with me? I mean, the guys at the station might talk."

He put his head down on his hands. "Oh God."

* * * * *

By the time we had finished eating, Gavin was back to his usual self. He crossed his arms over his broad chest, focused his light gray eyes on me, and asked what it was I had wanted to tell him. Unexpectedly, I found myself clamming up. My suspicions seemed too silly to voice aloud when he put me on the spot like that.

"Do you have any leads on who shot me?" I parried.

"No."

"What you mean, 'No'? It's been four days."

He sighed. "We're trying to trace the bullet, but so far we've come up empty. Forensics thinks it was homemade. If they're right, which it's looking like they are, we won't get very far with that piece of evidence."

"What about the other evidence?"

"What other evidence?"

"I don't know, didn't you guys find something?" I threw up my hands.

He shrugged. "What was there to find? Someone took a shot at you in an otherwise deserted parking lot and took off."

I stared unblinkingly at him until he continued, rather irritably. "We're working on witness testimony, but that isn't much to go on. You're the only one who could have seen who shot you, and you've told us nothing. The rest of the statements are just a bunch of conflicting, vague after-the-fact reports."

"That's it? That's the best America's Finest can do?"

His calm demeanor was starting to fray at the edges. "I didn't say that. I'm merely trying to explain why we can't provide a quick turnaround for you. We have to do it the long, hard way—alibi, motive, opportunity. The one thing we have going in our favor is that silver bullet. Not everyone could've made it."

"How hard is it?" I scoffed. "All the ingredients for it are in the chemical room off the chem lab. You just mix up the stuff and brush it on. Becky has her basic chemistry students silver-plate stuff in one of her labs right before Christmas vacation." I stared open-mouthed at Gavin as I realized what I had said. "Oh, no."

"Jo, relax. If that's how it was done, and it's as easy as you say, any number of people could have done it. The master keys let you in any room in the school, and there are enough of them scattered around that I would seriously recommend changing the locks at some point."

"You don't understand," I said miserably, forcing out the words I wanted so desperately not to say. "Becky was—I think—involved with Bob. Romantically I mean."

"Is that why you came to the station tonight?"

I nodded and produced both the e-mail and the letter I'd found, explaining hesitantly how I'd come across them.

"You should have told me about these earlier." It wasn't an accusation, but I felt guilty just the same. I wasn't helping anyone by withholding information only to blurt it out later.

"I know," I said wretchedly. "I guess I didn't want to accuse her—even tacitly—if I wasn't sure, and it's hard to imagine Becky and Bob as a couple—I wouldn't have thought him her type. Her story about the Grateful Dead concert seemed the more believable explanation."

He shook his head. "That's not what I mean. We've already been through Bob's e-mail—your headmaster gave us access the night he died—and Becky's Grateful Dead concert story does check out. I could've saved you some unnecessary hand wringing had you bothered to confide in me."

My cheeks turned pink. "Oh. What about the second letter?"

He picked it up and idly pushed the two halves back together. "It's not exactly the smoking gun we're looking for. From what you've told me, it's at least a year old, possibly as much as four—that's how long Bob had been running the Olympiad, right?—and frankly, unless you're sure the handwriting's Becky's," he looked to me for confirmation, but I just shrugged, "it could be from any number of old girlfriends. From what I understand, Bob was no slouch in the dating department. Chances are it's from someone with no ties to the school."

I sagged back against the chair as a wave of relief flooded through me. *Thank God it wasn't Becky.*

"Anything else you want to tell me?"

"Bob's assistant coach has accepted his coaching job, after all. And Chucky Farryll's been practicing with the varsity soccer team. He and his mother would have been on campus last Thursday night—when someone shot at me."

"I see."

"I don't get it. Why would anyone try to shoot me so long after Bob's death? If they hate me that much, why did they bother killing Bob in the first place? The whole thing doesn't make sense! Someone's trying to tie me in to all this, which means it's someone I know, and yet no one I know could possibly have done it."

Gavin was prevented a reply by the sound of someone pounding on the front door. In between pounds, a voice could be heard shouting, "Jo? Jo, honey, open this door! I mean it, right now!"

"Oh, no." I got up and ran to open the door before it was pounded in. Gavin was right behind me.

He reached forward and put a hand over mine as I would have unlocked the door. "Wait! Do you know who it is?"

I looked at him scornfully and opened the door to reveal a redheaded fury.

"Josephine Delilah Gartner! How dare you get shot at and not tell your mother!"

As my mother pushed past us into the room, I heard Gavin murmur, "Delilah?"

"I thought you and Dad were in New York for a conference," I said.

"We were. He's still there. I came back when I learned my only daughter had been shot at by some maniac. Not that you bothered to tell us."

Gavin discreetly tried to leave, but I grabbed him by his shirt and pulled him back inside. "Oh, no," I hissed. "You're not going anywhere. You're supposed to protect me from getting killed, remember?"

I prodded him into the living room, where he sat gingerly on the edge of the man-eating club chair. My mother had appropriated the couch and sat smoothing her cream colored suit skirt in rapid, jabbing motions. She looked up and a slight frown puckered her brow as she noticed Gavin for the first time.

Gavin jumped back up and offered his hand. "I'm Detective Gavin Raines, Mrs. Gartner. Pleased to meet you."

She shook it firmly and introduced herself, automatically flashing me a look of disappointment that I hadn't displayed manners enough to have introduced them properly, no matter that she hadn't given me the chance.

I sat down on the couch next to my mother and put my arm around her shoulders. "I'm fine, Mom, really. I didn't call because I didn't want to worry you guys. I know how important that conference is to Dad, and the whole incident sounds much worse than it was. It was just a silly accident, right Gavin?—I mean Detective Raines." I didn't wait for his response but continued on, "I didn't mean for you to find out from someone else—er, how did you find out, anyway?"

She sniffed. "Rafael."

"Him again? Does he have you on speed dial or something? I swear that man's had it in for me ever since I refused to let him give me highlights and an updo for the senior prom," I said irritably. "Didn't it occur to you that he might be overstating things a bit? The last thing he told you was that I was pregnant..."

Gavin looked up, startled.

"Which was pure crap. Why would you assume he was right about this?"

She blinked furiously. "I thought you might have needed me," she replied in a low voice.

"Oh, Mom, of course I do."

Gavin politely went back to examining the carpet is if it were the most fascinating thing he'd seen in a long time while we had a mother-daughter moment.

My mother dabbed away tears that somehow hadn't marred her impeccable makeup and then turned to Gavin and without preamble began to give him the third degree. He looked a little frazzled. After a while, I took pity on him.

"Mom, it's late, and I know you're on East Coast time. Why don't we have brunch on Saturday?"

By some miracle that probably had more to do with jet lag than anything I had said, as she is not even remotely a night person, my mother let herself be herded to the door. Gavin insisted on walking her to her car.

"It was a pleasure to meet you, Mrs. Gartner," he told her as she got into her Lexus.

"And you, Detective Raines. I'm glad to know my daughter is in such capable hands. I'm sure I can rely on you to keep her safe." She said it graciously, but there was no doubt it was an order.

Gavin nodded once briskly and moved back several feet to give us some privacy. Mom gave me a kiss and an affectionate hug that lingered rather longer than normal. As I was about to step away from the car, she touched her fingers lightly to my face. "Oh, honey, your skin is looking *so* much better. What did you do?"

"Um, just followed the doctor's orders." I spoke in a low voice, mindful I had told Gavin she had bought me a miracle cream in Europe. To my relief, she didn't pursue it and drove off with a cheery honk.

"So that's your mother," Gavin said. He sounded a bit faint. "We're both still alive so I guess that went okay. Can I go now?"

"Went okay? Are you kidding me? If you don't figure out who's behind all this, I'm going to have to start going to Rafael's for rumor control, though I'd almost rather be killed than spend time there. And when he turns my hair fuchsia because it's the new red, I'm coming after you."

He didn't respond until we were nearly at my door. "Speaking of Rafael, want to tell me about this pregnancy rumor?"

"No." But I let out a deep sigh and told him anyway.

He listened without interruption. "I see."

"What's that supposed to mean?"

He raised his eyebrows in surprise. "Nothing. Make sure you lock up." He turned away and managed to get almost all the way down the stairs before he burst out laughing.

Chapter Twenty-Seven

ဆ

For once, Roger started off our department meeting with something that concerned me. I was so surprised my hand stopped in midair over the cookie plate and Becky swiped the last of Mary Mudget's coveted brownies out from under my nose.

Roger was saying, in a rather self-congratulatory way, "And so it should come as no surprise to any of you that the Olympiad is now on the headmaster's radar."

"I'm surprised the Olympiad's on *anyone's* radar," whispered Becky through a mouthful of brownie.

"Shhh! Brownie thief. No one wants to hear your views."

Thanks to popular little Chucky Farryll, a lot of kids were involved in the Olympiad this year. Apparently enough of their parents had mentioned the Olympiad to the headmaster during the last soccer game that his High Mucky Muck had announced his intention to come watch.

That, of course, had sent Roger into a tizzy, and the rest of us were caught up in its vortex. No longer were Kendra and I to divvy up events and train whoever showed up to the meetings. Roger wanted the *entire* department involved. Each of us would pick one or two events and relentlessly train the delegates up until the Olympiad.

Amid the groans and protests, Kendra raised a hand to object. "I don't think that will quite work, Roger. We haven't picked the delegates yet. A ton of kids signed up this year. We didn't want to turn any of them away—discourage their interest in science..." There was a murmur of agreement around the table. "Right now, all the categories are open to whoever is interested in participating. We've got about ten teams building contraptions for the egg drop, and nearly as many working on Rube Goldberg apparatuses."

Mary Mudget nodded approvingly over her knitting, something in soft baby blue yarn this week. "That's nicely in keeping with the middle school spirit that events are more about participation than winning."

Roger didn't seem to have gotten that memo. For a moment I thought he was going to bang on the table to snap us all out of our callow idealism—and general laziness. "We're doing it differently this year," he all but shouted over the hubbub. His small, hard eyes raked over us, defying anyone to contradict him. We quieted down and he went on in a calmer voice. "The Olympiad is in six weeks. I'd like Kendra and Jo to arrange a practice Olympiad a week from now. The winners and runners-up in each event will practice one-on-one with their assigned teacher up until the Olympiad."

I opened my mouth to object, but Kendra caught my eye and discreetly shook her head, though I could tell she was just as annoyed as I was. She was right to stop me. Trying to make Roger change his mind when he was like this was a waste of time. She flipped open her daily planner with obvious annoyance. "How does next Monday work for everyone?"

Thanks to Roger's self-interested glory seeking, I spent a ridiculous amount of time after the meeting organizing the stupid, unnecessary practice-Olympiad, just so the headmaster could see how good an administrator Roger was. By eight o'clock, I was tired and hungry and cranky—and had barely made a dent in all the work. I left the top floor of the science wing and pounded down the stairs with as much venom as if they were Roger's head. *There just wasn't enough time*, I thought furiously. Not unless I stayed late every night this week. *Like I didn't have enough to do already!* I rounded the corner and took out some more of my aggressions on the hedge that ran alongside the science building. "Damn!" I kicked the hedge. "That stinking!" Kick. "Roger!" Kick! Kick! Kick!

"Something upsetting you?" A blast of musky perfume assailed my nostrils and the blood in my veins turned cold. *Oh, God. I'd forgotten about Natasha.*

I turned around to face her. She stood a few yards away near the small copse of trees outside the science building that the students like to sit under on warm days. As usual, she looked like a million bucks, in a lookin'-for-Sugar-Daddy sort of way, with a short tight skirt, a skimpy low-cut shirt and four-inch heels. I opened my mouth to reply, but instead of answering, I ran full tilt in the other direction toward the parking lot.

For once, luck was on my side. I got my car unlocked on the first try and was squealing out the gate before she'd made it even halfway across the quad in her tippy little heels. If I'd ever deserved a speeding ticket, it was that night.

A little way down the street from my apartment, I saw a blue Jetta parked in front of a hydrant and pulled up alongside. I honked, flicked on my hazard lights and got out. Gavin came around the car to intercept me.

"What's wrong? Did something happen?"

"Na-Natasha." My teeth were chattering so badly I could barely get the words out. "Sh-she was waiting for me a-at school. I d-didn't even see her."

Gavin plucked the keys out of my fingers, locked my car door, and steered me up to my apartment. "I'm going to park your car. I'll be back in a second," he told me. I nodded and sat on the couch, turning on the TV for comfort.

By the time he returned, I had mellowed out a bit and could form coherent sentences.

He listened patiently. "So…nothing happened."

"Because I got away!"

He shook his head. "No, I didn't mean it that way—"

"I don't know why you don't take her seriously. She scares the crap out of *me*." I stood back up and took a step closer to him. "I'm damned lucky I got away. You know, you spend all these resources watching my apartment, and half the time I'm not even here. How does that help me? Jeez, Gavin, do you want to help me or not? Don't you care if something happens to me? Don't you care if another person goes missing, if another person is found dead?"

His eyes blazed like molten silver. "That's a stupid question," he bit out.

"Is it?" All at once, my anger deflated. "Never mind. Go back to your car. I'm inside for the night. You don't have to worry." I headed toward the door.

"Where are you going?"

"To get my phone out of my purse," I said tiredly. "I want to call my mother. Is that okay with you?"

He didn't reply, just fished his wallet out of his back pocket, pulled out a card and wrote a couple numbers on the back. "This is my private cell. And my home phone. From now on, I want you to call me every night by six and tell me where you are. I'd prefer it if you were home by dark, but I understand you have a life to live. Make sure you use it."

He turn and left, waiting long enough for me to lock the door behind him before heading back down the stairs to his car.

Chapter Twenty-Eight
ℰↄ

Because of Roger's stupid practice Olympiad, I stayed at worked until nearly dark every night that week and still had to go back again over the weekend to get things ready. Roger dropped by Sunday night as it was getting down to the wire. Not to help, to make sure I wasn't screwing up. After a little teeth gnashing, we came to an understanding — he would hover officiously over my shoulder giving advice on how I could organize things more to his liking and I would try very hard not to kill him.

As I stood there gratuitously rearranging supplies under Roger's micromanaging eye, I began to have trouble remembering just what my problem was with becoming one of the Undead. Vampires didn't have to work thankless jobs, or go home to tiny apartments. They wouldn't have to take it as Roger instructed them to move a box of paper six inches to the right. A *vampire* would have hauled off and killed Roger back when he complained how the paper clips were being laid out.

Unless he had some secret death wish, I didn't even know why Roger was here. Surely the whole point of dumping the prep work on me was to free him up. Did he have nothing better to do on a Sunday night than hang out on campus? *Silly question.* Of course he didn't. The real question was, *Why was I there*? I didn't have to be. *I* had options, one in particular that was pretty damn appealing right about now. Will was gorgeous and intelligent and his kisses turned me to jelly. How bad could an eternity spent with him be?

Luckily for Roger's continued existence — and my karma — Kendra popped by on her way to check her events, and Roger followed her out. I took a much-needed break. I felt wrung out like a dishrag and it was only seven o'clock.

I knew exactly what time it was because my cell phone rang with my daily phone call from Gavin. He had gone from being annoyingly hard to reach to annoyingly punctual. I didn't kid myself that his sudden attentiveness had anything to do with *me*. He was scared my mother would come after him if anything happened to me—and believe me, you don't want to be on her bad side.

He called to make sure I was safe at home. Obviously I wasn't, and after some mild abuse when I refused to go home immediately, Gavin informed me he'd call again at eight and slammed the phone with as much force as one can muster with a cell.

I decided I needed some company—the past hour with Roger hardly counted—and went down the hall to see how Kendra was getting on in the computer room where we'd stored the kids' entries. It was a risky move. If Roger was still with her he would cleave back onto me like a jumping cactus, but I really did need to touch base with my co-captain before I spent any more time on this thing.

Kendra was bent over one of the kids' Rube Goldberg apparatuses holding a clamp. She stopped her tinkering for a moment to greet me. "Hey, Jo. What's up?"

She'd gotten rid of Roger. I wish I knew how she'd done it. "Oh, nothing." I swallowed my envy. "Just taking a break."

"Been here long?" She adjusted the position of a lit candle that wasn't quite cutting it as a fuse. A chain of things went wiz and bang and a ping-pong ball shot off across the room and bounced off the whiteboard.

"Are you supposed to be doing that? I mean, if the project sucks, shouldn't you let it?"

She straightened up and regarded me coldly. "Plenty of them will suck tomorrow, believe me. But some of the kids have good ideas, and a project like this one here probably worked before it made the trip to school Thursday morning. You really think they should be eliminated in front of the headmaster and all their friends because the bus ride was little bumpy?" She expertly tightened something and this time, the ping-pong made it into the trash can.

I felt like the lowliest grade school tattletale. I left before I said anything I'd regret, but by the time I got back to my classroom I was so angry I had to splash cold water over my face until I calmed down. If I were honest, Kendra wasn't really the problem. She was merely the straw that broke the camel's back. But I was sick and tired of dealing with so many precious egos and being too low on the totem pole to do anything but take the abuse.

I patted my face dry with a couple of brown paper towels from the holder above the sink and took deep yoga breaths until I calmed down. As I relaxed back against the counter, I stared abstractedly at the pile of old textbooks, still stacked in that odd way. A faint smell of lit candles had followed me from the computer room and I was suddenly transported back to the last time I'd smelled candles in my room—the night Bob had died.

And then I knew. I knew how it had been done, how someone could have been two places at once. It was so simple, I couldn't believe I hadn't put it together before. I owed an apology to the kids who'd had a sword fight with those conjoined meter sticks. They'd been telling the truth about finding them duct-taped that way.

I pulled the meter sticks out from under the sink and re-created the makeshift sword as best I could, which wasn't hard because the boys had left on most of the tape. A piece of charred string dangled from one end, and I kicked myself for not having noticed it before.

I tucked the stringless end of the doubled meter stick between the long part of the T of those funny back-to-back book stacks, and re-adjusted the heavy books on top and voila! the base of the stick was secure. I grasped the charred string and slowly backed up toward the sink fixture, where I'd removed a matching bit of string the night of Bob's funeral, until the meter stick arched. When I let go the meter stick swung sharply forward, grazing the top of the nearest lab bench before clattering to the floor. If the bench had been closer to the back sink, as it had the night of Bob's death, any glassware on top would have been swept to the ground in a loud crash.

My mind raced as everything clicked into place. All that was missing was a way to break the string after a short delay, giving the killer time to race downstairs and establish an alibi.

A candle would work just fine. After a few minutes the flame would burn through the string, the arched meter stick would snap straight and knock the glassware to the floor. And the killer would be in the clear.

It was only natural for us all to have assumed Bob's death was coincident with the noise. But it hadn't been. He had died earlier. And now I had proof.

I reached for my phone, but before I could get a call through to Gavin, Roger came in, followed by Kendra. I jumped, nearly dropping the phone. I had been so engrossed in my thoughts, I'd forgotten they were still there.

"What's wrong?" Roger's raisin eyes anxiously scanned the neat supply piles. "I heard things falling up here."

"Nothing's wrong." I lifted my shoulders up in what I hoped was a careless shrug and forced a bland smile across my lips.

Kendra glanced at the meter stick on the floor near my feet and her lips quirked up in a smile. "What in the world are you doing in here?"

"Just trying out a new demo for class. It doesn't work very well."

"Aren't you doing the rock unit?" asked Roger. "Why aren't you using the rock trays? What do you need with a demo?"

For moment, my hands clenched into tight fist and I forgot all about Bob's murder. Why couldn't Roger just let me teach the way I thought best? How come everything I did to make earth science more fun for the kids was shot down? It wasn't as if I pulled stuff out of the air. I got my ideas from respected earth science journals, from the new lab books that came with the text, from the websites of master earth teachers all over the country. I carefully researched and tested every new lab, every new demo, every new bit of software. The kids liked it a hell of a lot more than listening to me talk and they soaked up information like sponges.

Kendra was standing behind Roger. She caught my eye and shook her head in silent sympathy, and my anger left as suddenly as it had come. "Do you need a hand?" she asked.

"No, that's all right. I'll just stick to my rock trays."

"If you change your mind, I'm happy to help. I've prepped all my events for tomorrow, but I'll be down in my classroom for a bit if you need me." Kendra turned and left. Roger, quieted by my unexpected agreement with him, glanced suspiciously once around the room and followed her out with a wordless grunt. I crossed the room and stood in the doorway, watching as they left the second floor to go down to their classrooms.

My hands were shaking a little as I called Gavin. He didn't pick up. I swore under my breath. What was the point of finally having his cell phone number if he didn't answer the blasted thing? I left increasingly addled messages on his home phone, his work phone, and with the dispatcher in case he was hiding from me at the station. Served him right if they thought I *was* hounding him like a jealous girlfriend.

As I hung up after my last message, I realized I didn't know the answer to the most important question of all. Which one of my colleagues had done it? Kendra was the obvious choice, but she and Mrs. Mudget had been talking in the hallway when they heard the glass shattering. Gavin would know for sure how long they had been there, but the fuse wouldn't have bought more than a few minutes' time, and I thought one of them would have mentioned it if the other had conveniently appeared, tired and breathless, just before the glass broke.

I thought I could safely rule out Rachel, who taught English at another school when she wasn't coaching soccer, and Mrs. Farryll as lacking the necessary skills to whip up a simple machine from odds and ends in an earth science classroom.

Alan was still in the clear. In order to be on the other side of Maxine's office around the time of the crash, he would have had to pass by Maxine's window in the other direction after setting off the fuse, and we would have noticed.

Becky had been in conference with the Campbell twins' parents for a solid half-hour before Bob's murder. Carol had had back-to-back conferences. Thankfully, I could rule them both out.

That left only one person — Roger.

He had come out of the men's room after hearing the glass break. The men's room was at the front of the building, near the foot of the stairwell. He could have come down from my classroom, ducked into the men's room, and waited there until he heard the beakers go crashing to the floor.

Those pictures I'd found of Roger receiving commendations by the Olympiad officials popped into my head, clear as day. Roger not only knew how to build simple machines, he was a whiz at it.

I had thought his motives too petty to lead to murder, but maybe his motives were just petty to *me*. For Roger, that horrible teaching review Bob was about to release really was everything. Killing Bob allowed Roger to salvage his reputation *and* put him in line for the biology job he so coveted. The fact that that job had been filled by someone else was immaterial; he'd already started a subtle smear campaign on Leah, a few more whispers and the job would be his for the taking.

The murder attempt on me had happened after I had recommended to the headmaster that Leah be hired as a permanent replacement. And Roger had been on campus during the shooting. I had assumed he hadn't shown up until after the police came because he was too concerned with saving his own skin to risk helping someone else, but maybe he had been slow to the scene because he was getting rid of the gun.

And when shooting me hadn't worked, he'd engineered a way to get me on campus late on a Sunday night! Kendra would leave soon and I would be left alone in the science building with him. I needed to get out of there. Now. I grabbed my purse, shook it once to make sure my keys were still in it and sprinted for the outer door.

I stopped before I crossed the threshold into the night air. What was I thinking? I couldn't go out there. The sun had gone down. Natasha was out there, waiting for me. And she scared me more than Roger.

I went back my classroom. It was the safest place for me. For now. I closed the door behind me and locked it.

My cell phone remained frustratingly silent. *Where was Gavin?* I paced the floor, my mind racing. I decided I was pretty safe as long as Kendra stuck around. Roger would hardly want a witness when he came after me.

I opened a window and stuck my head out, craning my neck to see if the lights were on in Roger's room. They weren't.

Where was he?

My teeth started to chatter. I told myself he was probably over bothering Kendra in her room, but since her room was downstairs on the other side of the building, I had no way of knowing if she was even still on campus unless I left my room to check.

What if he wasn't over talking to Kendra? What if she'd gone home? What if he was on his way back up to my room?

I left another, more urgent round of messages for Gavin, not caring if he heard the panic in my voice, only wanting him to come get me. I stuck my head back out the window to check if the lights had gone back on in Roger's room. They hadn't. I wedged myself in the corner facing the door and felt a tiny bit safer with two walls at my back.

I tried not to think about Roger coming upstairs and breaking down the door with an axe. *Think of something else.*

Dammit, where was Gavin when I needed him?

I looked over at the sink at the leftover bits of the device Roger had made. I wanted Gavin to eat crow. I wanted all the Is dotted and Ts crossed when I told Gavin how I had figured it all out.

Textbooks, meter sticks, duct tape, string. The only thing still missing from the scenario I had created was the candle itself. I hadn't actually seen one.

I forced my brain back to that night. I went in the room, I checked Bob's pulse, I went to stand in the back of the classroom. *Think, Jo, think!* The string had been tied around the faucet. The candle must have been in the sink. Had I looked in the sink?

I hadn't.

I had been looking at Bob. I had watched as Kendra tried to resuscitate him, and my attention had stayed on Bob when the paramedics took over. I cursed myself for being such a looky-loo.

But so what if I hadn't *seen* the candle. I'd smelled it. I knew it had been there. The police would just have to take my word for it. But would they?

What I didn't understand was why their crack CSI team hadn't put it together. It seemed so obvious. I know it's a little harder to sort out the relevant clues from the irrelevant ones than they make it look on TV, but this was too much. When you find a six-foot long meter stick with a bit of charred string at one end, a candle in the sink, and another bit of string tied to the sink nozzle near the candle, doesn't it occur to you that someone may have rigged a little timing device for themselves?

I hadn't put it together immediately, but then I hadn't seen the candle in the sink, and frankly, with all that had gone on I'd forgotten all about smelling one until tonight. But they had no excuse. Unless…

My anger dried up as suddenly as it had come, and my body froze with fear as I whispered the inevitable conclusion. *Unless they hadn't seen the candle either.* Without that, the rest of the pieces would just seem like innocent classroom props. And Lord knows I had enough crap around my classroom to overwhelm the best of CSI teams. I stared blindly at the sink as my mind wrapped around the truth.

I'd been too quick to blame Roger. He'd had the motive, opportunity, and ability to have killed Bob, but he hadn't done it. He hadn't been in the room. And so he couldn't have removed the candle from the sink. Only one person could have. The person who had spent several minutes at the sink washing the blood off her hands even though, come to think of it, there hadn't been much blood to wash off. Kendra. Kendra had pocketed the candle while we were distracted by the arrival of the EMTs.

I was an idiot and a fool.

A knock sounded on the door, breaking the silence. I held my breath, hoping against hope it was Gavin.

"Jo? Are you in there?"

It was Kendra. She rapped harder on the door. I remained quiet, not moving a muscle. If I was lucky, she'd think I'd already gone.

But I wasn't lucky, just stupid. I'd forgotten that if she had helped herself to Becky's chemicals to silver-plate the bullet, she must have a master key. I forgot, that is, until I heard the key turned in the lock.

I discarded my strategy of huddling quietly by the window and rushed toward the counter by the door where I'd left my cell phone. But before I'd gotten halfway, Kendra had the door open and blocked my way. I might have taken my chances and tried to push past her if it weren't for what she held in her hand—a long wooden stake, sharpened to a point at one end. It didn't take much to guess what it was for. It certainly seemed to confirm my theory that Kendra was behind everything, but I would have given a lot to be wrong just then. She kicked the door shut behind her and took a halfhearted jab at me with the stake, laughing when I banged my thigh on a table edge jumping out of reach.

We stared at each other, Kendra holding the stake with the comfort of an athlete, me crouched warily, knees flexed, ready to dodge her next move. Kendra broke the silence first.

She spoke almost lazily, as if we were discussing something no more important than tomorrow's lunch menu. "When I saw you with the meter sticks, I realized you'd figured out how I'd altered the time of Bob's death. I rather hoped you would have suspected Roger. Not that the man can make a simple machine to save his life, but you couldn't be expected to know how he sat back and let me do all the work while he schmoozed with the parents and accepted all the awards." She laughed again, a cruel bitter sound that sent shivers down my spine.

She gave the stake a meaningful caress. "I almost didn't bring this with me, but I'm rather glad I did. You as good as told me you'd figured it *all* out when you didn't let me in just now." Her mouth twisted. "It's a shame, I must say. Think how fitting it would be if Roger had gotten the blame because of all those years he had taken credit for my work."

She rounded on me suddenly, her temper flaring. "And don't think that officious little shit is going to come up and help you!" She regained control of her anger, though barely. Her fury bubbled just below the surface. "I told him I had things under control and sent him home. That worthless security guard is still resting in his booth after letting Roger out of the parking lot. It looks like it's just you and me." She advanced toward me, a cruel smile of pleasure sharpening her features.

My cell phone, sitting uselessly on the counter behind her, rang, and she laughed that my salvation was just out of reach.

I retreated until I was up against the windows, automatically shifting away from the one I had left open. "Why?" The word came out as a croak from my fear-parched throat.

"Why?" A fleeting look of sadness crossed her face and was gone, replaced by self-righteous condemnation. The sharp loathing in her eyes made me flinch. "It wasn't supposed to go that way. Bob and I were in love. We were keeping it quiet, of course. I didn't mind the secrecy, really. I knew he loved me, but Bob was very attractive. Women threw themselves at him. The students were easy, a kindly word to their parents stopped their nonsense. And that cloying little assistant coach of his took that job I arranged for her as I knew she would. None of them loved him the way I did. And then you came along!

"I saw the way you came on to him. Always over there between classes, pretending you wanted help, swinging your hair around." She mimicked cruelly, "Oh, Bob, teaching's *so* hard. My students *won't* listen, can't you help me?"

"We hadn't been able to spend time together for weeks. Then finally, on Parents' Night, Bob and I made plans to sneak off for a private drink together after our conferences were over. But you couldn't stand it, could you? You couldn't stand to see us happy together. So you tricked him into inviting you! You used some dark magic on him! You...horrible...vampire seductress!"

I gaped at her. A crazy image of myself as a red-haired Elvira rose unbidden in my head and I pushed it away. "Really, Kendra," I said earnestly, willing her to believe me, "it wasn't like that. Bob only invited me because he was being nice. I thought a bunch of people were going. I had no idea it was just the two of you."

"Liar!" she shrieked, coming so close I could see spittle forming at the corner of her mouth. "Do you have any idea how I felt when I went up to meet him and found him in your room, leaving you directions for *our* date? You stole him away from me!

"Your Little Miss Innocent act doesn't fool me! You were working on him long before you became a freak. Oh, I've seen you at work. Bob, that dark man everyone was goggling at during the Christmas party, even that detective is wound around your finger." She let out a high-pitched laugh. "But you got yours, didn't you? I saw you in that bar, with that man. I know what he did to you, what you are! And now you can go to hell where you belong!"

She raised the stake in both hands and aimed a sharp blow to my chest. I grabbed hold of her wrists and tried to push her away, but she was too strong. Little by little, the stake came closer. But my death wasn't coming fast enough for her. She began to kick ruthlessly at my feet, knocking me off-balance until I was forced to let go of her in order to keep myself from falling out the open window. She raised the stake and stabbed again. This time, I grabbed hold of the stake instead of her wrists.

It was a losing move. I had lost my leverage, and she knew it. She immediately adjusted her grip to take advantage of her dominance. Within moments, I was hanging on the stake, clinging to it rather than pushing it away, desperately trying to keep myself from going out the window.

With a cruel shriek of victory, Kendra let go of the stake and I tumbled backward through the window clutching the useless piece of wood as I hurtled toward the ground two stories below.

Chapter Twenty-Nine
🦢

As if moving in slow motion, I felt myself turning over in the air and I kicked with my hands and feet as if I could somehow fight my way to a soft landing in the hedge below. Then I felt the sharp stabbing pain of a hundred little knives and everything went dark.

Except it wasn't quite dark. I could see the moon through the leaves of the trees overhead. The dawning realization that I hadn't died brought not relief but confusion and fear. It didn't feel like I had broken any bones. Was I paralyzed? A wave of horror and self-pity washed over me, overwhelming me so completely that it was several moments after my hand automatically reached up to brush away my tears that I realized I hadn't been acutely injured, at least on the top half of my spine. After a moment of confusion and disbelief, I realized why.

Somehow, outrageously, amazingly, I had made the hedge. I tried moving one leg and was rewarded with a distant rustle as my foot popped out the side of the bush. The rest of me soon followed, and as I lay on the grass breathing air in gulps I realized that, save for a few nasty scrapes and some sore spots that would be lovely rainbow-colored bruises by morning, I wasn't hurt.

I climbed slowly and painfully to my feet and looked up at the window in confusion. It didn't make sense. I should be dead, or at least seriously maimed, but I was fine. I shouldn't have landed in the hedge—it was too close to the wall. I should have landed a good five feet farther out. And even with landing in the hedge, I should have broken my neck. Kendra evidently agreed—she hadn't even bothered to check to make sure I was dead.

"She pushed me out a *second-story* window," I muttered aloud in disbelief. "How the hell did I survive that?"

"You levitated," said a voice behind me.

Oh God. Natasha! The thought went as fast as it had come. I already knew it wasn't her. I turned to find Will leaning casually against the smooth trunk of a palm tree a few feet behind me, much in the same way he had stood against the wall in the club the first night I'd seen him. He was dressed, as usual, in black, and looked like another shadow in the night.

"Not very well," he continued, stepping forward with that combination of strength and grace that was uniquely his. "But you did it. As I expected, you are coming along quite nicely." He sounded pleased, satisfied, almost proud. As if I'd learned to ride a bike for the first time, all by myself.

I should have been glad to hear I had finally developed a *good* vampire trait. Thrilled even. I can levitate? Cool! But it wasn't. I didn't return his smile. I just stared at him, horrified. Everything had come together with an almost audible *thunk*. Gavin had said I was on a knife's edge, and I had kidded myself I could choose to what side to stay on, that I could choose to remain normal, human, I didn't have to succumb. But I realized now how naïve that was. And I knew why Will hadn't tried to turn me again. He didn't need to bother—I was slowly, irrevocably turning into a vampire on my own. The holy water had effected only a surface change. It had provided a pleasant delusion, no more.

For the first time, I truly grasped the fact that I was turning into something I didn't understand. Sure, I'd known it—I'd known it for months. But I hadn't accepted it. The idea that I was slowly becoming a vampire had been unreal. A horrible dream, a strange celluloid fantasy, a joke even—it was just too absurd to believe.

I'd had to come up with logical explanations for everything that had happened so far, little white lies, little cover stories to tell my friends. Skin changes? Allergy. Garlic? Food poisoning. Blurry image in mirror? Everyone's vision had to go sometime. But somewhere along the way, I had bought into them myself, just a little, just enough to keep the truth at bay.

But levitating out a second-story window was something I just couldn't explain away. There was no soothing rationalization for the fact that I had just defied gravity. Everything else I could find a way to accept and still keep the whole vampire thing at a distance. But this? This was different.

I backed away from him, stumbling a little, my voice shaking as I spoke. "What did you do to me?"

His pleased smile faded abruptly and his handsome face looked cold and hard without it. The charming suitor had disappeared and a stranger stood in his stead. When he spoke, his voice was harsh, his accent pronounced. "You should count yourself lucky my essence flows in your veins. It saved your life tonight."

A searing anger arose in me. "The hell it did! Kendra just tried to put this through my heart!" I held up the stake I still had, clutched tightly in my hand. "She thought I had lured away her boyfriend, that I had used some special trick to turn him against her because I was a vampire." Her accusations reverberated through my head like a physical blow. I felt sick, disgusted, as if I wanted to run screaming from my own self, from the demon I was inexorably becoming.

"That's absurd." Will's eyes glittered dangerously. He crept closer despite the stake I held before me until he seemed to tower over me, but I was beyond caring. What could he do to me now that time wouldn't do on its own?

"That's not the point," I said. "Kendra used to be my friend. Now she thinks I'm a monster!" My voice dropped almost to a whisper as I spoke the truth. "And she's right."

Something changed in Will's face. His eyes held sudden pain, as if he felt my own. "Jo—"

I backed away from his outstretched hand as if it were a skeletal claw reaching from the grave. I wondered if I'd ever really seen him before. Really seen him for what he was—something that preyed on humans to survive, whose nature it was to kill, as he had tried to kill me. Of course I hadn't, I hadn't wanted to look past the attractive packaging. It was so much easier to see only the wickedly handsome man who had picked me out of an envious crowd, who liked to read, and was considerate and had a sense of humor. Who was everything I wanted. But he was not that man. Not, in fact, a man at all.

"You changed me into something I don't want to be." My voice rose with every word, until I was shouting at him. "I didn't ask for this! I don't want to be this. I want to go outside during the day, to run, to hike, like a normal person. I want to enjoy food that is green and—and cooked! I want to go to sleep at night without worrying that I won't recognize myself when I wake up in the morning!" It was like a dam bursting. All the stress I had been feeling for the past few months burst out like an erupting geyser. The pain from all the indignities I'd suffered just poured out of me. The face mask. The mockery. The lies. The beautiful days spent cowering indoors. I leaned back against the stucco wall of the science building, unable to bear any longer the sheer weight of it all. Tears streamed down my face in an uncontrollable torrent and I pulled in air with big gasping sobs.

Will stepped forward, hands outstretched. "Jo," he said. He looked helpless, pained, as if he regretted every tear I shed, but I didn't care. It didn't matter. It was so far from enough as to be worth nothing to me.

"Get away from me." I raised the stake, prepared to drive it through him. "Leave me alone!"

He stood for a moment, hands poised awkwardly in the air where they had been stilled by my rebuff. He gave me a long probing look, and then with a funny little nod, turned on his heel and left.

I slid down the wall, and sat there, still clutching the stake, hugging my knees, staring blindly in front of me. I heard sirens, and the sounds of several police officers running up the stairs behind me toward my classroom. I didn't move. I couldn't.

Moments later a dark torso leaned out the window I had gone out of, and panned the area under and around it with a flashlight. I had moved too far out of range for them to see me. I noted the fact dumbly, as if watching it all from a great distance.

Gavin and another officer ran down the stairs calling my name, scanning dark patches near the building with their flashlights over the side of the stairwell as they moved. A light swerved over me, quickly returned and held steady. "I've found her!"

Gavin pushed past him, came around the side of the building and knelt down next to me. "Go get the EMT," he directed the officer sharply. His eyes remained fixed on me.

"Are you all right?" He touched me gently, as if I might break.

"I'm—fine," I said, hiccupping against the tears that started anew. I couldn't seem to stop them.

Gavin stared at me for a long moment, then murmuring something too low for me to catch, sat down on the ground next to me, put his arms around me and held me tight for a long, long time until I finally ran out of tears.

Chapter Thirty
ɛ͡ɔ

The EMT gently covered my scrapes with antiseptic and bandages, clucked over the many bruises I would have and then cheerily pronounced me otherwise free from harm. She handed me a cup of something hot and sweet, which after the first sip I recognized as Lipton filched from the faculty lounge just down the hall, sweetened with about five packets of sugar. It was disgusting, but I drank it anyway because she insisted and it was something to do, anything to keep myself from thinking.

The kindly EMT stayed with me chatting lightly about this and that until Gavin pushed open the door to the small utility room near the headmaster's office where he'd stowed me, and strode in. His face was drawn and there were shadows under his eyes. Once again I was struck by the thought that he looked older than his years, as if the burdens of sorrow and authority weighed heavily on him. His gray eyes were unreadable as they sought me out, silently assessing my scrapes and bandages. His mouth tightened slightly, but he said nothing to me. Instead, he turned to the EMT for an update of my status. She told him I was fine, admonished me to finish the second cup of sweetened tea she'd brought me and to take it easy for the next few days, and bustled out.

The small room was sparsely furnished, containing only those items necessary for its use as a place where students could take a makeup test or meet with a counselor or tutor when no other rooms were available. A couple of student desks were pushed against the far wall leaving the bulk of the space open for a pair of aging upholstered chairs that someone had arranged cozily around a coffee table, though the room was far too drab to be inviting.

Gavin sat across from me in the chair the EMT had vacated, shifting it back a couple feet so he faced me more directly, thought why he bothered I didn't know, for he didn't meet my eyes. When he'd finally arranged the furniture to his satisfaction, he informed me that, strictly speaking, my statement was unnecessary. Kendra had been forging my suicide note when the police had arrived.

He gently asked if I felt well enough to talk. It was an uncommonly nice if empty gesture—failing my suddenly going comatose, he'd have to get a statement from me. He was unusually awkward and self-conscious, and persisted in addressing the desk to the left of me.

"Oh for heaven's sake, Gavin!" I snapped. This sudden display of delicacy from him was absurd. "Surely in your line of work you've dealt with plenty of people who've cried on your shoulder. Just because you acted like a decent human being for once…"

"I see you *are* well enough to talk." His gray eyes turned flinty as they moved sharply to fix on mine.

I returned the glare. "Do you want to know what happened or not?"

He held up his pen and clicked it twice to indicate he was not just ready but waiting.

I told myself not to lose my temper. I told myself I was a bigger man than he and made myself do some silent yoga breathing. None of that worked, but the fact that I wanted to get everything out so I could begin forgetting it, did. In a low voice, I relayed everything that had happened, everything that Kendra had told me, even the nasty things. I managed to recount everything she'd said and done, reliving every moment up to and including the horrible terror of being pushed out the window. My voice shook, but I didn't break into tears again—dealing with Gavin had somehow irritated them out of me.

When I was done, Gavin flipped through his notes, apparently checking to see if there were any discrepancies between my and Kendra's statements. At least I assume that was what he was doing; he didn't see fit to explain his MO to me. His jaw was set and if he gripped his pen any harder it would break.

"So as I understand it," Gavin said finally, glancing over the pages in front of him as he spoke, "Kendra and Bob were dating—or had been dating. Reading between the lines, I'd say it looks as though he was trying to let her down easy after a spring and summer fling, whereas she was still very much in love with him and wanted the relationship to continue."

I nodded. "She was the blonde who wrote that love letter, you know. You probably didn't notice at the time, and her hair's grown back out to light brown since then, but she had been streaking it blonde."

He silently made a note of it and continued, "She mistook his invitation for a beer after the parent-teacher conferences as a date, a sign of his renewed interest. When she found him leaving directions for you in your classroom, she lost her temper in a fit of jealousy, picked up one of your display rocks and hit him with it. She blamed you of course…"

"What do you mean 'of course'?" I demanded, mindful of Kendra's accusation that I had been using my vampire wiles on Bob, like some tawdry romance novel vixen.

"She had to blame someone," he said reasonably, looking up from his notes. "You were the logical choice."

"You too? Just because I'm…" I remembered in time where I was. For all I knew ten people had their ears pressed up against the door, "I didn't try to *lure* him away."

Gavin raised his eyebrows in surprise. "Never said you did. Anyway, we're not dealing with reality here, we're dealing Kendra's reconfigured version of reality. She needed a scapegoat as much as an alibi, and you were good for both."

Oh. I'd had so many ugly missiles hurled at me that night that his bald statement of belief in my character was surprisingly warming. I smiled at him.

Gavin suddenly busied himself with his notes again. "So she arranged for the glassware to go crashing to the ground around the time you should have been coming back for your next parent conference, and then faked the teeth marks on his neck to implicate you further." He drummed his fingers thoughtfully on the arm of his chair. "I'm still not sure how she learned about..." he hesitated slightly, and then summed up Will, vampires, and my own vampness with a sweeping gesture, "all *that*."

"Pure darn luck. The coffee shop across from the police station was Bob's secret grading place. One night when I was there..." I casually glossed over the fact that I had been there to spy on Gavin, "Kendra stopped in. I think she was hoping to meet Bob, but found me instead, and jumped to conclusions. She began trailing me, thinking I was heading for a tryst with Bob. She followed me the day I learned... She saw everything." I stared at my shoe, willing myself not to think about that night.

If Gavin noticed my sudden reticence, he was kind enough not to make it worse by commenting on it. "You're probably right. It certainly explains what happened next. When you weren't arrested for killing Bob, she naturally assumed the police just didn't know to connect the teeth marks on Bob's neck with *you*—I wasn't among the officers who responded to the 9-1-1 call the night of Bob's death so she didn't know that any officer involved in the case *could* make the connection. So she tried to "out" you at the restaurant by ordering that garlic shrimp scampi for you."

"Yeah, and *that* worked smashingly."

"You might have found the pregnancy rumor embarrassing and ridiculous, but it really backfired on her. You got the attention and recognition she so desperately wanted. And when you denied it, she only became angrier. In fact, I think that's what turned her against you. She felt you didn't treat his memory with the reverence it deserved, and became frankly unhinged.

"The burden of guilt she felt over killing Bob must have been tremendous. I do believe it was an accident, but by not owning up to it, she turned it into murder, at least insofar as the community was concerned. I've seen what guilt can do. The stronger it got, the deeper she buried it, until it became too much for her. That's where you came in. In you, she saw the duality she despised in herself. Like her, you were trying to hide a part of you that you feared." His eyes met mine unwaveringly. In them was not censure but clean, clear logic. He reached forward and placed a hand over mine, gripping it fiercely as if to take the sting out of his words, to remind me it was Kendra's view he was explaining, not his. "You weren't lethal, but to her mind, you should have been. *You* were the one who housed a monster, not her. She rationalized her part in Bob's death more and more as the guilt became stronger, and you provided a way for the denial to become complete. She transferred responsibility to you. You were the one who was evil, not her. Therefore, you were the one who had killed Bob, who had set in motion the chain of events leading inevitably to his death, you were the chess master, she was the pawn."

I made a small noise in protest and tried to pull away, but Gavin gripped me harder. He leaned forward, pinning me with his eyes, forcing me to listen, not to look away.

"She needed to show the world what you were, what you had done. She brought a gun to school, a family heirloom, old and unlicensed. It had one bullet—for obvious reasons she couldn't buy more. She used her master key to sneak into the chemistry supply room, silver-plated the bullet and waited to catch you alone. She took the shot, and without waiting to see if she had succeeded or not, ran the back way to the gym, stashing the gun in the bushes somewhere along the way for later retrieval. Then she ran from the gym to the parking lot, as if she'd come after hearing the shot. She's a good runner, it probably didn't look as if she'd exerted herself more than the short sprint from the gym she'd owned up to."

Gavin stopped talking and waited for my response. His summary made a clear distinction between Kendra's actions and mine and should have made me feel better, but it didn't. I may not have given in to it yet, but as his tale made clear, the potential for evil was in me now, whether I liked it or not. For how much longer could I control it? He had used the word *monster* almost ironically, to highlight what *Kendra* had become, in contrast to my own probity. But wasn't she right at some level? I may not have done anything worse than unintentionally provoking her anger through my ignorance, by my careless treatment of her deep feelings for Bob, but what about next time? The monster was in me, wasn't its manifestation inevitable? By framing me for a murder I hadn't committed, wasn't she preventing me from doing evil in the future? *No!* Something in me rebelled. It didn't have to be that way. I wouldn't let it.

I became aware of Gavin's hands still gripping mine. His grey eyes regarded me quizzically, but as much as I wanted the relief that came with sharing the burden of my fears, I didn't tell him how much his words had scared me. My fears were my own to sort out. His belief that I would stay poised on that knife's edge, that I wouldn't give in, was too precious for me to risk. I needed him to fight for me. I was relying on it. Will was pulling me one way and I needed Gavin to pull back.

I swallowed on a dry throat and forced my voice to assume a lightness I didn't feel. "She must've been sorry to hear she missed. I'm surprised you didn't notice that—it was probably as good as a confession. You must've been off your game, Detective." I quietly slid my hand out from under his.

For a brief moment I thought he looked disappointed, but it was just a trick of the light. His light tone matched my own as he relaxed back in his chair, crossing his arms lightly across his broad chest. "Evidently she managed to control her dismay by the time we finally got around to questioning her, after prying you out from under that SUV."

That was totally uncalled for. I went back to glaring at him.

He resumed his narrative. "Since the shooting didn't pan out, she decided to try to kill you using a more direct method."

The stake, I translated silently.

"Apparently we were still doing a good enough job watching your apartment that she decided the next attempt would have to be at school again. She talked up that Olympiad thing to the headmaster during the soccer finals, knowing it would get back to your department head, and that he would demand you organize some sort of trumped-up demonstration for the headmaster."

Hah! I knew Roger was to blame somewhere in all of this. If he hadn't been such a glory-seeking jackass…well, she probably would have found some other way, but still…

"Kendra scheduled the mock Olympiad on a Monday and dumped all the extra work on you, knowing you would have to come to work Sunday night to get things ready. When your department head showed up, she simply told him to go home, she would take care of you."

"Nice word choice."

He ignored my comment. "Anyway, you know the rest."

I certainly did.

His eyes drilled into mine with razor sharpness. "You're lucky you landed on that hedge," he said softly.

I developed a sudden fascination for the school's carpeting.

"It's amazing you weren't more hurt."

"Yeah, lucky me."

I put down the paper cup I had been mangling for the past half hour and stood, swaying slightly on unsteady feet. "Can I go home now?" I asked rather plaintively. I wasn't just trying to avoid Gavin's probing questions. I was suddenly so tired I could barely see straight.

Gavin stood quickly and put out a strong arm in time to steady me as my knees began to buckle. "Maybe I should drive you."

Chapter Thirty-One

ഹ

We drove home in silence. Gavin maneuvered expertly into a tight parking space near my apartment and killed the engine. Neither of us made a move to get out of the car. I was too tired to so much as undo the seat belt and Gavin seemed to have been zombified.

After a few minutes, Gavin shifted suddenly in his seat as if to say something to me, but before he could get a single word out, we were blinded by the headlights of an oncoming car careening the wrong way down the one-way street. Its driver, a woman, screeched to a halt in front of my apartment building and got out in such a hurry she left her headlights blazing but forgot to switch on the hazard lights. She clicked briskly on high heels under the halogen streetlight, her hair glowing brownish-pink.

I watched her click halfway up the stairs to my apartment before realization dawned. I'm used to my mother's hair being an unnatural color, but never a shade close to brown.

"Halogen lights distort color!"

"What?"

"Oh, crap!" I jabbed a finger against the seatbelt button. When it didn't release, I started pounding it with my fist.

"Jo!"

"How do you get out of this thing? I have to get up there!"

Gavin grabbed my fist in mid-pound. He gently undid my seat belt with the other hand and I launched myself out of his car. He troubled to lock his car, and reach into my mother's to flick on the hazards, but was only a few steps behind.

When we caught up to her, she was banging on my door. "Jo? Josephine? Honey, it's your mother. Open the door!"

"Mom?"

She gasped in alarm, stared wide-eyed at me for a long moment, and then threw both arms around me in an unexpectedly prickly hug. "Jo, honey, I came as soon as I heard." Her voice caught and she squeezed me even tighter.

Something sharp was digging into my scalp, but I didn't complain. For little while, anyway. When she finally let me go, I saw she was holding a dozen roses. Odd. I hadn't noticed her carrying flowers when I'd spied her from the car.

"Oh, Jo, sweetie, how are you?" She hadn't completely relinquished me. Her hands remained lightly my shoulders and her eyes scanned me from head to toe, taking in every bandage, every bruise, every scrape. "You seem okay," she said. "I heard you got pushed out of a window?" She made it a question.

"I'm fine. Really. I didn't fall very far—and I, er, managed to break my fall by landing on a hedge." The last part was true. Well, mostly true.

Her teeth clenched in fury and her blue eyes seemed to emit sparks of rage. The only thing worse than pissing off a redhead, apparently, was pissing off a redheaded mother. Kendra was lucky she was behind bars.

Very gently, I detached her hands from my shoulders before they could add to the bruises on my frame. "Mother. Mother!" I met her eyes and said, "I'm fine."

She blinked. "Of course you are, dear."

Gavin eyed me speculatively, as if trying to fit what I'd said to my mother against what I'd told *him* in the hopes of filling the gaps in my story. I schooled my features into my best look of innocence and stared back at him. After a brief while, a slightly hazy look of acceptance replaced the suspicion in his eyes.

I kept myself from spiraling down into another I-am-Demon freak-out by telling myself that my success was rooted in a lifetime's worth of dissembling and no way vampire related.

"Jo, honey, why don't we go inside?"

"Oh. Right." I automatically reached for my bag before I realized it wasn't there. "My keys...in my classroom..."

Gavin pulled out his phone. "I'll have someone bring them over."

"That's all right," my mother said. She opened her capacious designer purse and withdrew a ring of keys that was the duplicate of my own, down to the tiny funny-shaped one that opened my bike lock.

"How did you get the one to my bike—never mind," I said.

Gavin follow me in, bending down first to pick up a small, rectangular package. He turned it over in his hands and then handed it to me. "I believe this is for you."

There was no note attached to the brown paper wrapping, just my name written in bold, unfamiliar script. "Odd," I said. "I wonder what this is?"

"Looks like a book," said my mother. She was right, of course. My mother could tell what was inside a package as effectively as an x-ray machine. I ripped off the wrapping and stared at the contents. It was a copy of Thomas Hardy's *Return of the Native*.

"Oh," said my mother, immediately losing interest. She went to the kitchen to look for something to put the flowers in.

I looked slowly up from the book and met Gavin's hard stare.

My mother came back in the room, still holding the flowers. "Jo," she said. Her voice had regained a little of its usual crispness. "Don't you have *any* vases suitable for long stemmed roses?"

Sure. On the shelf above the plastic containers, where I keep the crystal water goblets and brandy snifters. "No, Mom, I don't."

Gavin kept his eyes trained on me. "Mrs. Gartner," he said, "was there a card with those flowers?"

"Oh! I'm so sorry, Joey. I didn't think to check."

I looked at her in surprise. She must have been more worried than I thought. The warm familial glow that rose in my chest was abruptly cut short when she handed me a tiny card. It contained little more then a signature in the same bold and forceful script as had been on the package.

I dropped the book as if it burned. "I don't want the flowers," I said.

"What?" said my mother.

"Who's it from?" asked Gavin.

"Will."

My mother reached for the note but I ripped it into tiny pieces and threw it away.

"Oh!" she said. "Well!" She dumped the roses in the trashcan near my desk and the book followed with a satisfying thump. She brushed the dirt briskly from her hands as if to say *good riddance!* "Well honey, it's a terrible shame, of course, that you broke up with him, but frankly, dear, I didn't think he was good enough for you. I know you're young and have very noble feelings, but I can't believe you'd have been happy with Will in the long run, not with what he did for a living."

Gavin was, for once, absolutely speechless. I had forgotten I had told my mother that yarn about Will's occupation.

"Really, Mother," I said, "you shouldn't be so judgmental."

Gavin's jaw dropped.

"Well I'd hardly call it a *career*, darling, and he isn't even very *good* at it, now is he?" she sniffed.

I was so appalled at her snobbery that I automatically defended Will's occupation even though I had made it up. "Not everyone is cut out to be a banker like Dad, Mom. Being an assistant manager at the coffee shop is a good job for someone like Will."

Gavin let out a strangled snort. My mother looked curiously at him and he tried to turn it into a cough. Unfortunately he managed rather too well and I had to pound his back before he could breathe normally again.

When he could speak again, he said, "Whatever you do, don't let this, er — coffee shop manager — in."

"You don't think he's dangerous, do you?" my mother asked.

"I do." Gavin looked at my mother but his words were meant for me. "I've dealt a lot with men of his type, Mrs. Gartner. When a — er — jilted boyfriend sends something that has personal meaning, as I expect that book had, it usually means he's not ready to let go. They're the ones most likely to turn violent. The important thing is to make it very clear that the relationship is over. If you see him, go quickly in the other direction. And whatever you do, never ever let him inside. Even for a moment, no matter how nice he seems."

"Well! I can assure you that man will no longer be welcome here," said my mother, lifting her chin as if ready for battle. "In fact, I'm going to take those 'gifts' out to the dumpster right now."

I put out a hand to stop her. For all I knew, Will was hovering outside in the shadows, waiting to see my reaction to his gift. "I think that can wait 'til morning, Mom. Maybe you could make us some hot chocolate?" I let a little fatigue color my voice. It wasn't hard to do, I was bone tired and running on leftover adrenaline. She bustled off, pleased to be able to do something to mother me a bit.

Gavin headed for the door. "I'll need you to sign your statement tomorrow and I'll probably have a few follow-up questions."

"I'll come by the station on the way home from work."

"You're going to work tomorrow?"

"Trust me. It will be worse for me if I put it off." Plenty of teachers, students and parents lived within spitting distance of Bayshore, and had followed the police sirens to the school parking lot, like moths to a flame. I could only imagine what was swirling through the grapevine already. *Oh, no!* Had Kendra said anything about vampires in front of all those people?

As if reading my thoughts, Gavin said in a low voice, "Don't worry, we spoke to the headmaster tonight in the privacy of his office and I assure you, vampires were never mentioned. Kendra hasn't spilled the beans yet—and I'm quite sure her lawyer will advise against it. She'd have to admit how she'd been following both you and Bob—and how she'd nicked his neck in an attempt to frame you. 'Accidental homicide' is much more palatable to a jury when you don't add in those disturbingly premeditative-sounding bits."

"Hmph."

"It's only a tight little group at the station that knows about this, Jo, and I'll make sure nothing gets out on our end. As far as anyone will know, she attacked you with a regular old knife. I don't want to make things awkward for you at work."

"You mean any more awkward than the fact she hated me enough to try to kill me?" I said. "You know this is going to resurrect all those stupid rumors about me and Bob. I almost wish you would let the vampire rumor take its course—at least no one would believe that one!"

There was a loud crash in the kitchen. My mother seemed to be wrestling more pots on the stove than were necessary for a couple cups of hot chocolate. I put a hand on Gavin's arm to get his attention. "Thanks," I said simply.

I thought his expression softened slightly before he looked away. "So," he said. "What's the significance of the Thomas Hardy book?" Apparently I was wrong about the glimpse of humanity. Really! The man was made of stone.

Gavin waited for a response, but I didn't answer him. The truth was, I really didn't know what Will had meant in sending that book. I had told him about my weird Christmas ritual of reading Hardy books to distract him from what I had thought was some closely held regret about his career—as some sort of human resource manager. Talk about title inflation.

But while depressing Victorian literature might help put petty holiday complaints in perspective, I didn't think there was any frigate of a book big enough to take me away from the fact that I was turning into a vampire.

Will's victims usually experienced a quick transformation, but I was facing a protracted death. Not only did I know I was going to die (un-die? I'm still a little fuzzy on that part), but I knew what my fate would be. And unlike most people, I had no hope of wearing wings and a halo.

Had Will sent the book to underscore the supreme hopelessness of my situation or to help me face it? Was it a nice gesture or a cruel one?

Gavin's voice pulled me out of my dark study. "All right," he said, "Don't tell me. I'll guess. Let's see...Will was born in the 1800s and was a contemporary of Hardy. No?" He put his hands in his pockets and leaned casually against the door jamb. "Well then, perhaps he hasn't actually read the book and thinks *The Return of the Native* is about a nudist colony in Malibu. If that's the case, I'm all the more glad I told your mother to steer clear of him. That's not it either? Well, I'm out of ideas. I can think of no reason why he would give you a depressing book to read. I read that book in high school and am still getting over it. Don't look so surprised. I can read, you know. It's practically a requirement for graduating college these days."

He pushed himself back to an upright position with his shoulder so that he stood very close to me. He smelled good, an inexplicably comforting blend of wool and fabric softener. "Please, Jo, be careful." He spoke slowly and seriously. "Kendra may be in jail, but somehow I was never as worried about that threat."

"Really, Detective," I said with a lightness I did not feel, "you worry too much."

"Perhaps. But I'd rather you stayed alive. Because if you didn't—" His gray eyes burned into mine before straying briefly to my lips. I felt a heated rush down to my toes. "Your mom would come after me. And for some reason I'm more scared of her than anything else I've run across." He smiled that rare grin of his and his silvery gaze held mine for a brief, breathless moment. And then he turned and let himself out.

End

Why an electronic book?

    We live in the Information Age—an exciting time in the history of human civilization, in which technology rules supreme and continues to progress in leaps and bounds every minute of every day. For a multitude of reasons, more and more avid literary fans are opting to purchase e-books instead of paper books. The question from those not yet initiated into the world of electronic reading is simply: *Why?*

1. ***Price.*** An electronic title at Ellora's Cave Publishing and Cerridwen Press runs anywhere from 40% to 75% less than the cover price of the exact same title in paperback format. Why? Basic mathematics and cost. It is less expensive to publish an e-book (no paper and printing, no warehousing and shipping) than it is to publish a paperback, so the savings are passed along to the consumer.

2. ***Space.*** Running out of room in your house for your books? That is one worry you will never have with electronic books. For a low one-time cost, you can purchase a handheld device specifically designed for e-reading. Many e-readers have large, convenient screens for viewing. Better yet, hundreds of titles can be stored within your new library—on a single microchip. There are a variety of e-readers from different manufacturers. You can also read e-books on your PC or laptop computer. (Please note that

Ellora's Cave does not endorse any specific brands. You can check our websites at www.ellorascave.com or www.cerridwenpress.com for information we make available to new consumers.)

3. *Mobility.* Because your new e-library consists of only a microchip within a small, easily transportable e-reader, your entire cache of books can be taken with you wherever you go.

4. *Personal Viewing Preferences.* Are the words you are currently reading too small? Too large? Too… ANNOYING? Paperback books cannot be modified according to personal preferences, but e-books can.

5. *Instant Gratification.* Is it the middle of the night and all the bookstores near you are closed? Are you tired of waiting days, sometimes weeks, for bookstores to ship the novels you bought? Ellora's Cave Publishing sells instantaneous downloads twenty-four hours a day, seven days a week, every day of the year. Our webstore is never closed. Our e-book delivery system is 100% automated, meaning your order is filled as soon as you pay for it.

Those are a few of the top reasons why electronic books are replacing paperbacks for many avid readers.

As always, Ellora's Cave and Cerridwen Press welcome your questions and comments. We invite you to email us at Comments@ellorascave.com or write to us directly at Ellora's Cave Publishing Inc., 1056 Home Avenue, Akron, OH 44310-3502.

Cerrídwen Press
Monthly Newsletter

News
Author Appearances
Book Signings
New Releases
Contests
Author Profiles
Feature Articles

Available online at
www.CerridwenPress.com

erridwen, the Celtic Goddess of wisdom, was the muse who brought inspiration to storytellers and those in the creative arts. Cerridwen Press encompasses the best and most innovative stories in all genres of today's fiction. Visit our site and discover the newest titles by talented authors who still get inspired - much like the ancient storytellers did, once upon a time.

Cerridwen Press

www.cerridwenpress.com

Cerridwen Press

Cerridwen, the Celtic goddess of wisdom, was the muse who brought inspiration to storytellers and those in the creative arts.

Cerridwen Press encompasses the best and most innovative stories in all genres of today's fiction.

Visit our website and discover the newest titles by talented authors who still get inspired — much like the ancient storytellers did...

once upon a time.

www.cerridwenpress.com